LOST
WOLF

Other books by Rachel

The New Dawn Novels

Winter Wolf

Wolf Dancer

Wolf Sight

The Deadwood Hunter Series

Lexia

Whispers of Darkness

Holocaust

Betrayal

Surrender

Novellas

The Beast Within – Woodland Creek Series

Deaths Echo – The Complex Series

A New Dawn Novel

Rachel M. Raithby

Copyright and Legal Information

Cover Art, Interior Images & Formatting by

Rob & Kat Smith

www.Creationinspire.com

Editing by Hot Tree Editing

www.hottreeediting.com

Author Photo © Kat Smith of Creationinspire

Dedication

This one is for my parents and grandparents,

who held my hand in the dark when I, too, was barely surviving.

I love you guys, more than any words could ever say.

PART ONE

Set during the events of *Wolf Dancer*

CHAPTER 1

A buzz hummed through Regan's veins, and it had nothing to do with the bottle of cider she'd drunk. For the first time since her sister's death, Regan felt a little like her old self—the wilder, freer version of herself. The version she'd buried under grief and pain, then duty and obligation.

At sixteen, Regan had lost her twin sister. They'd been alike in all ways, but in personality they'd been opposites. Her sister, Megan, had been quiet and reserved, dedicated to school work and pack life. She'd been born to follow the rules, and Regan had been born to break them. In fact, Regan took great pleasure in breaking rules, and not once had she felt guilty for running her parents ragged. That was until after her sister's death, until Regan had to change who she was so that her parents could cope with life.

In some ways, it hadn't bothered Regan to change. She'd been struggling to cope, too, and living life to its fullest just didn't have the same appeal. It wasn't until she was in the middle of a secret party, laughter all around her that it truly hit her how much she'd changed.

"Pleased I convinced you to come?" Katalina asked her, a devilish grin on her face.

Regan couldn't help smiling back just as wickedly. "Yes! I so needed this."

"See, I told you. Every now and then it's good to break a rule or two."

"Aren't you the slightest bit worried about Bass finding out?"

Katalina laughed. "I can handle him. The packs needed this. Look around you. Friendships are being made, bonds formed. This is more than just a party. It's strengthening the alliance."

Regan gazed at Katalina, a little envious of the person she was. Regan had once been more like her. Now she was a shadow of herself.

No more.

Tipping back the bottle she held in her hand, Regan downed the last of its contents, a thrill stirring in her soul.

"That's the spirit," Katalina cheered. "Someone turn up the music!"

Cheering with her, Regan threw her head back, hands lifting to the sky as she laughed and danced along to the beat. Letting the mask she'd been hiding under slip away, and when a hand landed on her shoulder later in the night, his touch sending a shockwave through her body, Regan threw caution to the wind. Broke every rule in the book. Tonight, she was being the girl from her past. Tonight she was going home with a sexy blue-eyed wolf. Consequences be damned.

CHAPTER 2

After shift change, Tyler had headed to the pack kitchen to eat. Taking a seat with his plate of food, he scanned the room, noticing there was a distinct lack of younger pack members present.

John sat down next to him, mug of coffee in his hand and a sandwich on his plate.

"Not eating with the family tonight?" Tyler asked.

"No, she had dinner with her parents earlier. This saves her cooking for me. I'm surprised you're not at the party."

"Party?"

John laughed. "I'd have thought you'd be in the know."

"Just tell me what you're talking about," Tyler grumbled.

"I heard a few whispers. Kat's organized a party on the border for both packs."

"Wow, and Bass agreed to it?"

John's smiled grew wide, and he dipped his head. "Word is he doesn't know."

Tyler laughed, shaking his head. "Poor Bass. You going to tell him?"

"Hell no. You?"

"Fuck that. I'm going to join it. Coming?"

"Nah, I'm too old. But go, enjoy it while it lasts. Can't see it being a secret for too long."

Stuffing the last of his pasta into his mouth, Tyler headed out, grabbing a quick shower and changing clothes, before going to search for the party. It didn't take him long to hear the distant beat of music, and the closer he got, the clearer the laughter and conversation became.

Breaking through the trees, several people paused at the sight of him, but Tyler concentrated on one individual. Katalina. Silence fell as he walked toward her. Katalina watched him with apprehension.

"Tyler."

"Katalina," he responded, doing his best at keeping his tone indifferent.

"Look—"

"What's going on, huh?" he asked, deadly serious. Katalina's face fell. "Not inviting me. It's an outrage!"

"Ty!" She smacked him. "You ass. I thought you'd come to play enforcer."

"Not likely." He laughed. "Pass me a beer."

Relief flooded her face, and laughter erupted. Shaking her head, Katalina glared at him, but he could see the amusement in her gaze.

"Sorry, couldn't resist."

"Jesus, bro," Logan said, throwing him a beer. "You had me then. Thought we were busted."

Tyler caught the beer, popped the top off, and took a swig before answering. "Nah, was just too good an opportunity to miss."

Katalina poked her tongue out.

"You do realize Bass will find out about this, don't you?"

Katalina smiled sheepishly. "I'll handle him."

Laughing, Tyler clinked bottles with Logan. "Cheers. Long may it last."

Sipping his beer, Tyler surveyed his surroundings; there was a good mix of River Run and Dark Shadow, and while most seemed a little on the tipsy side, there were some he knew were there to protect, not party.

Logan, it seemed, had gone for the party side. Tyler had lost track of the conversation a few minutes ago, but Logan hadn't noticed as he babbled on.

"Logan, how much you drank, pal?"

Logan paused, his brow creasing as he studied the bottle in his hand. "Lost count." He shrugged.

"Not concerned about being around River Run, then?"

He pulled a face, shaking his head overdramatically. "Course not. Kat's as much theirs as ours. All's good, Ty. Let loose."

Yet it didn't sit right with Tyler. Not that he thought they'd hurt Katalina; it was just with Bass being absent, he felt obligated to watch out for Katalina in his absence.

She was clearly drunk, dancing giddily with a group of girls, equally as drunk as her. Some he knew, but there was one who caught his attention and kept doing so throughout the night. It was her hair he'd noticed first; it hung straight to her waist, black with the subtle hint of blue. It reminded him of a midnight sky.

"Dude, just go up to her already," Logan said, slapping him on the back.

"She's River Run, pal."

"Sooo?" Logan answered dramatically.

"So, I'm not nearly drunk enough to use it as an excuse when Bass finds out and murders me."

"Don't see what the issue is. Not like you're wanting to marry her." Logan shrugged. "I mean, if you're not interested… I'm all for fun."

Logan winked as he stepped away, tossing Tyler a wicked grin over his shoulder. It took Tyler all of two seconds for his brain to kick in and halt Logan in his tracks.

"I think not, *pal*," Tyler murmured, kneeing Logan in the gut. "She's too beautiful for you."

Logan grunted and doubled over, hands on his knees he let out a breathless laugh. "You're welcome."

Grinning back at Logan, Tyler winked at his friend before setting his sights on the black-haired beauty he'd not been able to look away from all night. Taking a deep breath, he allowed a charming smile to grace his lips before placing a hand on her shoulder.

She turned, her gaze locking with his, and whatever cheesy hook-up line that was on the edge of his tongue slipped away.

My God, you're beautiful.

His wolf cocked his head, rising to attention and right then and there, Tyler knew one night would never be enough.

CHAPTER 3

Regan flopped onto her back with an exaggerated sigh, hitting her duvet with a huff. Sleep was eluding her. When she closed her eyes, she saw his blue, blue gaze, and tight bronzed muscles moving above her; it made her anything but sleepy. She didn't regret her one night of freedom and rule breaking with Tyler, not even the next morning, but it had been a week and she was beginning to have them. And these regrets only stemmed from her inability to sleep without dreaming of him, without waking up the next morning feeling anything but rested.

With another sigh, Regan flung her duvet off and got out of bed. Creeping out of the room, she silently padded past her parents' bedroom and down the stairs, going to the back door. Pulling her oversized nightshirt off over her head, she dropped her panties and shifted, running out into the dark night.

The evening was clear and crisp, the slight breeze playing through her fur and wafting up the scents of the wilderness around her. For the first time in a week, Regan relaxed. Her body let out a breath, dispelling with it every frustration she'd been holding in. For the next blissful moments, her mind was that of her wolf, no human complications, no blue eyes, just the forest and the predator at her core.

Slowing her pace, Regan came to a small stream that ran along the River Run, Dark Shadow border. She didn't use Dark Shadow's land for running, not like many others in her pack did. And while Regan didn't hold the same negative feelings toward the other pack as her parents, there was still a small part of her that felt like she was breaking her loyalty to her sister by accepting the pack alliance.

Emotions were complicated and messy, and part of the reason she'd not been sleeping. Because not only had she been breaking the rules going with Katalina to her illegal party, she'd ended the night sleeping with one of the Dark Shadow wolves. Yet she couldn't bring herself to wish otherwise, and that brought on a whole mass of complicated emotions. To make matters worse, her body craved more of the blue-eyed wolf.

Taking a breather, Regan lowered her head, drinking from the stream. Her ears twitched, listening for any threats, her mind relaxing yet always on alert. Detecting a rustle from the other side of the water, she snapped her head up, scanning the Dark Shadow land ahead. Slowly out of the bush walked a wolf, his dark brown fur highlighted with auburn. Piercing blue eyes met hers, and while Regan had never met him in wolf form, she knew it was Tyler. She'd never mistake those eyes for anyone else's. He'd been haunting her dreams, he'd chased her from her bed, and now he was gazing at her like she'd been doing the same to him.

They both froze, looking at one another as if one of them might have been conjured up. Regan's heart boomed through her body, the human mind she'd come to escape awakening. Minutes stretched out as they stayed frozen, caught between dream and reality. In the end, Tyler made the first move, stepping hesitantly into the stream.

Fear clawed its way through Regan's body; she wasn't ready. She hadn't unraveled her feelings around their one night of passion, and she definitely wasn't ready to meet his wolf face-to-face. Taking a step back, and another, Regan only paused when Tyler did. Gazing at him for a heartbeat longer, she dashed away, running alongside the steam that meandered back and forth over the border.

Looking toward Dark Shadow, Regan found Tyler was doing the same. Only he wasn't chasing her, he was joining her, and Regan found with the water between them acting as a barrier, she could cope with that. In fact, she could more than cope; she quite liked it.

CHAPTER 4

Regan

Night after night they met at the same spot, running the same route in wolf form. Each time Regan snuck from her home, she silenced her guilt, fed herself lies—they weren't speaking, weren't even crossing onto each other's land. It didn't mean anything. They were two wolves enjoying each other's company, that was all. It didn't matter that she forced herself not to shift each night. That their silent runs where filled with unanswered questions and feelings.

Tyler surprised her with his patience; it was as if he was perfectly happy to spend forever doing the same thing. That he didn't want to shift and talk at all. Regan wished her own body was as patient, that her hormones would get on board with her head. As time went on, Regan found herself counting down the hours until they'd meet again. But being in his presence wasn't enough; she wanted, *needed* more, until the point it could no longer be ignored. As much as she battled with her conscience and the jumbled feelings surrounding her sister's death, it wasn't enough to stop her giving in and meeting in human form.

Fidgeting with nerves, Regan waited for Tyler to arrive. She clenched the commandeered jeans in her hands as she wondered what he'd say. She had no idea herself what to say. Her plan went as far as throwing the jeans at him, and from there, her mind went blank.

With nothing to do as Regan waited, she found her mind wandering into the past and recalling a time when she'd not been as nervous, when her first instinct was to jump and build her wings on the way down. Her younger self would approve of the jeans move. Only she'd have planned out and imagined what followed afterward. At sixteen, Regan had been confident, carefree, and just a little reckless. Boys had found her nature very alluring, and Regan had kissed a different boy each month with not much thought or care. Megan, on the other hand, had been shy and awkward, tending to spend her nights studying or watching TV rather than rule-breaking with her sister. Regan often wondered if she'd become more like her sister to try to fill the giant hole Megan had left behind. Or maybe it was simply she viewed her reckless behavior as the reason for her sister's death. Either way, Regan had changed, and it wasn't until Katalina's party that she'd realized it maybe wasn't for the best.

When he appeared through the trees, Regan's heart gave a leap. Smiling, she threw the jeans at him, happy with the look of surprise in his blue wolf gaze. Yet when he returned, the jeans hung low on his hips, his sculptured chest bare and oh so tempting, her bravado faltered.

What was I thinking?

He smiled softly, settling her nerves a little. "Want to go for a walk?"

She agreed though she asked him to come to her. Crossing over to Dark Shadow somehow made the betrayal she felt toward her sister worse.

You're just walking, Regan. Stop with the negatives already.

Yet when he jumped the stream, stopping mere inches in front of her and resting his hands on her shoulders, Regan knew they'd be doing much more than walking. Her hands moved to his chest as heat bloomed at her core, the memories from their first night reminding her of all she was missing.

"I should have brought you a T-shirt," Regan said, her fingers flexing over his bare skin.

Tyler laughed. "Who'd you steal the jeans from?"

Stomach flipping, Regan filled with sadness as she answered, "Cage. I figured you were both similar sizes, and… he won't be needing them."

"I'm sorry," Tyler murmured, cupping her face briefly. "Were the two of you close?"

Her eyes closed briefly, savoring his touch of comfort, soaking in his warmth and concern. "Not really, but he's pack… you know. Family. We all feel the loss of his absence."

"He'll come home."

Regan broke the contact between them, wanting Tyler's words to be true but knowing that in reality, Cage wasn't coming home until he found what he was searching for… until he could sort through the tangled mess of emotions inside of him. She could relate; her mind was like a spider's web at that moment.

"I hope so," she replied softly, taking a step back. "Shall we?" She inclined her head.

They walked and talked, and Regan found herself relaxing, that was until he touched on subjects that were far too close to home.

Do you like to please them…?

The way he'd spoken, as if he knew just how much she'd changed to do that. To please her parents. What scared Regan the most, though, was how easy it was to spend time with Tyler. She was purposely keeping walls between them because she knew just how far it would go if she didn't. Yet that knowledge hadn't stopped her from coming in human form. From taking the next step in whatever was developing between them.

She was playing with fire, walking a fine line between the past and the present, and when Tyler pulled her to a stop and pressed his lips to hers, Regan gave up erecting walls and smashed them down.

A groan left her throat as she truly gave in to the lusty need humming through her veins. They clawed at each other, their mouths greedy. Regan held on, her body alive for the first time since the night of the party, but as Tyler tumbled her to the floor, she was hit with all she'd been holding back.

Her sister's face entered her mind and dread replaced the desire she'd once felt.

"What's wrong?" Tyler whispered as she froze. "Regan, talk to me."

Tears pooled in her eyes. She wanted to talk, but Regan had no idea how to explain what was going on inside of her. She didn't understand it herself.

"I can't. I shouldn't." She wiggled, pushing to get free. She needed space, needed to not see the hurt in his eyes.

Tyler sat back, and Regan shot to her feet, backing away. His confused and pained gaze created a war inside herself. The loyalty to her sister fighting against the compulsion to soothe him.

"Regan?"

Shaking her head, Regan saw no other choice but to run. If she stayed any longer, she'd cave and, come morning, be filled with regret, and she never wanted Tyler to be a regret.

"Hey!" he shouted after her. "Regan, wait."

She didn't so much as glance back as he gave chase. All her focus was on outrunning him, but in the end, it was a useless effort. He was an enforcer; he'd outrun her every time.

"You can't just run away from me, Regan," he snapped.

"Please," she begged, breathless. "Just leave it." Desperately building her mental defenses to push him back out.

"Regan? You feel this too, don't you? Tell me you feel this too?"

The despair in his voice gave her no other choice but to answer with the truth: "Yes, Tyler, I do."

"Then why?" He shook his head. "Is it Jackson? Because—"

"It's not Jackson."

"Then who? Your parents? Surely we—"

"You don't get it!" Regan said abruptly. All of a sudden, she felt too tight, full of so much emotion she might burst.

Tyler squeezed her hand, smiling encouragingly. "Then help me get it."

"It's not Jackson or my parents," she yelled. "It's… it's…" She snatched her hand from his, needing distance. "It's my sister."

"Sister? But you don't have a sister?" He frowned.

Regan's hands balled into fists, her anger over her death pushing forward. "I don't, I mean I did. I do…. She's dead. Killed. Killed by Dark Shadow," she finished with a whisper, almost relieved to have the truth out in the open.

"Regan, I…."

"Do you see why now? Why it doesn't matter how much I want you? I shouldn't want you. The guilt is tearing me up, and even if I could deal with that, my parents would never bless what's between us. Never. I'm sorry," Regan whispered, her voice raw, tears rolling down her face. "I'm sorry."

Tyler stumbled back a step, his face unreadable, and Regan took her chance to escape. He didn't follow her this time, and she couldn't help but admit just how much that hurt. How much she'd truly hoped he'd tell her it didn't matter, that they'd somehow find a way around it.

She raced away, her heart constricting painfully as she refused to look back. Her hope dying as tears spilled from her eyes.

CHAPTER 5

For weeks they'd been meeting by the stream. Never talking, never crossing the water, but simply running together in wolf form, enjoying each other's presence. Tyler desperately wanted to cross onto her side. The dominant wolf in him imagined doing so, then chasing her down, and making her face him. Yet the softer human side sensed there was something troubling Regan, some deep hurt she wasn't ready to confront, and until she was, she wouldn't come to him. He'd never waited this long for a woman, never been this patient, but with Regan, he really didn't mind. Not that he'd ever admit it aloud; he had a reputation to uphold. He didn't want people thinking he was a pushover, who pined after a woman for weeks.

Today, as he padded up to the stream, Regan was already waiting, and she wasn't in wolf form. She held a pair of jeans in her hands, and when he paused, she smiled, her gaze one of daring, before throwing the jeans across the water at his feet.

He stared at the jeans, his heart beating faster as he picked them up between his wolf teeth, going a short distance away to shift behind the cover of trees. When he reappeared and walked to the stream, his bare feet touching the edge of the water, the bravado in Regan's eyes faltered.

Smiling warmly, Tyler said, "Hey."

"Hi," she replied quietly.

They spoke for a few moments across the river. The whole time Regan seemed as if she wanted to bolt and take back her offer. He didn't understand the reservation and it frustrated him that she wouldn't tell him what was truly on her mind. It wasn't until they were finally walking that their conversation eased, and Regan relaxed a little.

They walked in silence for a few minutes, and even though the stream was no longer between them, Tyler felt no closer to her. He didn't understand the walls she'd built up around her. He didn't understand her hesitation when it was clear she wanted him as much as he wanted her.

Unless I imagined our first night?

"Hey, Regan? If you're worried about what people will say… there's no need. I cleared it with Bass."

"You did what?" she gasped sharply.

"Wow." Tyler held up his hands. "He's alpha, Regan. He knows what happened at the party. He caught you sneaking off pack lands the next morning."

"Gwad," she groaned, rubbing a hand to her face.

"Anyway, he didn't specifically say I couldn't see you again. So, if that's what's bothering you, don't worry—"

"It's not that."

"Then what is it?"

She glanced at him. "Can we just enjoy our walk?"

Tyler suppressed a frustrated sigh, forcing a smile on his lips. "Of course."

They followed the same route they'd ran as wolves, only this time, Tyler was on her side of the stream, and they were traveling a much slower pace. After a while, Regan slipped her hand into his, sending a jolt of electricity up his arm from the connection. He couldn't take the silence between them. The unasked questions. So he asked less dangerous ones instead.

"Regan, what is it you do?"

"I'm studying accounting and finance, and when I'm not

doing that, I work shifts at a café."

"Do you enjoy it?"

"Studying or work?"

"Both."

She glanced at him, a small crease between her eyebrows like she'd never actually considered it before.

"I guess I like work. The humans I've met there are cool. Jada, who often has the same shifts as I have, has become a good friend. Studying… I'm good at it, but it's boring if I'm honest."

"Then why study it?"

"It was safe I guess…. Gives me the opportunity to find work easily nearby. And it pleases my parents."

The way she said the last sentence had Tyler studying her as he asked his next question, "Do you like to please them?"

She paused, gazing at him with an unreadable expression. "I didn't always," she replied after a long pause. "Anyway, enough questioning me. How about you?"

Tyler wanted to press her further, but sensing her shutting down, he chose to let it go and answer her questions.

"Pack work takes up most of my time. I'm in charge of the dominant teens."

"Tough age."

"They're a good group. Drive me crazy half the time, but I like training and guiding them."

"They're in good hands."

"Thanks," Tyler murmured, bumping his shoulder to hers. "And when I'm not doing that, I'm working with my dad. He owns a tree service company. A few of the pack members work for him. My mom does the office work."

Pulling Regan to a stop, Tyler took hold of her other hand and looked into her eyes. Her hesitation lasted the barest of seconds before desire flooded her gaze. Breathing her in, Tyler lowered his head and gave into the need he'd had for weeks. Her lips were as soft and delicious as he'd remembered. They opened for him, her grip on his hands tightening as he dipped his tongue inside.

Regan groaned, closing the space between them, their bodies becoming flush against one another. Fire ignited, the air around them charged with unacknowledged desire. The slow, gentle kiss grew intense, their linked hands separating and clawing at flesh. Tyler lost all rational thought, his one and only need being Regan.

His hands roamed her body, finding skin and grazing up her spine. Regan returned the favor, her own hands just as greedy as his, but when they fell to the ground, never breaking the kiss, she froze up.

"What's wrong?" Tyler whispered, stilling. He studied her, double-checking he'd not imagined the passion between them. "Regan, talk to me."

Tears pooled in her eyes. "I can't. I shouldn't." She wiggled, pushing for him to get off and his stomach dropped, hurt and confusion churning inside of him.

Tyler sat back, and Regan shot to her feet and backed away.

"Regan?" he whispered, wide-eyed and holding a hand toward her.

She shook her head and began to run.

"Hey!" Tyler jumped to his feet, irritation filling him. He was done with being patient. Tyler wanted answers. Needed answers. She desired him as much as he did her; he could feel it. "Regan, wait."

She didn't so much as glance back. He gave chase, surprised at how fast she was, but Regan was no enforcer, and within minutes, he was pulling her to a stop.

"You can't just run away from me, Regan."

"Please," she begged, breathless. "Just leave it."

"Regan? You feel this too, don't you? Tell me you feel this too?" he asked desperately, gripping her hand, anxiety growing within him.

She sagged, sadness filling her face. "Yes, Tyler, I do."

"Then why?" He shook his head, trying to grasp the situation. "Is it Jackson? Because if it is—"

"It's not Jackson."

"Then who? Your parents? Surely—"

"You don't get it!" she said shortly, her face hardening..

Tyler squeezed her hand, smiling encouragingly as he squashed his frustration, for fear she'd close up and leave him more confused. "Then help me get it."

"It's not Jackson or my parents," she shouted. "It's… it's…" Regan snatched her hand from his, her eyes hardening. "It's my sister."

Shock rolled through him. "Sister? But you don't have a sister?"

Regan went rigid, the walls she kept around her rising up. "I don't, I mean I did. I do…. She's dead. Killed. Killed by Dark Shadow."

Tyler stumbled back a step, horror coursing through him. Regan's words echoed in his head. Her pain, her sorrow like daggers to his heart.

"Regan, I…," he began, but Tyler had no idea what to say.

"Do you see why now? Why it doesn't matter how much I want you? I shouldn't want you." Her shoulders sagged forward, pain filling her features. "The guilt is tearing me up, and even if I could deal with that, my parents would never bless what's between us. Never."

Tyler felt like a bucket of ice-cold water had been dumped over his head. There was nothing but a painful ringing in his ears.

"I'm sorry," Regan whispered, her voice raw, tears rolling down her face. "I'm sorry."

Tyler wanted to ask why she was sorry. *It's I who should be sorry. I'm Dark Shadow.* But as she walked away, he voiced nothing, did nothing. And when she was no longer visible, when her footsteps could no longer be heard, and her scent had been erased from his lungs, Tyler continued to do nothing. Standing in the same spot she'd left him on, his heart slowly cracked.

CHAPTER 6

Dashing through the trees, the pain she'd been holding took over. Stumbling, Regan wrapped her arms tightly around her middle as if to keep herself together. Her clumsy steps turned frantic, and before long, she was running into the forest, blindly racing through the dark night. Her broken heart beat a relentless drum through her skull, and Tyler's sorrow-filled expression haunted her every step.

It wasn't until she fell to her knees that Regan registered where she'd been going. Pressing an unsteady hand on the small headstone, she dropped her head, her tears rolling from her cheeks and onto the earth.

"Hey, sis," she whispered, sucking in a breath. "God, how I miss you."

For a few minutes, Regan did nothing but cry; no sentences could form from the jumbled mess inside of her mind. Instead, she allowed everything she couldn't string into words to be washed away with her tears, her pain, and sorrow and regret, emotions she'd been keeping locked away inside until meeting Tyler had stirred them back to life.

"I've made a mess of things, Meg," Regan said quietly. "I'm so lost, sis. I'm not even sure how I'm supposed to go back.... I guess I can't. If I could, I'd go back and make sure I never went out that night. Then maybe you'd be here in person listening to me, telling you all about this crazy hot guy I slept with."

Regan dragged in a few breaths, laughing emptily as she traced the carved letters of her sister's name.

"It's probably not all that shocking to you hearing I slept with a hot guy, but after you... well, I haven't exactly been acting like the sister you knew. But the thing is, I actually really like him, enough that I've felt a little like me again with him. The thing is, Meg, he's... he's not from this pack. He's Dark Shadow, and I hate myself for falling for a guy who's from the same pack that took away my sister. It would never work, even without the potential problems with the alliance. Mom and Dad would never forgive me if they knew. I'm so stupid, Megan. What was I even thinking? I wasn't, that's what. I wish you were here. I wish I could just speak to you for one minute.... I wish I could just speak to someone. I'm all alone.... I'm—"

Regan's head whipped around as she braced to spring to her feet, but as the person who'd disturbed her came into view, Regan relaxed just a little.

"Mia, what are you doing here?"

Mia hesitated, her eyes flickering from her face to the gravestone behind her. She lifted the flowers that were in her hand in answer.

Regan swiped at the tears on her cheeks and rose to her feet. "I didn't know you visited her."

"I can come back," Mia murmured, turning away.

Regan thought she should possibly say something, but as she opened her mouth, nothing came out.

Mia paused, then walked a couple of steps before pausing again and turning around. "I didn't know you'd be here, and I didn't mean to hear what you were saying, but I did. Some anyway, and I guess I just wanted to say..." She halted, biting her lip in deliberation. "You can talk to me. Well, you used to talk to me, before... well, before everything. Before it all went wrong."

Regan stared silently.

"We're friends, well, we were. We are.... I lost her too, Regan. She died because of me too."

All the air knocked out of her. Regan's knees buckled, and she slid to the ground. Mia was beside her a second later, a hand gently rubbing circles on her back.

"Regan? Regan, are you all right?" Mia gasped.

"I'm so sorry," Regan sobbed. "I'm so, so sorry."

"It's okay, Regan. She was your sister. Your twin."

"But you're right. She was your friend. We both lost her, and I just...."

"I didn't say those things to make you feel bad. It's just you sounded so lost, and I couldn't walk away without reminding you that I'm still here if you want to talk. If you need someone to confide in."

Regan shuffled back and sat on her butt. Running her hands over her face, she dragged in a few breaths before facing Mia again. "Do you ever feel like you've been walking down the wrong path, and you've been walking down it for so long that you no longer have any idea how to get back?"

Mia sat down, her expression thoughtful as she answered, "You can't go back. But you can change course."

Regan laughed softly. "You make it sound so simple."

"It won't be, but I think it's a hell of a lot better than living a lie."

"A lie?"

Mia pursed her lips, a tiny crease appearing on her forehead.

"Just say it," Regan urged.

"I'm a little worried about upsetting you."

"That never stopped you before."

"You've lost your twin, Regan, but you've lost a lot more than that. You've lost the very essence of who you are. Megan was the quiet sister, and you were the loud sister. Her wolf was submissive, while yours is dominant. You were opposites in so many ways, yet two halves of one whole."

Regan knew where Mia was leading. She knew she'd changed in more ways than one, and possibly not for the better. There was grief and mourning, and then there was hating the very core of herself. Loathing the wild, free, teenager she'd been, because she'd gotten her sister killed.

"That essence killed her, Mia," Regan whispered. "I killed her."

"Oh, Regan." Mia took hold of her hand. "If you killed her, then so did I. So did everyone at that party."

"If I'd just stayed home, then she'd never been out there to be found."

"If Megan had just stayed home, then she would never have been there to be found."

"She was worried about me."

"I know. And I'd be lying if I didn't admit that the very thoughts you're having haven't haunted me, but the truth of the matter is; Megan's death is the fault of the man who killed her, and no one else. And if Megan were here, she'd tell you herself that it wasn't your fault, and she'd also tell you to stop hiding from yourself."

"My parents need me to be sensible."

"You're not a silly teenager anymore, Regan. I'm not suggesting you start partying and being reckless, but maybe it's time to remember you're a dominant female, not a submissive maternal."

"So, I should start training like you?" Regan mumbled.

Mia placed a hand on her shoulder, looking her in the eyes. "Only you can decide what *you* look like, and if that's the person you are right now, then that's fine, but I don't think you're fine with that. I'll leave you to be with Megan, but remember, there was once a time you told me as many secrets as you told her."

It was in the early hours of the morning when Regan returned home. She crept through the house, each careful, silent footfall taking tremendous effort. Her legs were like lead weights and her soul even heavier. By the time she reached her bed, Regan could do nothing more than collapse forward, falling to sleep diagonally across the bed. She didn't have the willpower or inclination to change into her pajamas. The day had been hard. She wanted nothing more than for it to end, for every doubt circling her head to quiet, and every emotion pressing against her bones to ease.

Sleep came, but it didn't bring relief, and when she woke the next day, Regan realized she had no choice but to face the music, to change direction. She'd known in the back of her mind that she was walking the wrong path for some time, from before she'd even known the name *Tyler*. Yet that didn't make the realization any easier or mean she knew which direction she should now venture in. The truth was, she'd ignored the inevitable wall she was racing toward because she'd had no idea how to smash through it, or climb over it. Instead, she'd waited until she stood before it, gazing up, feeling very small, and rather lost.

Change wasn't going to be easy, but it was better than hiding, than living the lie she had been since Megan's death. She'd take one small step at a time and hope somehow, she'd find herself again.

CHAPTER 7

Bass rolled over in bed to answer his phone. Katalina groaned beside him, slapping his back as she mumbled, “Make it stop.”

Chuckling, Bass answered with a whispered, “Nic? What’s up?” then climbed out of bed and stepped quietly from their bedroom.

“I was out taking a run after my late shift and came across Tyler on River Run’s side,” Nico explained.

“And?”

“And he was just standing there, Bass, looking like his entire world ended.”

“Has he sensed you?”

“No, and I haven’t approached. This is an alpha situation.”

“Where are you?” Bass asked, his body filling with a killing calm. He had no idea what had happened, but whatever it was, Bass would be keeping his cool.

“He’s not far from the stream cutting along the border. Follow the outer border, then track down the stream. You’ll soon sense him.”

“I’ll be there soon, Nico.”

Bass ended the call and headed back into the bedroom. Pulling on the jeans and T-Shirt he’d discarded before getting into bed, he walked over to Katalina’s sleeping form. “Baby?” he murmured, brushing her hair off her face. "I've gotta go deal with something."

She became alert immediately. "What's wrong?"

"Something's up with Tyler."

"Intruders?"

"No, I don't think so. Go back to sleep, I'll be home as soon as possible."

"'kay, love you."

Bass bent, kissing her softly. "And I you."

Not long after, he reached the stream and picked up Tyler's scent, following the trail until he reached Nico. "Hey," Bass said. "Any movement?"

"No."

"Okay, thanks, Nic. I'll take it from here." Bass placed a hand on Nico's shoulder. "Go get some sleep, pal, you look tired."

Nico smiled, but it didn't reach his eyes. "I don't sleep much these days. Too busy worrying about Olivia."

"Try," Bass urged. "Try." Parting ways, Bass walked the short distance to Tyler. He was staring at the ground, not moving a muscle when Bass approached. "Ty? Tyler are you all right?" he murmured.

Tyler looked up, and Bass studied his gaze but there was nothing there. Tyler was empty, vacant, as if something had stalled his brain.

"Tyler, are you all right?" Bass repeated a little firmer.

His eyes focused, recognition lighting Tyler's features before they filled with rage.

"Hey, Ty? Tyler, what's going on?"

Tyler began to shake.

"Talk to me?" Bass urged, making sure his tone was soft, comforting, his body language open—shoulders rounded, hands up, palms out.

"I thought I found it. I thought I found it," Tyler whispered roughly.

"Found what, Tyler?"

For a moment, the anger on Tyler's face lessened. His mouth opened as if to speak, but then he closed up, his features hardening, body straightening. Head shaking a mere fraction, he replied, "I can't."

Bass braced himself, ready to act on a moment's notice. "I can't make you talk to me, but I'm your alpha, Tyler, your friend, and something has filled you with this unhealthy rage. Anger like that, Ty, it eats at you, turns you into something else. Let me help you."

"I can't," he repeated. It took visible effort, but minutes later, Tyler had reined in his anger; his face and body relaxed, as he eyes softened. "I'm okay," Tyler insisted.

Bass studied him before deciding the danger had passed, and took a step forward. When Tyler didn't react, Bass closed the distance between them and placed a gentle hand on his shoulder. "Are you sure, Ty? You had me a little worried there."

"I'm sure.... I received some news I wasn't ready to hear, but I'll get over it."

"Whatever it is, it's okay if you can't," Bass reassured him. "You can talk to me, or Nico...."

"Really, I'm fine. I don't want to talk about it."

Bass released him. Taking a small step back, he debated whether to push Tyler further, whether not knowing would jeopardize the rest of the pack. Tyler was one of his inner circle, an enforcer. The man had earned Bass's loyalty and trust, yet lately,

Bass was questioning the very foundation on which he stood. Bass wondered how many more snakes laid in the grass waiting to strike. What danger awaited around the corner. But thinking like that wasn't healthy and certainly wasn't in the best interests of his pack, so Bass saw no other option than to trust Tyler, and hoped the man would come to him if the need arose.

CHAPTER 8

Tyler held his breath as Bass studied him.

"I want to respect your privacy, Ty, but I've gotta ask. Does whatever it is that's troubling you endanger Dark Shadow?"

Tyler's chest tightened uncomfortably. Bass had asked the one question that he wasn't sure he could answer truthfully, the one question that highlighted just how a relationship between wolves from both packs could strain the alliance. Because as Tyler gazed at Bass, his allegiance to his alpha was blurred by his feelings for Regan.

Regan's sister had been killed by a Dark Shadow wolf. For all Tyler knew, it could have been one of his friends who'd done the deed, and while Tyler knew Bass didn't condone such cruelty, he also wasn't sure if he'd approve of their relationship anymore. Whether he'd go back on his original word. The complications it would bring could put strain on the alliance. Bass had said be discreet, and Regan's parents' reaction would be anything but… And if there was one thing Tyler was certain of, it was that even with the information Regan had given him, regarding Megan's death, it didn't change anything.

He still wanted her.

He still craved to know her mind, body, and soul.

"No, it doesn't," Tyler answered, not feeling the least bit guilty for the potential lie.

Bass nodded, smiling softly. "Good. Join me for a run."

It wasn't an invitation, so Tyler didn't bother mentioning

he wasn't really in the mood for company. Instead, he forced a smile on his face and dropped the jeans he wore to the ground before shifting into wolf form. Bass did the same, setting off along the river. Tyler wished Regan was accompanying him and not his alpha, but having no choice, he shook his emotions aside and followed.

The run was long and tiring, Bass sticking to a pace that meant when they returned home, Tyler could do nothing more than collapse into bed, his muscles sore from exertion. And while Tyler might not have wanted to join Bass for a run, it did accomplish the very thing he was certain Bass had intended it to do. To tire him out enough that his mind and his body could do nothing but sleep, and for that, Tyler couldn't help but be thankful.

The next night Tyler waited by the stream. A lone wolf waiting in the darkness hoping for his light to return, but Regan didn't come, and as each night passed without her presence, the dark anger in him grew.

It was a week later that Tyler realized the rage inside of him wasn't directed toward Regan's absence but at the nameless killer who'd destroyed their chance before it'd had time to grow. It was that realization that had him hiding in the trees, waiting for Katalina to walk by on her nightly walk with Arne. She wasn't always alone on these walks, but luck was on his side that night.

Dropping from above a good distance ahead so not to scare Katalina, Tyler smiled at the dog that growled the moment he appeared.

"It's all right, boy, come here," he called brightly.

The dog ceased growling but didn't approach until Katalina ruffled his head and whispered something Tyler didn't hear.

"Is there a reason you're dropping from the trees frightening dogs?" Katalina asked as she continued to walk.

"Didn't scare you though?"

"Only for a second, I recognized you before you hit the ground. Still prefer not to meet wolves falling from trees on my walks though." She smiled, her eyes creasing with amusement. "Do you need something, Ty?"

Tyler fell into step beside her, scratching Arne on the head as he rubbed against his legs. "Actually yeah," he admitted, taking a deep breath before explaining, "I need you to find out who in Dark Shadow killed Regan's sister, Megan, and I need you to not tell Bass or Jackson it's me who wants to know."

Katalina stopped. Facing him, she studied him warily. "What? I…" She shook her head. "I was under the impression what happened between you and Regan was a onetime thing. Night of drunken fun and all that."

Her answer had Tyler closing up. He'd expected her out of everyone to understand.

"It was. It's just… it's been weighing on me. That someone in this pack might be wandering around when blood needs to be repaid."

Katalina frowned. "Ty, I'm surprised Regan told you about Megan at all. She didn't tell me until we'd become close friends, and I'm not sure I agree with the whole blood needs repaying thing. We've no idea what truly happened because we weren't there. It was a different time back then."

"Please, Kat, I'm not saying I'm going to do anything with the information. It's just bothering me. I've tried to move past it, but I can't without knowing the truth."

"Then why not ask Bass or Jackson? Why me?"

"Because I don't want to cause any problems between the packs, and risk upsetting people."

"But let me guess, I won't cause the same issues?" Her hands landed on her hips. "You know I sometimes hate being the girl from both packs."

Tyler grinned. "I know you do, but it does come in handy."

Katalina shook her head, a reluctant smile gracing her lips. "I'll think about it, but I'm not promising anything."

Tyler touched her shoulder. "Thanks, Kat, I knew I could rely on you."

"Yeah, yeah. Now disappear and let Arne and I get on with our walk. Unless you care to join us?"

"Actually." He grimaced. "I'm late for my shift."

"Tut, tut, tut, can't promise I won't rat you out to the boss." She smiled playfully. "I think you should run."

Tyler followed the order, laughing as he did. For the first time in a week, he felt just a little lighter; the anger in him soothed, if only for a short while.

CHAPTER 9

The conversation with Tyler weighed on Katalina, enough to have her changing direction and walking off Dark Shadow land and toward Jackson's.

"Come on, Arne, we've got a question to ask."

She wasn't sure she believed Tyler when he said there was nothing between him and Regan, and it wasn't that she'd detected a lie, but that she couldn't quite believe Regan would have told Tyler more than she'd told her. Not unless they were more than just a casual fling. Because up until a few moments before, Katalina hadn't known it was a dark shadow wolf who'd killed Megan. Regan had never explained further than to say she had a twin sister who'd died, and Katalina hadn't questioned as it was clear the subject hurt Regan deeply.

But as she approached Jackson's home, it was all she could think of. What exactly had happened, and was she now friends with the very person who'd robbed someone of her life before it had even had a chance to begin?

"Kat," Jackson greeted as she walked in. "Did I forget you were coming over?"

"No, it was a last-minute decision."

"Oh, good. Was worried I was going senile for a minute."

Katalina laughed. "Hmm... not so sure you're in the clear on that one."

Jackson scowled. "Did you come here for a reason then, or to just insult me?" he grumbled.

"As much as I love a good insult, I actually wanted to talk." Katalina inclined her head toward the door. "Want to walk?"

"I'm not going to enjoy this conversation, am I?" he asked, striding for the door and holding it open for her to exit first.

"Probably not," Katalina admitted. "But look on the bright side, you get to take a stroll with your amazing daughter."

Jackson rolled his eyes, slamming the door closed behind him as he followed her across the grassed land leading to the trees ahead. Katalina eyed him warily, nervous of his reaction to the question she was about to ask.

"Well, I guess there is no easy way to put this so, I'm just going to go right ahead and ask. I'd like to know what happened the day Megan was killed."

Jackson faltered, gazing at her for a moment before speaking, "Megan.... Have you been talking with Regan?"

"Yes," Katalina lied.

"She doesn't talk about her often. That day took away more than just one life. Regan is fundamentally changed. I'm not sure she'll ever heal from the consequences of that day. What did she tell you?"

"Not much, but I couldn't go on not knowing if the person who did it is part of Dark Shadow."

"He's not, and if he was, I'd demand blood. Megan's death was more than just a casualty of war. It had nothing to do with power or land, and everything to do with the joy of killing. Megan wasn't outgoing. She was submissive while her sister dominant. When they hit the rebellious teenage years, Regan got into trouble, and Megan preferred to stay in with a book. I honestly don't think it bothered her. The two were opposites, yet as close as two sisters could be. It was a Saturday night, the usual group had met up for a bonfire and drinks. Nothing new. I'd let it go on long enough to make them feel like kings and queens before sending enforcers to break it up. But on that night, Dark Shadow attacked. The call was sounded. The group weren't stupid and were already on their way home, but as far as I could tell, in the chaos, Regan didn't answer Megan's call, and so Megan went out looking for her sister. Only she never found Regan. His name is Richard. A nasty, narcissistic wolf. He lives for the hunt, for the game, and when he found Megan on her own, he killed her."

"I don't know a Richard," Katalina said quietly. Relief momentarily easing the turmoil rolling through her.

"As far as I know, he left with Castor and the others the day Bass took over. If he ever crosses onto my land again, he won't leave alive a second time, that's for sure."

"God, poor Regan. No wonder she doesn't talk about it."

"She blames herself, and no matter how many times I tell her that's not true, she won't believe me. Regan was on track to becoming a powerful wolf. Instead, she hasn't even finished her training, refuses to fight."

"Yeah, I'd thought she was a maternal." Her heart hurt for Regan and how lost she was.

"She's not though. At her core, she's a dominant wolf, meant to lead not follow. With time, I thought she'd get back on the right track, begin her training, find who she should be, but it's been three years."

"Aren't her parents concerned?" Katalina asked.

"I think they're part of the reason Regan is the way she is. Her parents haven't recovered either. They became overprotective, worried every second Regan isn't with them. It eats at me that I not only failed Megan but her family too."

Katalina paused and, turning toward Jackson, she closed the space between them, wrapping her arms around him, holding him tightly. He stiffened for a second before relaxing and returning the hug. Katalina wondered if he let anyone comfort him, or if he too held all his pain inside like so many others. The wolf inside of her pushed forward, sensing her father's distress and wanting to soothe it with the touch of pack, of family.

"The only person to blame for any of this is Richard. You've done all you can, and you'll be there if or when Regan is ready to remember who she was."

Jackson let out a deep sigh. "You are so much like your mother," he murmured. "Sometimes it's like I can almost touch her."

Katalina pulled back, swallowing the sudden grief lodged in her throat. She didn't often mourn the loss of her birth mother; it was hard to miss a person she'd never met, but there were moments like these that she longed to. That she wished she had more than a just a picture.

"Am I?"

Jackson smiled, his gaze taking on a dreamy look she'd not seen before. "You have her heart."

"Bass says I have a human heart," she answered, beginning to walk again.

"You have her heart, which was made bigger by your human parents."

"Sometimes I think it's my biggest weakness," Katalina admitted quietly, staring at the ground.

Jackson stopped her with a touch of his hand, tilting her chin up so she had no choice but to see the conviction in his eyes as he spoke his next words.

"Never. You are all I hoped for and more. Don't let anyone ever make you feel as if you are less, Katalina. It is us who are less, *us* who must adapt."

She had no words to respond with, only a swirl of emotions awoken inside of her. Katalina often struggled to see Jackson as her father, to connect with him as such, but then he'd say something or look at her a certain way, and it would hit her deep in her soul. Almost painful in the realization she wasn't parentless. She had, in fact, been lucky enough to have four, and one of them was still alive, while the other three she'd carry within her, in memories and heritage.

Katalina took his hand, pulling it down from her chin and squeezing it. "We should get back. I didn't tell Bass where I was going."

He nodded, before squeezing her hand in return and turning on his heel.

"How is that mate of yours? He's not been to bother me in a few days."

"He's busy helping Nico."

"How is the he?"

"His wounds have healed. Though I worry he's going to have wounds of the heart to contend with soon."

"Lady troubles." Jackson chuckled. "Nothing worse."

They reached the house, and Arne clambered up onto the porch, slumping himself down with a huge sigh.

Katalina laughed. "Have I worn you out, boy?"

He gave her a half-hearted tail wag in answer.

"Could you give us a ride?" she asked Jackson.

"Sure," he answered, rolling his eyes. "I swear you love that dog more than Bass."

Katalina nudged him in the side. "Shush, don't tell him."

Laughing in answer, Jackson looked at Arne, then his truck. "Come on then," he huffed, as if the short trip was a hassle.

Katalina hid her smile as she climbed into the truck after her dog. Heart to hearts with Jackson were good, but she much preferred it when they went back to their usual banter. Bickering and teasing were much less emotionally draining.

She'd found the information Tyler had asked for, information that weighed heavy on her heart, yet something inside of her said now wasn't the right time to tell Tyler what she'd learned. That maybe it wouldn't ever be the right time because Regan's past was only hers to tell.

Chapter 10

Each night Regan forced herself not to leave her room. She'd gaze out of her window, eyes scanning the darkness and wondering if Tyler was out there waiting for her, and secretly hoping he was. But she never went to find out, never gave in to the burning desire to track him down, to kiss him again.

It was as if her very soul called for him. As if he had a direct link to the core of herself that she'd tried so hard to bury.

Days merged into weeks and though she knew she had to make a change, she'd not yet figured out how. Mia's words haunted her as much as the echo of Tyler's touch. Regan knew a lot of what she'd said had been the truth: she was living a lie. But was Tyler part of that lie or a small link to who she used to be?

"Regan?"

Regan jumped at the sound of her name been called loudly.

"Sorry, honey, but I called your name three times before you heard me. What's the matter?"

"Nothing, I'm fine," Regan lied. It fell so easily from her lips; she'd told it that many times.

Her mother sighed. "Regan, you are not fine. What's so interesting out of that window?"

Regan turned her gaze back to the dark night. *A blue-eyed wolf.* But instead of mentioning him, Regan asked about another subject she was sure her mom wouldn't be happy about. "Do you ever think I made a mistake giving up on my training?" Regan looked back at her mom as she took so long in answering.

"No."

"That wasn't all that convincing, Mom."

"What's brought this up? Has Jackson said anything to you?"

"No, of course not. He'd never make me train if I didn't want to."

"Do you want to?" her mom asked, so quietly Regan knew she was afraid of the answer.

"I'm not sure. Sometimes, yes, I think I do." *I'm just afraid of what you'll think.*

"You're safer doing what you're doing."

Regan looked back out the window, unable to say her next words to her mother's face. "Yes, but is what I'm doing actually living?" Her frustration grew. It was hard trying to move forward when the people she needed to talk to were as stuck as she was.

"You look very much alive to me, Regan, which is far more than I can say for Megan. I've already lost one daughter. I don't want to lose another."

"The war's over now," Regan whispered. Hurting for her mom's pain, but at the same time angry that she couldn't see what she was doing to the one daughter that was still alive.

"The alliance won't hold," she spat. "Dark Shadow are nothing but a bunch of savages. They'll show their true colors eventually."

Regan's door slammed shut, signaling her mother's departure. She looked at the space her mother had vacated, felt the residue of her hatred and grief, fueling Regan's anger further. Deep down, Regan didn't think her mom truly believed all Dark Shadow were bad; instead, her mom had held onto the hatred like an anchor. She'd used it as a tool to survive, to keep going, and Regan had done the same in a way, but Mia had been right. Megan would never have approved of the way any of them were living. It saddened Regan how lost she and her parents were. Yet she couldn't allow grief to hold her back anymore. Even if that meant leaving her parents behind, stuck in their sorrow and hatred.

Decision made, Regan pulled up her window and leaped to the ground. As she took off into the darkness, time, at last, began to tick forward. It had taken years, and she still had no idea where she was heading, but the important thing was she'd changed course. She'd taken that first small step forward.

CHAPTER 11

Tyler had literally just collapsed onto his bed after a long day and an extra shift on the late afternoon patrol when there was a faint knock at his door. Too tired to even bother moving or scent who it was, Tyler mumbled, "Yeah?"

I'm not doing another shift, he thought as the door opened and closed as quietly as the knock sounded. Tyler forced himself to lift his head and see who'd entered; he'd expected whomever it was to open the door and speak, not silently sneak in.

He did a double take. Sitting up, Tyler rubbed at his eyes just to be sure he wasn't imagining her. "Regan?"

She smiled softly but didn't speak a word.

"Wha—"

"Shush." Regan brought her finger to her lips as she spoke, stepping toward him and climbing onto his bed.

"Bu—"

Tyler's words were cut off as Regan's mouth connected with his. Her body pinned him to the bed, her hips straddling him as her hands pushed him backward. Suddenly fueled with energy as his blood pounded through his veins, hunger stirring in his soul. He'd stopped waiting by the stream, but never once had he given up his hopes of having her again, of seeing her smile, of feeling her soft body on his.

Questions needed to be answered, feelings discussed, but all of it could wait. The whole world could wait for all Tyler cared because she'd come to him. She was here, and in that moment, *his*.

It was the middle of the night when Tyler woke. For a second, he thought he was dreaming; Regan was asleep, her head on his chest, face peaceful and relaxed. Slowly, he ran his fingers through her hair, brushing it softly from her face. She was so beautiful. He'd never met a woman who took his breath away as much as she did. Her skin was pale, like milk, a complete contrast to her midnight-black hair, yet her lips and cheeks had a permanent dusting of rose.

Her nose twitched, and her lips lifted at the corners a faction. "You're tickling me," she whispered.

"Sorry," he whispered back, almost frightened that speaking louder would shatter the illusion.

"What time is it?" she asked quietly.

"3:00 a.m."

She sighed. "I should go before my parents find me missing. That's if they haven't already."

"What will you tell them if they did find you missing?"

Regan was silent for a good few breaths. "If I were brave… the truth."

"And what's the truth, Regan?" Tyler murmured, holding his breath as he waited for the answer.

Her hand found his. "That I like a blue-eyed wolf… a lot, and that I don't care he's from Dark Shadow."

"Don't you?" he asked nervously, holding his breath.

Her eyes opened and found his. Tyler searched her dark-blue eyes for the truth he was afraid of, looking for some shred of hatred she must feel for the pack he belonged to. It had to be there; he hated himself for the death of her sister.

"I thought I did, but I think the truth was, I was using it as an excuse because the way you made me feel scared me. You make me remember the person I used to be, the person I was before I lost my sister."

"I'm so sorry that the pack I belong to did that to you, to her."

She shook her head gently, eyes filling with such sadness it hurt Tyler's heart to see. "It wasn't your fault, Ty. Bass is different. Things are different."

Silence hung between them, their eyes locked, unsaid emotions passing between them before Tyler asked the question he'd needed to know from the beginning, yet feared. If she said a name he recognized, he knew without a doubt, he'd be killing a member of his own pack. Tyler wasn't sure he understood the knowledge, or where it came from, only that it was there. That this fierce protection came from the deepest depths of his wolf.

"He's not in the pack anymore," she whispered. "It doesn't matter who he is."

A he then....

"I need to know."

"Plenty of wolves died in the war between our packs, Ty. Why does Megan's death matter so much?"

"Because you matter."

"Richard. His name is Richard," she whispered.

Relief washed through him and Tyler expelled a breath. He recognized the name. He'd been an enforcer and had left with Castor.

"Will you tell me what happened?" Tyler whispered, brushing his thumb over her cheek.

A single tear slipped from her eye as she squeezed them closed and sucked in a deep breath. "I will but not now. I can't now."

Reaching forward, Tyler kissed the tear away. "Whenever you're ready," he breathed.

"I really need to go," she whispered some time later. She'd been quiet for so long Tyler had thought she'd fallen back to sleep.

It was four o'clock in the morning, he had to be up for work in two hours and had only had a few hours sleep. Not that he regretted the missed sleep.

"What happens from here, Regan?"

Pushing up, she shuffled until she was sat up one hand rested on his chest, the other brushing her hair from her face.

"I can't tell my parents, not yet. They'd never understand, and for all we know you'll be bored of me in a few weeks."

"Not going to happen," Tyler answered, running his hand up her thigh and squeezing. He wished Regan could see the woman he did. Could see just how beautiful and strong she was. It bothered him that she couldn't. Made him determined to show her just what he saw.

"I'm quite boring," she said, trying not to smile.

"Me too." He grinned, in an attempt to lighten the mood.

"I really need to go."

Please don't. "So, you've said." Searching his gaze, Regan closed the space between them and kissed him softly. "Bye, Ty," she murmured.

Tyler watched her climb from his bed, not bothering at all to hide the fact he was watching her as she searched his room for her clothes.

"I'll sneak you home," he said, about to get out of bed.

"Stay," she instructed, holding up a hand. "I used to be quite good at sneaking about."

"Did you?" He lifted a brow, intrigued to know what other secrets she held.

She raised an eyebrow in return. "Let's hope sneaking in here wasn't a fluke."

Her hand landed on the door handle.

"Wait!" Tyler gasped, afraid the entire night had been some incredible dream and he'd never see her again. "When will I see you again?"

She shrugged. "Not sure." With a wink and a wicked grin, Regan slipped from his cabin, leaving Tyler in bed. He was hooked. She was his new favorite drug, and tonight had not nearly been enough. He didn't care when she planned on seeing him again because he'd hunt her down himself. Rolling over, Tyler smiled, sighing happily. *Let the games begin.* He closed his eyes, settling deeper into the sheets that now held her scent. *The fun has just begun. Tomorrow, Regan, I'll be seeing you tomorrow.*

PART TWO

Set after the events of *Wolf Sight*

CHAPTER 12

"This is lovely. We should do this more often," Olivia said, before taking a sip of her latte.

"I agree." Katalina sighed. "I've missed human things."

"Wolves drink coffee," Anna stated.

Olivia giggled, and it was such an unexpected sound Katalina couldn't help staring.

"What?" Olivia asked, blushing from the attention.

"New York suits you," Katalina said.

"I left."

"But it's stayed with you."

"I've changed," Olivia agreed.

"For the better," Katalina assured her, squeezing her shoulder.

"I've never visited New York. I'd love to," Anna added, popping a piece of her muffin into her mouth.

"We should all go. Girls' weekend," Katalina suggested.

"Stop rocking the boat, Kat," Olivia warned.

Katalina's smile turned wicked. "Why? It's my favorite hobby. Do you miss New York?"

Olivia's face turned dreamy, her gaze far away. "Yes, I do. At first, the hustle and bustle frightened me, but after a while, I loved to walk the crowded streets, watching people. Plus, I wasn't the weirdest person there. That's always a bonus. Oh, and the shops! I seriously miss the clothes."

"We should go then," Anna said.

Katalina smiled. Anna hadn't yet fully grasped what she'd let herself in for. Mating a wolf meant a simple girls' trip turned into a total meltdown for all men involved. A few months ago, she'd have probably been able to convince Bass… most likely. But not anymore. Not with the constant attacks and never-ending threats. They'd been lucky to make it out to coffee, and that hadn't been allowed without secret protection.

Shaking her head, Katalina glanced across at Luke, who sat trying to look inconspicuous in the car down the street. To be fair, he wasn't doing a bad job for a recently promoted novice soldier, but he wasn't the only one who'd been training. If Katalina had any hope of ever having any freedom, she had to not only train as her peer wolves had but become better than all of them. Even then she wondered if Bass would ever loosen his hold. How good would she have to be for him to trust she could protect herself?

"Maybe we should start with coffee, and when the guys trust us alone, we'll work up to New York," Katalina suggested.

"How very reasonable of you, Kat." Olivia smiled, nudging her. "What happened to rocking the boat?"

"I've done that enough lately. Bass is going to turn gray from stress at this rate."

"What makes you think they don't trust us?" Anna asked, frowning.

"It's not that they don't trust us." Katalina paused, deliberating how best to explain to Anna. "Our type of men doesn't trust others easily. Leaving us unprotected goes against their natures."

"Do we need protecting at a café?" Anna's frown deepened further.

"Of course not." She sighed. "But if we did, I'm more than capable of protecting us," Katalina added. "They are just being overprotective fools," Katalina shouted.

Anna jumped, looking around. "Who are you yelling at?"

"Kat," Olivia groaned.

"Cage," she explained. "I mean honestly, white? Why are you wearing white?" Katalina continued louder.

Cage stepped from his hiding space, a sheepish smile on his face.

"You were spying on me?" Anna asked, shocked.

"No, not spying," Cage replied as he joined them.

"Well, then what would you call it?" Anna asked, her voice tinged with anger.

"Protecting, I was protecting you," he explained, smiling sweetly.

Not that it worked. Anna didn't sound convinced. "And what exactly are you protecting us from? Hmm, I don't see any danger."

"You're in my world now, Anna. Danger can't be so easily seen."

"Hmm," she huffed. "Well, I don't see Nico and Bass acting like cavemen. We're having coffee for God's sake."

"Actually, Anna, our men are acting just as cavemanish," Katalina said. "It's just Cage was the most obvious. He seems to have forgotten what to wear in his months away." Katalina grinned up at Cage, sticking out her tongue. "Losing your touch."

"Actually, I told him to wear that shirt today," Anna added in his defense, looking guilty.

"Yeah. Was there a reason for that?" Cage asked, disgruntled.

"If you're implying I foresaw you spying on me, and decided to tell you to wear white, then the answer is no. I just like you in that shirt."

"So, where's Nico?" Olivia asked, scanning the vicinity.

"Actually, I haven't spotted Nic yet. But that right there—" Katalina pointed to the car parked down the street — "is Luke."

"Luke?" asked Olivia.

"He's River Run, just moved up in rank. And as for Bass and Nic, well, I can't see them, but I can sense Bass close, so Nico isn't far behind."

Olivia bent down and rummaged in her bag. Retrieving her phone, she swiped the screen and called Nico. "Hey.... Where are you? Really.... Oh, right.... Well, you tell me."

Nico appeared seconds later.

"Busted." Katalina laughed.

Bass followed next; he didn't look pleased.

"I'm not sure why you're looking so disgruntled. It's our girls' outing that's been disturbed," Katalina told Bass as he walked up to her.

"You could have quite easily gone along ignoring us, as you did for the first twenty minutes."

"No, I couldn't. I'm surprised there isn't a hole burned into my back, you've put that many eyes on us," she argued.

"Well, now that everyone is here, you might as well get a drink and pretend to look normal," Anna suggested.

"You should have got changed," Nico grumbled to Cage.

Katalina hid her smile, taking a sip of her tea. "Your mistake, Nic, was allowing Bass to come. I sensed him following us from the moment we left."

"I told you," Nico said, slapping Bass on the back.

"Well, it's too late now. We might as well join them," Bass said. He didn't look that bothered. In fact, Katalina suspected he'd hoped that she'd spot them. Protecting them was far easier when sitting with the person in danger. Not that she was in danger or incapable of protecting herself.

"Yes, stop loitering and sit." Katalina smiled slyly. "Now, what were we talking about? Oh yes, our trip to New York."

All three men snapped to attention, protesting in unison.

Olivia buried her head in her hands, groaning. "You had to go there, didn't you?"

"I don't need to be psychic to know you most certainly do not care about Bass's gray hairs," Anna said.

"I don't have gray hairs!" Bass protested, his hands subconsciously touching his head.

All three girls burst out laughing. Katalina laughed so hard tears formed in her eyes and rolled down her cheeks. Glancing up at Bass, her face hurting from the creases in her cheeks, she nudged him in the side. "We're joking, babe. Don't look so serious."

"Come on, pal, let's go get the drinks. What are you having, Cage?" Nico asked.

"Coffee, black, two sugars," Cage answered.

As Nico and Bass stepped away, Cage's phone pinged. Katalina caught movement out of the corner of her eye. Sitting straighter, she made eye contact with the old man who'd been watching them from the moment they'd arrived.

"What's wrong?" Bass asked Cage, pausing en route to ordering the coffees.

"We've got a tail. Luke says he's been watching the girls since they got here," Cage answered.

Drinks forgotten, Bass and Nico moved to block the girls from view. Katalina climbed to her feet. "Bass, wait."

"Just stay here, Kat, please." Bass sounded tired. Katalina had noticed the tone creeping in far too often lately, and she didn't like it.

"He's human and looks more frightened than aggressive. Maybe this could do with a more human approach." *Not a possessive alpha one.*

"I agree," said Anna, pushing her way to the front. "I've been waiting for him."

"What? Who is he?" Cage asked, grabbing Anna before she could walk off. Katalina was even more intrigued now she knew about Anna's vision.

"I'm not sure. That's what I'm going to ask him," Anna answered, trying to shake Cage off.

"Wait, Anna, sweetheart." Cage moved in front of her and lowered himself so their eyes were level. "Talk to me, honey. What have you seen?"

"Just that someone was looking for us. Well, Katalina to be exact. He needs her help. He means no harm."

Shock rolled through Katalina at Anna's words. She studied the man, wondering just what he needed from her. "Bass," she murmured, taking his hand. "Maybe we could do with his help. Look at his van."

Phillips construction was printed down the side, along with a logo.

"Shall we?" Anna asked, glancing back.

"We'll see what he wants first," Bass instructed, meaning for Katalina and the other girls to stay behind.

"I don't think so," Katalina said, staring Bass down.

"He means us no harm," Anna repeated.

"I trust Anna," Cage said, taking her hand and preparing to move.

"Well, I can't tell you what to do, but Kat, Nic, and Olivia will stay here," Bass instructed.

"Pfft." Katalina scoffed. Stepping forward, she danced out of Bass's reach as he lunged for her. "I'm River Run and Dark Shadow. I don't take orders. I'm Switzerland."

"Kat," Bass growled, going after her.

"We may as well all go. Not like a human is going to do much damage with all of us around," Nico suggested.

"Not got much choice now, have I," Bass grumbled.

Guilt wormed its way into Katalina's mind as Bass joined her. She didn't like been treated like a fragile princess who needed protecting at all times, but that didn't mean she didn't understand where Bass's actions were coming from. It frustrated her. Made her wish for a simpler life with less complications and threats.

The six of them walked toward the man. What remained of his hair was speckled with gray. Katalina pegged him at mid-fifty. The young woman in the van slipped into the driver seat as they approached. The man glanced at her briefly, nodding at her as they spoke a silent message to one another. Katalina didn't for one-minute think that the man meant them any harm. If anything, he looked like he thought he was the one in danger. The young woman also looked frightened. Her knuckles were white as she gripped the steering wheel while the engine idled, ready to leave at a moment's notice.

Katalina couldn't understand what he was frightened of. To anyone else, they were just six young adults. He couldn't possibly know how dangerous they truly were.

"Hello," Anna said before anyone else had chance to speak. "You've been looking for us?"

Yeah, not the human touch I was thinking of. Katalina shook her head, smiling slightly. Anna's innocent hello didn't calm the man much. In fact, he looked even more terrified.

"I… well."

"How about we start with hello, I'm Katalina, and you are?" Katalina said.

"T-Tim, and that's my daughter, Eva." Tim gestured toward the woman in the van.

Bass tensed beside Katalina. He expected the worst from people, and Katalina couldn't blame him. The caution was warranted after recent events, but she couldn't quite bring herself to be afraid. She had no idea what he wanted, but she was certain it wasn't a fight.

"What can we do for you, Tim?" Bass asked, voice cool, face impassive.

Tim visibly gulped. "Are, are… you the one in charge?"

"Katalina is the one who can help you," Anna said, smiling helpfully, with a faraway look on her face that Katalina had already gotten used to. Though she didn't quite appreciate her words at that moment. Dread was slowly building inside of Katalina as she speculated at just what Tim wanted.

"Honey, I'm not sure you're helping," Cage said, wrapping his arm around her shoulder and bringing her close.

"Well… I…. How about I just show you?"

"Show us what?" Bass asked.

Tim gestured toward the back of the van, stepping toward the rear doors.

Katalina then heard what she'd missed over the rumble of the engine, the heavy breathing and scrape of what she was sure were claws. Her eyes widened as she glanced at Bass. "We'll stay here," she whispered, reaching out for Anna.

Anna frowned at her as Cage nudged her in Katalina's direction.

"Kat will keep you safe," Cage murmured.

"I don't need keeping safe," she mumbled.

Bass, Nico, and Cage followed Tim to the van. He eyed them for a second, sweat clear on his brow, then opened the doors.

"Well, shit," Nico swore.

Anna broke free and ran to Cage.

"Anna," Katalina gasped, reaching for her.

Anna went into Cage's arms and peered around the doors. "Well, I didn't foresee this."

Katalina looked to Bass. On his nod, she moved closer and looked in the van. There, in a cage, was a small wolf, fur dull and matted. It looked crazed. Its snarl was savage as it took them in.

How am I supposed to help with this?

"Is it wild?" Katalina asked quietly.

"No, it's bitten," Bass said. "And out of control by the looks of it."

"Can you help?" Tim asked.

"How did you get it in the cage?" Nico asked.

"Him. He's my son, Zackary. And he put himself in the cage."

My God.

"When did he last take human form?" Bass asked.

Katalina was out of her depth. She had no knowledge of bitten wolves, or how to help them.

"A week ago, maybe, but not for very long. He's been a

bit… wild since being in the cage. I was afraid to let him out."

"Not surprising. It goes against the wolf's nature. I'm shocked he went in, in the first place," Bass said.

Poor thing. Katalina studied the wolf, the desperate, crazed look in his eyes, and filled with sorrow. Hurt for the boy trapped inside the wolf's mind.

"He attacked me. He felt he had no choice." Katalina spun around as Eva spoke. She'd been so engrossed by the cage that she'd not noticed the sound of her door opening. A mistake she didn't intend to make again.

"I told you to stay in the car," Tim gasped, rushing toward his daughter.

"Where?" Bass asked, directing his gaze to Eva.

"Where, what?"

"Where did he attack you? Were you injured?" Bass explained further.

Eva lifted her arm, the underside of which were covered with gauze. "He threw a glass at me. It shattered, some of the glass cut me. I'll live."

"So, he wasn't in wolf form? He hasn't scratched or bitten either of you in wolf form?" Bass questioned.

"No, why?" Tim asked.

"Because that is how the gene is often passed on. A simple scratch isn't often enough, but a serious injury where flesh is exposed is another story."

"W-we could become one as well?" Eva asked quietly.

"Yes. It is a good thing Zackary volunteered for the cage. Otherwise, it is highly likely you'd have both been injured, or worse," Bass explained. "But what I don't understand is why and how you found us?"

Katalina thought it was obvious why Tim had found them. He clearly loved his son, so much so he hadn't freaked out by him shifting forms and instead had locked him in a cage, managing to track down the very kind he hoped would help. But she kept her mouth shut, because as much as it pained her, Bass was alpha, and she needed to show him respect.

"Isn't it obvious? He needs your help?" Tim said, his eyes widening.

"I'm not sure what you think it is I can do? Putting him out of his misery would be kinder."

"Bass," Katalina hissed, hitting his arm. "Have a little sensitivity."

Once the initial shock of Bass's words wore off, Tim moved to the van doors and closed them, spreading his arms out as if to shield his son.

"I'm sorry, Katalina, but we have enough on our plate without bringing a bitten rogue onto our lands. Where would we even put him? He can't be allowed to run free. The state he's in he'd attack half the pack, and if you've forgotten, we're not exactly overflowing with living arrangements at the moment."

Bass was right, she knew that. Yet it didn't seem right to turn him away, or lessen her frustration at Bass's lack of compassion.

"How did you find us?" Bass asked again. He had on his cool, calm mask, but Katalina could feel the tension vibrating below his skin. Bass had stopped talking to her, and she didn't like the fact that he had. Katalina suspected Bass was feeling overwhelmed with all his responsibilities and he was taking the attack on Dark Shadow as his own fault. He didn't need the added stress, but she also couldn't turn Tim away. Plus, Anna had said she was meant to help Zachery, and Katalina believed in Anna's gift.

"It was a fluke," Tim said, looking frightened again.

"You're not another elaborate trap?" Bass ground out.

God, I'd never even thought of that!

"It's not a trap, Bass. He's meant to help you. Just as you are meant to help him," Anna assured.

"And what exactly did you see, Anna? More cryptic bullshit?" Bass snapped.

"Hey!" Cage growled, moving in front of Anna. "Take that back before I make you!" Anger hummed through Cage, vibrating through tensed muscles into clenched fists.

Damn it. Katalina moved between Bass and Cage. The two had been getting along since Cage's return but Bass wasn't acting like himself. His mask had slipped. She'd never seen it slip. "A little help here, Nic," she rasped, putting two hands on Bass's chest. "Hey, look at me," she growled. "That was uncalled for."

After another few tense seconds, Bass's gaze dropped to hers and his face relaxed. "You're right." Bass looked up. "I'm sorry, Cage, Anna. I shouldn't have said that."

Katalina breathed a sigh of relief, then turned back around. Nico moved back from Cage's path. Tim had watched the whole exchange with wide, fearful eyes.

"I-I s-swear I found you myself. I've been looking for weeks for some sign that others like you exist. We were going to move on today. I didn't see any wolves in the week here, and then I saw her," Tim glanced at Katalina.

"And how exactly did I make you think I was a wolf?" Katalina asked, surprise flitting through her.

"I'm not sure.... I was desperate. It's your presence. You're always on alert. The other two sat relaxed chatting, but you, you had at least half of your concentration on your surroundings, and you noticed me the second you arrived. Most teenage girls aren't looking out for danger."

So, I'm not as subtle as I'd first thought. Her face must have dropped because Tim added, "I only noticed because I was looking. For anything really. I knew for sure you were different when these three turned up. You're not like teenagers at all, more like bodyguards."

Katalina laughed quietly.

"I'm sorry, but we still can't help you. Maybe we could have a few months ago, but now is not the best time," Bass said.

"We'll put him in the barn at Jackson's," Katalina suggested. "That's secure enough."

"That is not my call," Bass answered.

"No, it's Jackson's, and he won't say no to me," Katalina said triumphantly.

Nico laughed. "First time for everything."

"Yes. But that day will not come today. It's far off in the future," Anna added.

"Really, what does he say no to?" Katalina asked.

Anna smiled knowingly. "Some things aren't meant to be said, Kat."

"If you say so," Katalina grumbled.

"Are you one too?" Tim asked Anna quietly.

"A wolf? Oh God, no. I'm psychic." She smiled brightly.

"Psychic… right." Tim looked a little more concerned.

"Okay, well, Cage, do your thing," Katalina said.

"Me? I thought you were calling him?" Cage answered.

"I will if I need to, but I'm obviously using up all my 'you abandoned me' guilt, so we'll try the normal way first."

Cage smirked, then stepped away to make the call. He returned ten minutes later. "That took some convincing. I think I just used up the last of my 'you promised me your daughter and she dumped me' guilt."

"Ha! That so isn't a thing, and you've met Anna. If it was a thing, it shouldn't be now," Katalina said.

"Whatever." Cage pulled a face. "He's at home. I said we'd see him soon. Anna, you can go in the car with Luke." Cage pointed to the car down the street.

"Kat, go with Anna and Luke. C—" Bass instructed. He then paused, his mouth opened as if to speak but didn't.

Cage made eye contact with Bass for the barest of seconds, then looked away. Katalina inwardly sighed. Everyone was trying hard to find their footing within the pack alliance, but it wasn't easy, and it wasn't always in the wolf's nature, especially Bass's. Pausing instead of giving Cage an instruction must have taken a lot of effort. Katalina took his hand and squeezed, silently telling him she loved him for trying so hard for her.

"Go ahead," Cage said quietly. Katalina met his gaze and smiled.

"Cage, lead on foot, Luke next, then I'll follow the van behind." Bass turned and met Nico's eyes. "Take Olivia home."

Nico nodded his agreement.

"That all right with you?" Bass asked Cage.

"Yup. Come on, Anna. I'll walk you to the car," he replied.

"Is it far?" Tim asked.

"No, not far," Katalina answered.

"Okay, Eva, get in," Tim instructed.

Once Tim and Eva were in the van, Katalina focused her attention on Bass. He was having a quiet word with Nico. She caught the tail end of it, "...stay alert, just in case. Make sure everyone takes it seriously."

"On it, Bass. For what it's worth, I believe the guy," Nico said.

"I do too. But I won't make a mistake again."

"You haven't made any mistakes, Bass," Nico insisted.

"I've made many," Bass said sadly.

Katalina bit off her reply. He wouldn't listen, no matter how many times she told him Indiana's attack wasn't his fault. It worried her the amount of responsibility he was putting on his shoulders. That he held himself to such high expectations. Everyone made mistakes; it was a part of being human.

Chapter 13

After kissing Bass goodbye, Katalina walked over to the car. Anna and Cage were having a hushed conversation, which ceased when she neared.

"Talking about me?" Katalina asked.

Cage ignored the question, and when Anna had climbed into the car and closed the door, he gave her an instruction. "Keep her safe, Kat."

"We'll be right behind you, Cage."

"She's my heart, Kat, and we live in uncertain times."

Katalina's chest tightened; she loved seeing this side to him. The vulnerable, breakable side that only Anna brought out in him. "I'll protect her with my life if I have to."

Cage frowned. He opened his mouth to say something, but Katalina spoke before he had the chance. She understood the confliction on his face, the sudden shift in expression. He was at war with himself. Anna was his mate, but Katalina was his alpha's daughter. "Cage, Jackson would never ask me to leave those weaker than myself in order to save my life. It's not who I am. So please don't feel wrong about asking me to protect her. Okay?"

Cage smiled softly and cupped Katalina's cheek. "You're important, Kat. Never forget that. You're more than just his daughter. You are the link."

Katalina didn't like the direction this conversation was heading. She had a hard enough time with being an alpha's mate and daughter. "Then it's a good job I'm tough," she said brightly, opening the car door. "Go and do your job, or Bass will start complaining."

"I make it my daily mission to irritate your mate," he said with a wink, then jogged away.

Jackson was waiting for them out front of the barn when they arrived. His face held his usual expression—like everything Katalina did was a hassle. "What trouble have you found for us this time, daughter?"

Katalina smiled darkly. "Wishing you hadn't had me yet?"

"Never," he replied without pause.

"I must try harder then."

Jackson shook his head, trying to contain a smile. "You'll be the death of me, girl."

Tim had backed the van up to the barn door. Cage opened the barn and looked to Jackson for instruction.

"So, we're taking in strays now, Bass?" Jackson asked.

"Don't blame me. This is your daughter's and Anna's doing, not mine."

"Anna's?" Jackson turned, finding Anna. "Did you see something?"

"Just that he needed Katalina's help," Anna answered.

"Well then, let's get him out."

Tim, who'd been quiet up to this point, opened the van doors and stood back. He watched as the cage was lifted with his son inside with a mixture of hope and horror on his face.

"So, you can help him?" Tim asked Jackson. "I mean… You're the a-alpha right?"

Katalina's heart lurched unevenly. *Why do I keep finding more trouble for them?* Bass and Jackson got along pretty well considering their history. She wasn't sure whether they liked each other or whether they just cooperated for her sake. It wasn't something she liked to think about; enough people had changed for her.

Jackson glanced at Bass before answering. "One of them, yes."

"There's more than one?" Tim asked.

"There's more than one pack, yes," Jackson said.

Tim didn't look any less confused. Katalina jumped in before tensions rose. "Right now, you are on Jackson's land. Cage and Anna are his pack. I'm Jackson's daughter, but I'm mated to Bass. He's alpha of the other pack. We're allies."

"Mated, as in married?"

"In shifter terms, yes."

Tim nodded, but Katalina wasn't convinced he understood the situation, and she couldn't blame him. After all, she was still getting used to the shifter world, and she'd been here months.

Bass and Jackson put the cage down at the back of the barn. Zackary was snarling and snapping at the bars. He didn't look as if there was any humanity left in him.

"How we are playing this?" Jackson asked, stepping back and eyeing Zackary. "He yours or mine?"

"W-what do you mean?" Tim interrupted.

"Well, if we've any chance of reaching your kid, we've first got to control the wolf. To do that, he needs an alpha and a pack if he's going to survive this," Jackson explained.

"He won't ever be able to go home?" Tim gasped, the color draining from his face. "What about school? He's fourteen. He's got his whole life ahead of him."

“Let’s worry about that later. Right now, we need to establish whether there is a part of your son left to save.” Jackson turned his attention back to Bass. “So, yours or mine?”

“He’s on your land,” Bass began.

“Actually, if I could just interrupt, Zackary belongs to Dark Shadow,” Anna stated.

Bass sighed softly before turning to look at Anna. “My plate is quite full, Anna. Does it really make much difference?”

“Katalina is the one who can get through to him,” Anna said, as if that explained everything.

“Kat’s connected to both packs, Anna. So I don’t see the issue. I can take him,” Jackson said.

Anna’s determination amazed Katalina. It had been present from the moment they’d met. She followed her gift blindly into danger, always having faith that it was meant to be. If someone protested what she saw as the right way, she wouldn’t let it go. This time was no different.

“Katalina’s wolf draws its strength from Bass at the moment. She is connected to both, but for this occasion, she will need the strength Dark Shadow gives her, not River Run.”

And here I was thinking Dark Shadow brought me nothing but anxiety.

They all stared at her, and Katalina wondered what they saw. She didn’t often feel strong. Mostly she felt as confused as Tim. Cracking under the scrutiny, Katalina plastered a smile on her face and moved toward the cage. “Well then,” she said overly cheerful, “welcome to Dark Shadow, Zac, let’s get you out this cage, shall we?”

“Actually, Katalina, I think it’ll be best to open the cage with just me present,” Bass instructed.

“Oookay, let’s clear the barn then,” she replied.

Chapter 14

Bass eyed the wolf who foamed at the mouth as he snapped at the bars like he intended to eat him for lunch. He wasn't afraid. Zackary wouldn't get near enough to take a chunk from him. What he was, was tired. Tired of fighting for a simple life. Tired of letting his mate down. Of letting his pack down. He only wanted to give them a better life, one with the simple human joys his father had despised. One where everyone felt welcome and accepted. But mostly, Bass was tired of himself.

He hadn't realized it, but some of his father's arrogance had worn off on him over his life. He'd seen his father's death and Dark Shadow's takeover as the only option to bring Katalina happiness. He'd promised he'd change their world. But what had changed? They were still at war but just with another pack. Changes had been made, fear had slowly been leaving his packmates, but it had taken one stupid mistake to bring it all crashing down.

Bass had never doubted himself before. He'd never felt lost or out of control. His mask had been an easy thing to wear for as long as he could remember, so why did he feel as if it was slowly draining the life from him?

"You're not going to make this easy for me, are you?" Bass asked the crazed wolf. "Hmm? I mean, why would you? Nothing else in my life is simple, so why would I think this would be?" Snapping his mouth shut, Bass glanced back at the doors and worried if anyone had heard him talking.

"Get it together, Bass," he muttered to himself. "You don't need to be Sabastian Evernight. Plain old Bass is good enough for Kat, so it's going to have to be good enough for everyone else."

He flicked the latches, and the cage door crashed down.

Zackary came barreling out and, as Bass suspected, went straight for him. He was small and nimble, his thin scraggily appearance not showing any of the boy's true potential. Jumping out of the way, Bass spun and waited for the wolf's next attack.

"I suppose"—Bass slid to the right, dust from the ground creating a cloud around them— "you'll bring a little more humanity into my pack," he continued. Zackary leaped for him again. Bass stood his ground and snarled. His foot connected with Zackary, which sent the young wolf tumbling to the ground. "That's if you have any left."

Bass's snarled, allowing all of the dominance of his wolf forward in his mind, but it had little effect on Zackary. While the wolf got to his feet, Bass quickly dropped his jeans. His shirt fell to the ground next as he again maneuvered out of Zackary's way.

Shifting, Bass met Zackary head on. They slammed into each other, but Zackary went down. Bass's growl echoed around the barn, his teeth found Zackary's throat, and although he didn't bite down hard enough to break skin, it was enough of a warning for Zackary to freeze. Releasing him, Bass rose above him as Zackary cowered, a low, deadly rumble building in his chest. The growl Bass unleashed, vibrated through his own bones, yet it wasn't enough to make Zackary shift back.

It wasn't a good sign, but Bass would give the boy a few days to calm down. He'd been trapped in a cage for weeks. It would have made anyone crazed. Turning, Bass left Zackary cowering on the ground and padded over to his jeans. He shifted, keeping the boy in sight, just in case he was stupid or crazy enough to have another attempt at hurting him.

But the boy made no attempts to move, merely watched him with wild wolf eyes. Slipping from the barn, his shirt in his hands, his jeans covered in dust, Bass came face-to-face with many hopeful eyes. He met Jackson's first out of respect and because he, out of all of them, already understood Zackary's chances weren't good. Bass shook his head slightly, letting Jackson know the outcome.

"He respond at all?" Jackson asked.

"Only when I shifted and put him in his place," Bass answered.

"What does that mean?" Tim snapped. "Did you hurt my boy?"

"Not as much as he intended to do to me."

"He's a kid," he shouted.

"Not anymore," Bass answered, his voice hard but level. He hadn't needed to raise his voice; several low growls had sounded at the same time as his answer. Bass hid his smile and glanced quickly at Katalina. Did she realize her father and several other wolves had reacted in his defense, another alpha's defense?

Do you realize the power you hold, my Winter Wolf? Of course, you don't, you never have.

With each day their world shifted, their packs became ever more intertwined. Two alphas getting along; it was unheard of. Yet, both Jackson and Bass suppressed their base instincts for Katalina. Because she mattered more than their animals' need to be on top. She mattered more than anything.

"You need to accept the possibility that the son you once knew may never come back. Your loving, reasonable boy has changed forever."

Eva, who'd stayed silent and out of the way since arriving, laughed bitterly from her position leaned against the front of the truck.

Bass paused and gazed at her.

"Eva!" Tim scolded.

"What was so funny?" Bass asked.

"The loving, reasonable part."

Tim's face grew red as he snapped at Eva. "Stay out of this!"

"What does she mean?" Katalina asked, attempting to catch Tim's attention, but he was avoiding her, avoiding them all.

"I mean, my brother wasn't exactly a saint," Eva piped up.

"He's been through a lot," Tim said in his defense.

Eva pushed off the truck, the first bit of real emotion passing over her since they'd met. "I lost her too, Dad! She was my mom too, and I didn't feel the need to drown in drink and drugs." Turning on her heel, she stormed to the van and wrenched open the door. No one said a word until her door slammed shut.

"I think we need to hear the whole story," Katalina said softly.

Tim looked from his daughter to them and then spoke to the floor. "My wife, their mother died from cancer four months ago. Zac didn't take it very well."

"That's to be expected," Katalina said.

"Yes… but Eva's right. Zac started drinking at all hours. He was hanging out with older kids and I never knew where he was. When I found drugs, he didn't even care that I knew he was using. I guess he didn't care about much after losing his mom. He came home late one night, bleeding. This great tear in his side. I wanted to take him to the hospital, but he was so out of it, and I didn't want him to get into any more trouble. You've got to understand, he was a good kid before all of this, always tried hard in school, respected his mother and me…. Come morning, his wound didn't seem so bad, and he said he was sorry about everything. I really believe he meant what he said, but then later, he just lost it… over nothing. He ran out the house, didn't come back until dark. When he did, he was sweating, and his wound had more or less healed. He kept telling me to help him, then he just, well, he turned, right in front of me into… into a wolf."

Silence hung in the air. Bass wasn't sure what he felt, the practical half of him wanted to go into the barn and put the boy out of is misery. The other half, the half that had also lost a mom and knew the grief it could cause, that half wanted to help Zackary no matter how long it took.

It was Anna who broke the silence. "Your son will get over this. Katalina will help him."

Katalina looked at him in alarm. "Kat isn't going anywhere near him until he's gained some control."

"Agreed," Jackson said.

It wasn't always they agreed, but when it came to Katalina's safety, Jackson and Bass were on the same page.

"Cookie anyone?"

Bass let out a breath and turned toward Karen. She was on the porch of Jackson's house, a tray of cookies in her hands.

"I've made a pot of coffee and tea also," she added, gesturing for them to move.

"Good idea," Katalina said. "Tim, does Eva want to join us?"

"I'll go see."

Bass wrapped an arm around Katalina's shoulders and tucked her against his side. Kissing her face, he asked, "You okay?"

She sighed. "I love Anna," she whispered. "But God, I wish she'd keep her all-knowing wisdom to herself sometimes."

"Zac isn't your responsibility."

"Isn't he? I kinda of made him just that, didn't I? Me and my big mouth," she grumbled.

Bass laughed softly. "Your big heart, you mean."

"Yeah, that gets me into trouble too."

CHAPTER 15

Sneaking from Dark Shadow to River Run had become somewhat of a habit for Tyler. It wasn't one he was proud of, and he dreaded to think of the outcome if he were caught, yet he continued, day after day, night after night. At first, it hadn't been that often but as time went on, Tyler found himself sneaking out every night, and even that wasn't quenching his thirst.

Adrenaline coursed through him as he slipped under the cover of darkness through the trees and across the River Run-Dark Shadow border. Doing so wasn't considered wrong anymore. Though many didn't dare do so, more and more of the Dark Shadow pack were becoming accustomed to using River Runs land to run on, as they did their own. Yet Tyler wasn't using River Run's land for running. His intentions involved an open bedroom window and the gorgeous girl lying between warm sheets waiting for him.

Dashing from tree cover, Tyler moved on silent feet and made the jump upward toward her window. Fingers finding a hold in the wood slats, his foot found traction and pushed off the bracket holding the drainpipe to the wall. Within seconds, he climbed onto her window ledge and rolled with a soft thud into her room.

Springing to his feet, Tyler froze, listening for any movement inside the house. When he picked nothing up, his gaze fell on Regan, her bare shoulders visible beneath the thick duvet, midnight black hair spilling out over white sheets. Her skin was pale, her frame slight, and the scent of her in his lungs sent his wolf wild. Tyler had never anticipated one night of drunken fun to turn into an addiction. Yet here he was, standing in her bedroom while her parents slept down the hall.

His conscience grew heavier each day, yet he continued to come anyway. He'd tried to tell Bass a hundred times, the words always on the tip of his tongue. Surely his alpha would understand; he was mated to a River Run wolf himself. But his fear that Regan's parents wouldn't understand, that their relationship would cause Regan more pain when she'd already suffered enough, had the words dying in his throat.

He was lucky her parents were submissive. That their place within the pack wasn't based in defense. Had Regan's parents been dominant, there wasn't much of a chance at all he'd get in and out undetected. As it was, Regan was washing her sheets almost daily for fear they'd scent him on them. It wouldn't last. Someday soon, someone would notice, but until that time, Tyler would continue to come—feeding his addiction and praying for another day, another second.

She was asleep tonight. He'd had to work overtime on patrol. Since the recent attacks, everyone was on alert, and that meant the stronger members of the pack putting in extra work to make sure they were safe. He pulled his T-shirt over his head and dropped it to the floor, then unbuttoned his jeans and dropped them too. Padding over, Tyler gently climbed into her bed, sliding between the sheets and up against Regan's warm body. She didn't wake, but instinctively shifted so that she was cradled perfectly against him, like two pieces of a jigsaw fitting together. Kissing her on the curve of her neck, Tyler stroked her hair out of his way then wrapped his arms around her, holding her tightly. She murmured softly in her sleep, her arms interlocking with his, and as his tired muscles relaxed, the heat of her body seeping into him, Tyler nodded off, content, even though he was living on borrowed time.

"Ty. Tyler?"

Her soft words roused him, but he didn't open his eyes or move, he was far too comfy for that.

She giggled quietly, placing delicate kisses over his face.

"Come on, lazy bones. I know you're awake."

"I don't want to be," he murmured, refusing to move.

"My parents will be awake soon," she warned.

"I don't care." Tyler pulled her down and pinned her against him, wrapping his arms tightly around her so she couldn't move.

"Me neither," she whispered. "I'll call them in now, so you can meet them for the first time in your boxers with an erection."

Tyler snapped open his eyes. Her smile creased her cheeks, the twinkle in her gaze doing things to his insides. "You wouldn't dare."

"You're right. I wouldn't. I'm not one for brave and daring anymore."

"I'm pretty certain," he said, kissing her nose, "that allowing me into your bed each night—" He kissed her cheek. "—is classed as brave and daring," he finished, kissing her other cheek.

"Or stupid and reckless," she answered quietly.

"Brave and daring," he whispered, closing his mouth over hers.

Getting lost in her wasn't hard. Kissing Regan made time stand still. As his hands skimmed her body, and their mouths and limbs entwined, all thought of her parents left him. He didn't think of the ticking clock toward sunrise, or the early morning shift he'd promised to cover for John. His entire being was focused on Regan; the soft sounds she made in the back of her throat when he touched her just right, the silkiness of her hair between his fingers.

She was dragging his boxers down, her movements frantic and desperate when the sound of a creaking floorboard from her parents' room had Tyler snapping back to reality. Their wide gazes met as his heart boomed in his ears, fear dousing all traces of lust.

"Ty?" she whispered, terrified.

Jumping from her bed, Tyler pulled his boxers back into place and haphazardly dragged on his jeans while snatching up his discarded T-shirt from the floor. He moved swiftly to the window, each step not making a sound, and eased the frame up. Pausing for only a second, Tyler scanned the immediate area outside of Regan's home then leaped, landing nimbly in a crouch before racing into the trees.

Looking back, Regan could be seen watching him from her bedroom window. A pang of sorrow hit him; he didn't want to do this anymore. Running away from her each morning as if she was a dirty secret was wrong, but his fear of being denied her overruled all other emotion. Their packs might have an alliance, but interpack mating blurred lines Tyler wasn't sure they were ready for, add in Megan's death and Regan's parents dislike of Dark Shadow, and it made their situation impossible. Swallowing his pain, Tyler smiled before blowing Regan a kiss and melting into the trees.

He was thirty minutes late by the time he arrived at the handover point for his shift on patrol. His heart sank when it was Bass waiting for him, expression angry and gaze stern.

"Please tell me you have a good reason for being late," Bass said in place of a greeting.

Tyler grimaced. There was no way he'd tell Bass the truth. "I overslept," he offered, shrugging.

Bass didn't look impressed. "If I were my father, you'd be hung, drawn, and quartered for this, Ty. We're at war. Oversleeping isn't allowed."

"I know. I'm sorry, Bass. I swear it won't happen again."

"Make sure it doesn't. I'm not my father, but lately, I'm beginning to understand how he managed to fall so far from the path."

Bass walked away, leaving Tyler with an uneasy feeling in the pit of his stomach. Being late for patrol when they were attacked not so long ago wasn't good, yet Tyler sensed Bass's mood was caused by far more than that.

"Bass?" he called.

"Hmm?" Bass answered, half turning.

"Everything all right?"

Silence followed. Bass stood rigid. "Just do your job, Ty," he answered, forlorn.

CHAPTER 16

With a deep sigh, Regan turned away from her window and began to strip her bed of its sheets. Her parents hadn't emerged from their bedroom yet, so with a bit of luck, she'd get her bedding in the washing machine and be the first in the shower.

Regan allowed the hot water to wash away the heavy feeling in her stomach, taking far longer in the bathroom than she needed. That done, she exited the bathroom dressed and ready for her day. She had an afternoon shift at a local café where she'd worked for the last year, so her morning would be spent studying. At one point in her life, she'd wanted to go away to college—leave the shifter world behind for a while and see what it was like to not have to live in fear of attack. But since her sister's death, she'd changed yet another plan; instead, she was studying online for accounting and finance degree.

"Morning," her mom said brightly as Regan entered the kitchen. "Tea or coffee?"

"Coffee please," Regan answered.

Heading for the bread bin, she took out two slices and put them in the toaster. Her mom handed her a mug of milky coffee seconds later, and she sipped the warming liquid as she waited for the toast to pop.

"Do you need a lift to work later?" her mom asked.

"Yeah, please, if you don't mind."

"Of course not. I need to go to the store later, so it's not a problem. 2:00 p.m., right?"

Regan's stomach flipped. She was starting work at two, but she'd made plans to meet Tyler at half past one before her shift started. "No, actually, one of the girls needs to leave early so I said I'd cover. Could you drop me off at one fifteen?"

"Sure."

"Thanks, Mom."

Regan turned her back to her mom, facing the toaster. It wasn't just the lying that bothered her; it was how easily she did it. At fifteen, she'd lied guilt free. She kind of missed those days. They made life a whole lot simpler.

"I'm going to take my breakfast upstairs, get an early start on studying," Regan explained, as she took her coffee in one hand and buttered toast in the other.

Regan didn't look back as she left. She already knew what she'd see on her mom's face. And it was becoming harder and harder to live with.

CHAPTER 17

Tyler was well aware he was going to be late to meet Regan, but while the thought was in his mind, he wasn't allowing it to control him. He should have finished his session with the dominant teens in the pack thirty minutes ago, but two of the boys had clearly had a falling out, and while this wasn't abnormal behavior for teenagers, shifter teenagers sometimes took a bit of guidance so that the temperamental wolf didn't solve the situation with violence.

Tyler had set a task that required teamwork and a lot of effort. He'd then divided them off into pairs, putting the two boys with grievances together. The winning pair got to accompany him on a night patrol, and while that might not seem like much of a prize to some, dominant teens jumped at the chance to feel strong and important.

The winning pair had already finished, but second place was going to be close. Tyler watched the boys who'd started the obstacle course with hostile glares and no teamwork, begrudgingly work together so they wouldn't come last. The final part required one person to boost them up and on top of a wall, then the other to pull the person on the ground up and onto the wall with them. There were three walls, and the last two pairs were neck and neck on the middle wall.

"Come on! Come on, you can do it, Max!" yelled Cooper from the sidelines.

Max gritted his teeth, dragging Cory up the wall in one tug. The boys scrambled over, leaping to the ground and springing to their feet for the wall. They had the lead by seconds.

"Go, go, go!" Tyler yelled, clapping his hands to cheer

them on.

Cory bent over near the base of the wall as the other team ran for the last hurdle. Max ran, jumping and using Cory's back as a base to propel himself up. In seconds, he was straddling the top and reaching down for Max.

Tyler couldn't call it; the pairs were so close together.

Max and Cory hit the ground a second in front of the other team. The boys jumped to their feet racing for the finish line, but Max tripped going down on one knee.

"Awww!" Cooper cried from the sidelines.

A grin spread over Tyler's face; his tactic had worked. Instead of leaving Max behind, Cory turned back, dragging him upright, and they both raced for the finish line, arm in arm, helping each other along, winning by a spilt-second.

The teens burst into cheers, and Tyler gave high-fives all around.

By the time he'd finished up with the group, he had five minutes to get to the meeting point, which was a fifteen-minute drive away, and signing out a pack car could take as long as that as well. For a second, he thought about texting Regan that he couldn't make it, but his need to see her, if only for a few minutes, was a desperate thing.

Tyler – Regan, I'm running late. Be as quick as poss xo

Deciding to ditch the car, Tyler instead took off at a run, dashing through the trees. His wolf at the surface, he let the animal inside of him take over in every way but skin. When he reached a point where it was no longer safe to run at wolf speed, Tyler slowed to a jog, arriving at Regan's work fifteen minutes late, which meant they only had fifteen minutes together instead of thirty.

"Hey," Regan breathed, flinging her arms around him as she opened the back door to the café she worked at. "I didn't think you were going to make it."

“Sorry, babe,” Tyler rasped, panting from exertion. “Had a few issues to sort before I could leave.”

“Everything okay?” she asked, pulling back to gaze into his eyes.

“Yeah, just boys being boys really. Fourteen to sixteen is a tough age.”

“They're learning from the best.” She smiled, then pressed her lips to his, and for just a few moments, Tyler thought of nothing but Regan and the feel of her lips on his.

“God, I missed you,” he whispered as she pulled away.

“You saw me this morning,” she said with a giggle.

“I know,” he sighed.

“Come on,” Regan said, taking his hand, “Come inside, and I'll fix you something to eat before my shift starts.

Tyler followed her inside, speaking as he went, “I don't want to waste our time together eating.”

“You need to eat, Ty.” She frowned. “Besides, I like feeding you. It's my job to make sure you're fed and happy.” Her words sent a wave of warmth from his heart. He'd happily spend the rest of his life only being fed by Regan.

Leaning on the door frame, Tyler watched Regan work swiftly as she fixed him a quick sandwich. The cook, Johnny was in there also. He nodded briefly at Tyler before going back to his work. Tyler nodded back with a smile, thankful no other pack members worked at the café. Spending time with her while she was at work was the only time he got to interact with her in a public setting. The only time he was able to show off what was his, to show how lucky he was. And from the way Johnny always reluctantly nodded in greeting, Tyler knew the man was jealous. Not that it mattered. Regan had no clue how the human male gazed longingly at her.

“Here,” Regan said, facing him. “Come eat in the staff room.” She glanced at her watch. “We've got seven minutes left.”

Seven minutes. His heart ached with the knowledge. He had the late shift on patrol later that day, so the next seven minutes would be their last for the day, and it pained Tyler to know this. To be apart from her for so long.

In those early days, the feelings between them had been excitement and lust. Their interactions full of fiery desire and insatiable hunger, and as time went on, Tyler and Regan spent a little less time kissing and a little more time talking. Their hunger for each other didn't fade but evolved, becoming more than just a base sexual need.

"Are you okay, Ty?" Regan asked him quietly as he ate.

Looking up, Tyler met her gaze and searched her perfect dark-blue eyes. He wanted to say no. *No, I'm not okay.* But he saw her fear, knew Regan wasn't ready to tell her parents. It was more than just her worries over what her parents would say. Tyler knew she also needed to deal with her own guilt. They'd never said the word *mates* to each other, yet they both knew that's what they could become. If it were up to Tyler, he'd have said be damned what the packs thought. Regan was his, and he wasn't giving her up for anyone. But Regan had to work through her own tangle of emotions, had to deal with the fact she'd fallen for a wolf from the very pack that was responsible for her sister's death.

They'd talked about her sister's death—Regan's guilt over it and over falling for him. But they hadn't discussed everything. Tyler knew not to push her on certain subjects and was happy to wait until she was ready to give him all her heart, all of her troubles. In the beginning, he'd wanted to desperately know why a dominant wolf didn't train as such or even have a role within the pack as she should. But when he'd touched on the subject, Regan had closed up immediately.

Forcing a smile, Tyler pushed down his emotions and answered with a half-truth, "I'm just going to miss you, that's all."

"Me too, so hurry up and finish that sandwich." She glanced at her watch. "You've got five minutes to make sure I don't forget you overnight." She grinned.

Tyler gulped the last of his sandwich down, taking in the wicked gleam in her eyes. God, he loved this side of her, the untamed, reckless wolf within. "By the time I'm finished kissing you, you'll be feeling me on your lips for at least a week."

Her gaze heated, breath catching. Tyler grabbed her hand, tugging her into his lap. Regan gasped, her hands finding his shoulders, legs straddling his thighs. Pulling her flush to him, Tyler slid one hand to her nape, the other around her back. Their lips met with wild desperation, hands roaming each other like they may never get the chance to again. And by the time Tyler left her, Regan's lips were deliciously swollen, and he could feel her heart pounding as if she'd run a marathon. Tyler was almost certain she really would be feeling him on her lips for a week.

CHAPTER 18

Cage drove from his and Anna's home, Anna in the passenger seat beside him, music playing from the radio station she'd tuned into. His mind was half on the road and half on the pack meeting he was on his way to when Anna cried out, "Turn left!"

Glancing in the rearview mirror to check it was clear before slamming on the brakes, Cage just managed to make the corner at the last minute. He didn't question Anna or grumble at being asked to change direction at the last minute. Having a psychic as a mate meant these types of things happened often.

"Right," Anna continued, her voice far away.

Cage obeyed, studying her for a second. Her gaze looked on, unseeing, her expression relaxed. He'd become used to this over the months; the fear he'd once felt gone. Anna's visions weren't the same as they'd once been. After mating, the link between her and Cage seemed to have created a barrier somehow. It was as if Anna simply observed the vision now, instead of being consumed. She was no longer overwhelmed, no longer at risk of never returning. Anna had mastered her gift; she wasn't ruled by it anymore.

"Up ahead," Anna said quietly.

Cage search out the window screen, spotting a figure walking along the side of the road.

"Pick him up, he needs a lift home."

"Home?" Cage questioned.

Anna focused on him for the first time since the vision hit.

"Dark Shadow, not River Run," she clarified.

As the car neared, Cage recognized the person walking, and when he slowed next to him, rolling the window down to offer him a lift, Cage registered the exhaustion on the man's face. Yet he was pretty certain the universe, or fate, or whoever sent these visions to Anna, hadn't done so because the man was tired. He guessed time would tell. Sometimes Anna's visions made no sense to him at all.

"Hey, Ty, want a lift?" Cage asked.

Tyler paused, his mouth opening as if to say yes, before caution filled his gaze and he faltered.

"Get in the car, Tyler," Anna said, no room for argument.

Cage hid his smile. It wasn't often his mate gave orders.

Cage idled, waiting for Tyler to react. Tyler ran a hand through his hair, sighing before he climbed in. "You look beat, pal," Cage said as he put the car back into drive and headed for pack grounds.

"Pulled a few double shifts lately," Tyler replied. "Thanks for stopping."

"Thank, Anna, she's the one who directed me to you."

"Oh?" Tyler frowned.

"He's tired," Anna answered.

Cage met Tyler's gaze in the rearview mirror. Chuckling, he shook his head. "So, Ty, what's new?" Cage asked.

"Nothing much," Tyler replied, turning to look out of the window. "How about you? Settling in your new place?"

"Yeah, it's great. Don't tell Jackson, but I like being away from prying pack eyes." Cage chuckled. "Keeps my mom from being a busybody at least."

"Yup, parents can be a pain in the ass," Tyler agreed.

Cage kept polite conversation going as he drove, every now and then glancing at Anna and wondering when she was going to explain the detour to pick Tyler up. It wasn't until they pulled up to let Tyler out and he'd half stepped out the door that she turned in her seat and reached out a hand to stop him.

"Tyler," she said softly.

Tyler peered back, hesitant.

"Tell them," Anna continued.

His eyes widened slightly. "Sorry?"

"You need to tell them. Someone."

"Anna… I…."

A breeze blew into the car, and Tyler's scent filled Cage's lungs, along with another. His eyes locked with Tyler's, and fear filled the man's gaze.

"Regan?" Cage whispered. Tyler's whole demeanor changed. Cage wasn't sure if the man was going to bolt or make sure Cage wasn't able to speak Regan's name again.

Anna gripped Cage's knee, all while never taking her gaze from Tyler. "He's not going to tell anyone," she promised Tyler. Only Cage couldn't, shouldn't keep that promise.

"Anna, I can—"

Her fingers dug in further. "He's not going to tell anyone," Anna repeated. "But you should."

"We can't," Tyler breathed, terror on his face. "Please…."

Anna smiled sadly. "It's not our secret to tell."

Tyler let out a rushed breath. "It's just her parents… the alliance… how will they react? How will everyone react?" Desperation replaced fear. "Can you see? Can you see how they react?"

She shook her head sadly. “I only see what I’m showed.”

“And what do you see?”

“Pain. It will end in pain.”

“If we tell them it will.”

“No, Tyler,” Anna whispered solemnly. “It will either way.”

His features cleared of fear, replaced with frustration and a thread of anger. If Cage didn’t feel so sorry for the guy, he might have growled at him for looking at his mate that way.

“Then what’s the point? Might as well just enjoy what I have left with her.”

“I pass on what I’m told, Tyler. And I’m telling you, tell someone. Someone you trust. Someone who will listen. Someone from Dark Shadow.”

“Kat?”

“I don’t know. Sorry.”

Tyler’s attention drifted from Anna to Cage. “Can I trust you?” he snarled.

“Threatening me?”

With a frustrated sigh, Tyler rubbed a hand over his face. “Don’t push me.”

“Do you love her?” Cage asked.

“More than the world.”

“Then my lips are sealed, but please consider what Anna said.” Cage smiled, running his fingers through Anna’s long red hair. “I know it might not seem like it, but she really does know what she’s doing.”

With a nod and a grim smile, Tyler shut the car door and slipped into the trees, disappearing moments later.

"Little heads up next time would be nice," Cage murmured, putting the car back into drive and pulling away.

"I gave you what I knew at the time. And I meant it when I said you'll tell no one. We can't interfere with their fates beyond what I've already said."

Cage shook his head. "I'm not supposed to keep things like this from my alpha."

"Jackson will know when the time is right."

And even though it went against what he'd been taught growing up, Cage trusted Anna, trusted his mate, and hoped the universe made it right. He hoped Regan and Tyler walked away with two whole hearts and not two broken ones.

CHAPTER 19

She'd been coming to see him for two weeks. If Bass and Jackson knew she was coming into the barn alone, they didn't let on. Slipping quietly through the door, Katalina was running on silent, nimble feet before Zackary noticed. Jumping, she reached the beam above her and swung up into the rafters of the barn.

Peering down at the growling and snapping wolf below her, Katalina noted he gave up after a few minutes today and crouched down, silent but wary.

"Not in a barky mood today?" Katalina asked from her perch, legs dangling into thin air as she straddled the beam of the barn. "Bored of me already?"

He growled low in response.

"See, that right there is the reason I keep coming back. What wild wolf answers a human question with a growl? You understand me, don't you?"

Silence.

"You don't have to answer. I already know. I can see it in your eyes. There's a little human left in you. You're just too chicken to admit it."

That earned her a growl.

"Don't like been called chicken? It's the truth. You're scared. You reek of it. That's another cool wolfy power—being able to scent emotions. Took me some time to master."

His growled ended in a loud disgruntled bark.

"See, I was once like you. Human. Scared. Still get scared if I'm honest, but I've accepted my new life… for the most part at least. It's actually pretty cool being a shifter. Take me sitting up here for example. No way I'd have been able to do this before I turned. If you shifted back, you'd probably be able to climb up here too. Might even be able to get a punch in before I had you on your ass."

Silence. Not even a low growl.

Katalina let out a frustrated sigh. Anna said she'd be able to help Zackary and that she was meant to, but day after day she came, and there was little change.

"Come on, Zac. What are you waiting for?"

Nothing.

"Screw it!" Swinging her leg over the beam, Katalina dropped to the barn floor and crouched before Zackary.

The wolf jumped to his feet and froze. They eyed each other.

"What are you waiting for?" Katalina whispered. "Come get me, chick, chick, chick, chick, chicken."

His answering growl vibrated through her bones, and there was no chance of the noise going undetected, which meant Katalina was out of time. If she was going to get Zackary to shift back, it was now or never.

They danced around each other, dust from the barn floor billowing clouds around them. Katalina was working hard but not hard enough to have her worried; she could handle him. Just. Zackary was reacting with the primal rage of his wolf; it was how she'd first fought, but over time, she'd learned how to use human instincts to calm the wolf's. And if she could, so could Zackary.

"What are you so afraid of, huh? I know you're in there, so why haven't you taken back control?" Katalina leaped back, dodging the snap of his teeth, her feet nimble as she avoided each strike. "Unless you'd rather not take back control? Unless you'd rather be this mindless beast?"

Emotions clouded the wolf's eyes. For a second, they'd appeared human.

Katalina smiled. "So that's it. You're hiding. Hiding from reality, from humanity."

Zackary snarled savagely, confirming she'd hit the nail on the head. He'd lost his mother, he'd turned to drugs and alcohol, attacked his family. Zackary would rather hide in the primal mind of the wolf than face those very human problems.

"Kat!" The barn door opened a fraction, spilling a bright shaft of light into the barn, momentarily blinding Katalina.

Zackary leaped, teeth bared. She saw him coming too late. Her eyes adjusted to the new light a fraction of a second too slow. Teeth met flesh.

"Katalina!"

"No! Stay back, Jackson."

Taking hold of the wolf, Katalina flung him off. He hit the ground and immediately sprang back up.

"Are you insane?" Jackson shouted from the open doorway.

Without taking her eyes of Zackary, she answered, "I can reach him. Anna said it was me, so I must try."

"Anna isn't always right."

"Isn't she?"

Zackary stared at her, the eyes of his wolf full of pain and fury. She'd felt what he was hiding from—the grief of losing a parent, the disgust of what being a shifter allowed you to do, the strength of the wild animal fighting for a say within your body. She'd tried to hide too, just not in the body of her wolf.

"I get it. I know your pain," she said gently.

He didn't move, but a rumble built in the chest of his wolf.

"I lost my parents. I wanted to hide too."

He released his howl, the sound full of agony. Katalina gazed at his face. She could almost see the human mind hiding behind the animal's.

"But you can't hide forever, Zac," Katalina continued. Yet it wasn't working. Human emotions faded from the wolf's amber eyes. "Hey!" Katalina yelled, racing forward, ignoring the pain from her bite wound. "Don't hide from me!"

He growled in warning.

"I'm not afraid of you. I'm not afraid."

His eyes flickered.

The last thing Katalina wanted was to be cruel, but kindness wasn't working. Zackary's only hope was for his human anger to surpass the wolf's. "Not like you. You're a coward, hiding behind the mask of a wolf so you can forget your family."

It was working. He was trembling.

"What would your mother think? Would she want you to be a coward?"

Collapsing, the wolf's body trembled and convulsed.

"Come back, Zac. Stop hiding. Don't be a coward."

"I. AM. NOT. A. COWARD," Zackary yelled. He looked up, his human face clenched with emotional pain.

Smiling softly, Katalina stepped forward. "No, you're not," she murmured, holding out a hand for him and pulling him upright. "You're brave. Now let's get you in the house and into some clothes. I bet some food wouldn't hurt either, huh?"

Zackary smiled hesitantly, before nodding and walking beside her out of the barn. His eyes darted in all directions, equal parts of curiosity and fear in his gaze.

"It's going to be all right," Katalina assured him. *I've got you to shift back. That has to be the hardest part.* She hoped so anyway.

Chapter 20

"Kat. A word," Bass ground out, his anger on a tight leash that was threatening to snap.

Laying a soft reassuring hand over the boy's, she squeezed and spoke to him in a gentle whisper. "I'll be right back."

When Katalina's gaze met his, all the gentleness she'd shown Zackary was gone, replaced with annoyance and the slightest bit of rage.

"I ordered you to stay away from him," Bass snapped, the second she stopped in front of him.

The annoyance vanished, replaced with cold, vicious fury.

Ordered… what was I thinking? "I—"

Katalina cut him off before he managed to attempt an apology. Bass half expected her to hit him. He deserved for her to; she wasn't his to order. She was his to love, to protect, and care for, and sometimes that entailed allowing her near danger because he wouldn't cage her. Katalina wasn't weak. She could protect herself. Yet sometimes, the wolf in him didn't like that fact.

His wolf had been riding him hard lately. With the constant threat to his pack and mate, he was struggling to think straight. Riddled with guilt and self-doubt, Bass was ashamed to admit he occasionally wondered if he'd made a mistake becoming alpha.

"Order? Order?! Are you kidding me?"

"I'm sorry. I—"

"Save it! I'm not interested in your excuses. Yes, you asked me to stay away from him, and yes, I ignored you. Be pissed if you like, but Anna said it had to be me. I couldn't ignore that even if there was a chance I could be hurt."

"You could have been more than hurt, Kat."

"Give me some credit, Bass. I've faced more than one wolf before."

"I know and I'm sorry. I truly am. It just slipped out. I was worried."

"Well, I'm right here, alive and everything. So step down from your high and mighty alpha horse and just be my Bass, will you?"

Running a hand through his hair, he let out a frustrated breath and met Katalina's hard stare. "Forgive me?"

"I'll think about it," she murmured.

Leaning forward, Bass risked being snapped at and went for her lips. She resisted for all of two beats, then melted. Her rigid stance dropped, her crossed arms came undone and wrapped around him.

"That's cheating." She smiled against his lips.

"When it comes to you, my Winter Wolf, I'll cheat, I'll lie, I'll kill if it means you are happy."

"Less killing would be good."

"Unfortunately, I think that isn't going to be very achievable."

Her hands moved upward, gentle in their touch. Cupping his face, she looked at him, and Bass's heart expanded, full of so much love he often thought it might burst. Her smile was soft, but the look in her eyes was anything but—stern, insistent. Bass was almost afraid to hear what she had to say.

"Just don't let it change you, Bass. You're mine, remember? Not this world's, not this war's. Be the guy I fell in love with."

The guy she fell in love with. Bass was so far from that point—from the love-sick teenager who thought removing his father from the equation would solve all his problems. It wasn't all that long ago, but it felt like years. Yet he'd do anything for Katalina. Even if he thought it wasn't possible, he'd try. Because she was all that mattered.

"So, what do you plan to do with Zac?" he murmured, quiet enough the boy wouldn't hear.

Turning in his arms, Katalina leaned her head back against his chest and pulled his arms around her front. Bass kissed the top of her head and inhaled the scent of her hair into his lungs, the act distracting enough he was sure he didn't hear her correctly.

"Did you just say bring him home?"

"Yes."

"Kat, he's not a stray puppy you found on the side of the road."

She pulled away from him, her face telling him all he needed to know. She was pissed, and she'd do as she wished anyway. She always did.

Swallowing the sudden urge to growl, Bass attempted to explain why her idea was so terrible. "He's a newly bitten wolf. They're dangerous and unpredictable, Katalina."

"Well, what would you do with him, then?" she snapped.

"Keep him in the barn until he's learned control."

The noise that left her mouth was a mix of growl and sigh. "We are not keeping him in the barn."

"You do realize I can hear you, right?"

Bass looked up from Katalina's beautiful but angry face

and met Zackary's gaze with the full brunt of the wolf within him. The kid held the contact for three beats before looking away.

"Ugh, how do you do that?" Zackary ground out, his fists tight balls.

"I'm alpha. Holding my gaze for as long as you did is impressive, if not a little worrying."

"Worrying? Why?" Zackary asked.

"Because not only are you a wild, unruly teenager who's been bitten, but you're one with dominance. And frankly, I have enough on my plate without needing to babysit you."

"I don't need babysitting, and I'm not unruly! Try losing your mom and see how you take it." His voice rose, and as it did, Zackary began to tremble, anger on every rigid plane of his face.

"I did."

"Oh." The anger drained from Zackary. "Still, I don't need babysitting."

"You do, actually."

"Okay, I'm going to jump in here," Katalina said, stepping toward Zackary. "We know you're not a kid, but that doesn't mean precaution doesn't need to be taken."

"The barn," Bass replied.

"Get lost," Zackary spat.

The growl that left Bass was deep and savage, full of the dominance of an alpha. Zackary stumbled backward, even Katalina flinched from the sound. Bass hadn't intended to sound as he had, but as much as he didn't want to admit it, the attack from Indiana had affected him deeply, and he was struggling.

"What the hell is going on in here?" Jackson growled, barging into the kitchen.

"Bass was just about to go for a walk and cool off," Katalina answered, her expression hard.

"I'm—"

"Sounds like a good idea," Jackson interrupted.

Bass contemplated arguing. It wasn't in his nature to take orders, especially when backed up by another alpha, but he squashed the instinct and left Jackson's house without another word. Another line blurred, another instinct suppressed. While the man understood, his wolf was becoming more and more agitated. Katalina didn't understand the changes he was making for her. The lengths both him and Jackson sometimes went. As fierce a wolf as she was, at her core, Katalina was human. Nothing would change that, and he'd never want her to. It was the consequence of having a human upbringing, and Katalina's human heart was what he loved most. She reminded them of all the dangers of forgetting your humanity.

So he left, ran until the primal instincts of his wolf calmed, until he could once again be in Jackson's presence and not feel like ripping out his throat.

CHAPTER 21

"All right, son?" Jackson asked.

Tearing her gaze from where Bass had vanished, Katalina put her worries for him aside and focused on Zackary. "Zac?" she said softly, stepping closer to him.

"Kat," Jackson warned. "Give him space."

"He's okay. Aren't you, Zac?"

He pulled in a few more deep breaths before turning to face her. His wolf was in his eyes, the amber fracturing with the deep brown of his human color. "I'm okay," Zackary confirmed.

"You sure? The wolf is in your eyes?" she explained.

Zackary frowned.

Waving a hand toward the mirror across the room, Katalina said, "Why don't you take a look for yourself?"

With a hesitant glance at Jackson, Zackary made his way to the mirror. "Wow, that's cool."

"Cool, yes. But not so good for blending in," she answered.

"Are they always like this?" Zackary asked.

"No. Only when your wolf is close to the surface, when it has more control than the human half of you," Jackson answered.

"Oh." Zakary looked away from his reflection. "So how do I get them to turn back?"

"It'll take time," Katalina reassured him. Her exchange with Zackary brought back memories from when she'd been a newly turned wolf. How out of control she'd felt. How terrified. She didn't envy the kid at all.

"Yes," Jackson agreed. "But I must warn you, Zackary, most wolf shifters are born. Being turned by the bite is very different. You might never learn control. There's a possibility you'll always be a danger to those around you. Always a breath away from shifting and causing harm, or worse."

Zackary's face paled.

"All right, Jackson, that's enough scare tactics for one day," Katalina instructed.

"I'm not saying it to scare him, Kat. He needs to know. And so do you." Jackson walked over to the kitchen bench and helped himself to coffee. "Zac is of course more than welcome to stay in my barn until he's under control."

"Ugh," she groaned, exasperated. "He is not staying in the barn."

"No, Katalina, I think I should," Zackary said.

"Zac—"

"Honestly, it's fine. Your boyfriend was right. I did kinda go off the rails after Mom died." Zackary rubbed his neck, his expression ashamed. "I've already caused so much trouble for my sis and dad. The last thing I wanna do is hurt them." He headed out the kitchen, head down, shoulders slumped.

"Zac?" Jackson called. Zackary paused. "You can finish your food first. You're not that dangerous."

"Aren't I? I could hurt you, or Kat."

Jackson chuckled, the sound deep and rumbling. "I've faced far worse things than you, son. Take a seat, eat your food, then we'll find you a bed for the barn."

"And Katalina?" Zackary quizzed, looking at her like she was a breakable doll, annoying Katalina to no end.

"She's leaving," Jackson said casually.

Katalina gritted her teeth to keep from yelling. "She is not, and she can take care of herself."

"Her ability to take care of herself was never in question. I only guessed she'd be going after her mate and making sure he was okay," Jackson said, calm and appearing disinterested. Though his smile made Katalina want to slap him.

"Fine," she huffed. "But I'll be back later, Zac. Should I bring your family?"

For a moment, Zackary's eyes shone, then the light vanished. "No… not yet."

Glaring at Jackson before departing, Katalina set out to find Bass, her frustration evident in every step. It wasn't that she didn't understand how unstable Zackary was; she'd been there herself when she'd first turned. Yet what she didn't want to happen was for Zackary to be afraid of himself. Fear wouldn't help anyone. He needed to believe in himself, believe he could have a normal life, even while being a shifter. If Zackary didn't have faith in himself, then it wouldn't matter the time that passed by or the control he gained; he'd never move on.

Unable to track Bass down, Katalina headed home. Arne greeted her with glee as she walked in, his tail wagging in earnest. "You seen grumpy face?" she asked him, rubbing his body as he leaned against her. There was no fresh scent in the air so Katalina knew he'd not been home in a while. "Wanna go for a run?" Katalina asked her dog as she pulled off the first layer of her clothing.

Jumping up and down, Arne whined in excitement. There was nothing the dog loved more than going for a walk with a wolf. Katalina smiled. She could always rely on Arne to treat her the same. It didn't matter if she were human or wolf, in danger or not. To her dog, Katalina would always be the same.

"Come on then." She laughed as the last piece of clothing dropped to the floor. Once at the door, she opened it and shifted.

Arne barked at her as she leaped from the porch, and barked back. They headed for the trees, a snow-white wolf and German Shepard loping side by side.

Passing Nico, she glanced at him as he called, "He's by the lake. Go easy on him, Kat. He's in a foul mood."

Making a low howl in response, Katalina headed for the lake. She didn't go at full speed, or else Arne wouldn't have been able to keep up. Still, it wasn't long until the lake was in view and the speck of a lone black wolf could be seen by the water's edge.

Shifting, Katalina waited for Arne to catch her up. "Go play," she said, before approaching Bass. "I thought this place was my refuge, not yours." The black wolf looked up with such sadness in his eyes, it sent her to her knees. "Talk to me," she pleaded softly.

He shifted. Sitting beside her, Bass looked out over the water and spoke, "I like anywhere that reminds me of you."

"What's going on with you, Bass? You haven't been yourself since the attack. Kyle's dead. We survived…." It upset her that he continuously shut her out when it was clear Bass was feeling troubled.

"If only Kyle had been our biggest problem. And I'm not so sure we survived."

"What do you mean?" Her anxiety grew. Bass sounded defeated. Tired of life.

"Castor isn't going to stop, and when Bill is ousted, it will send a shockwave through the pack I'm not sure we can handle."

"We'll get through this. You'll get us through this," Katalina assured him, taking hold of his hand. Bass had stumbled lately, but that didn't mean she didn't believe in him. She had faith in their love. Had faith both packs would come out whole if they stuck together.

"I used to think that, but lately…."

"Bass, stop this. Stop doubting yourself."

"Why? Ever since I took over this pack, bad things have followed."

"Because before you became alpha everything was sunshine and unicorns." Katalina moved so that she was in front of him, blocking his view of the water. He looked to the ground. "Look at me," she ordered, frustrated. Irritation crept into her tone.

He met her gaze.

"Yes, things are bad. But they were bad before. Don't forget that. One step at a time, Bass."

"And what's my next step, Kat? Because I've never felt so lost."

She sighed, sorrow for Bass washing away her annoyance. "First off, you need to stop hiding from me. You're not my alpha. You're my mate. And you're not alone."

Bass sighed deeply. "I know…. I'm sorry for shutting you out."

Leaning forward, Katalina kissed him. When she pulled away, she pressed her hand to his cheek. "And as for Bill, I think it is time we set a trap for him and put an end to this once and for all."

"Could be risky," he warned, though his expression picked up a little.

"Not as risky as being stuck in limbo. Our pack needs to move forward. We need to rebuild. Living in a broken ruin serves as a reminder of what happened, and it's affecting everyone," she said, her tone leaving no room for doubt. It was time justice was served and the traitor caught. No more waiting. Action had to be taken.

Bass sat up straighter, smiling as the uncertainty left his gaze. "What do you have in mind?" Bass asked, pulling her down on top of him.

She laughed, willingly falling into his arms, pleased to see him looking more himself. "Haven't a clue, but I'm sure between the lot of us, we'll come up with something."

"And who might the lot of us be?"

"You know… the gang."

Shaking his head, Bass laughed for what must have been the first time in days. The sound like music to her ears, warming her heart. "We'll assemble the Scooby gang later. At this moment in time, I have more pressing matters."

Giggling, Katalina kissed him before coming up for air. "Wait. Since when do you watch TV?"

"I don't, but my best friend does. I've picked a few bits up over the years."

"Scooby gang." She laughed.

"Stop talking and kiss me."

And though she didn't take orders often, this one time she obeyed. When it came to kissing Bass, nothing in the world could stop her.

CHAPTER 22

Regan gazed out of the window, her mind on the wolf disappearing into the darkness. He wasn't visible anymore, but she could feel him all around her. The absence of him, the loss of his touch, the whisper of his breath over her skin. He was nowhere and everywhere. She was lost to him. He was her everything. Yet he was her biggest secret. Her greatest threat.

"What are you looking at, sweetie?"

Regan visibly jumped. "Oh," she gasped, her hand landing on her chest to keep her heart from escaping. "Mom… I didn't hear you open the door."

I thought the door was locked? Her gaze traveled from her mom's face to the lock. *Was I really that careless? That stupid?*

Regan always locked her door. She was careful, overly so… yet she'd begun to slip. Her fear and caution replaced with excitement and need. She hadn't locked the door; she'd been running late, Tyler had already been in her room when she'd entered. It was a miracle she'd shut it.

Her heart pounded at the thought of what could have happened. If her mom had walked in, if she'd found him there…. A shudder rolled down her spine.

Her mom noticed. "Close the window, Regan, a storm is blowing in."

And there was, in more ways than one. What had started out as a gentle breeze, a bit of fun, had grown into a full-blown tornado. They were hurtling along, and sooner or later someone was going to get hurt from their destructive path.

Shutting the window, Regan then turned and faced her mother fully. "Did you need anything, Mom?"

"Just coming to see if you'd eaten yet."

"No, not yet." It was late, and she was hungry, but she'd been hungrier for things other than food when she'd first arrived home. Tyler's shifts meant their time together over the last few weeks had been limited.

"There's leftover lasagna in the fridge. I was just going to heat a plate for myself. Shall I heat one for you?"

"Thanks, Mom, that would be great."

Her mom smiled before turning away and heading for the door, but she paused in the threshold, half looking back. "Are you okay, Regan?"

No. Regan gazed at her mother's face, taking in the little crease in her brow, the wide, concerned eyes. She wanted desperately to tell her, to admit she was falling for someone, and that keeping it a secret was killing her. But her mother was one of the reasons Regan and Tyler were sneaking around. Neither of her parents could ever find out. Yet it was inevitable. She was living on borrowed time, going through the motions until she could be whole again. If Regan was smart, she'd have held back, protected her heart from the possibility of being torn apart.

Being smart was something she was known for—smart, reliable Regan. It was why having a secret relationship was so easy, why Tyler climbed in through the window at all hours. Her parents would never expect her to do what she was doing; she was a good girl. She followed the rules. Yet Regan hadn't always been that way. There was a time in her life when letting a man in through her window wouldn't have been the most scandalous thing she'd have done. Another life, another time, when things were simpler, when she'd had a mother, father, and sister. But those times were gone. Her sister was gone, and not only had her sister's death changed the course of her life years ago, but it was also haunting her future.

Tainting the love that she and Tyler had.

Regan hoped for a happy ending, a way out with her heart intact, but she knew all too well, life didn't often go as planned.

Forcing a smile, Regan swallowed the guilt lodged in her throat and answered her mom with what she hoped was a happy tone. "All good, Mom. I'm all good."

Her mom turned away, buying the act, and Regan let out a heavy breath, thanking the universe for granting her more time. For another day where she could pretend a future with Tyler as her mate was a possibility.

CHAPTER 23

Tyler was on edge, the wolf inside of him pacing. Grinding his teeth, he looked up, seeing a sprinkling of stars through the canopy of trees above.

Really? This isn't funny anymore. A little break would be nice! Tyler wasn't sure he believed in a god, and if there was one, he had a cruel sense of humor. Yet he believed in fate, that the universe had a plan. Anna had confirmed just as much. He just wished that plan had a fewer mountains to climb.

He was on night patrol, expecting William as his River Run partner, but instead, Noah—Regan's father—had appeared through the trees. His heart had stalled, dread flowing through his body like a thousand tiny needles. Regan had filled his mind, and the panic coursing through him almost had Tyler running to find her, be damned the consequences of their secret relationship. But Noah had held out his hand, a cross between a smile and a grimace on his face.

Confusion had replaced dread. When Noah introduced himself, it took Tyler a few seconds to respond, for his heart to beat again and his brain to compute. Noah hadn't been there to confront him; he was covering for William's shift.

Tyler had never expected to cross paths with Regan's father during pack duties because the man wasn't dominant in the least, but River Run didn't have as many packmates as Dark Shadow, and Tyler guessed sometimes Jackson had to make do.

A text had come through from Bass seconds after Tyler had shaken Noah's hand, explaining the change in people. But that didn't ease the turmoil inside of him, didn't lesson the fear and guilt churning in his gut. Or stop Anna's words from ringing through his skull.

"You're late," Noah said, voice sharp, and clearly telling Tyler he hated Dark Shadow.

Tyler dropped his gaze from the night sky and plastered a smile on his face. Turning to face Noah, he said, "Sorry, I was held up." *I was in your daughter's bed, her naked skin beneath mine.... Oh, fuck I'm doomed. It's gonna be a long night.*

Noah's answer was a glare and he said little else for the rest of the night. Leaving Tyler with the knowledge that Regan's father's hatred ran deep. So deep he feared it would never be changed.

In the murky gray light of early morning, Tyler made his way home. Passing the charred remains of several Dark Shadow homes, he came to his own cabin and jogged up the steps onto the deck out front. His had also been damaged in the last battle with the Indiana pack, but with the limited space available, he'd decided to cover the hole in his roof with a tarpaulin and put up with the scent of burnt wood. Dragging his T-shirt over his head and then unbuckling his jeans, Tyler crawled into bed, his heart heavy and soul weary.

It had been a long night. While Noah hadn't outright voiced his opinions, it had also been clear the man wasn't planning on making friends with any Dark Shadow members. So not only did Tyler feel guilty spending the night patrolling with the father of the woman he was having a secret relationship with, it was also a reminder that Regan's parents would never approve. Even if Tyler managed to convince his alpha pair their relationship wouldn't threaten the alliance, there was just too much bad blood between Regan's parents and Dark Shadow. He understood why, but that didn't make it any easier to swallow.

Falling into a fitful sleep, he dreamed of Regan, but it was anything but peaceful. Tyler tossed and turned, his conscience eating at him. His troubles haunting his every breath. He kept telling himself they'd be all right eventually. That somehow, someway they'd find a way through with their hearts intact, yet as days slipped by into weeks, it was becoming clear that not all dreams were a possibility.

CHAPTER 24

Katalina took a pastry from the many plates on offer in front of her. "All pack meetings should be here from now on," she said, before taking a mouthful of cinnamon danish.

"I had wondered why Anna brought home so many cakes and pastries," Cage said. "But as much as I love you, Kat, my house is not a meeting room, and since when did pack meetings involve both River Run and Dark Shadow?"

"I'm grateful for you allowing us to meet here," Bass said.

"Didn't have much choice," Cage grumbled.

Katalina smiled at the not-so-discreet jab to the ribs Anna gave Cage.

"Of course, Bass. You're our friend. You're more than welcome any time," Anna reassured.

"So, what are we all doing here, Kat?" Cage asked.

"Not everyone is here yet," Anna replied before Katalina could answer.

"Do you know what this is about?" Cage asked Anna quietly.

"No," Anna answered.

"Then how do you know everyone isn't here?" Cage quizzed.

"Because Nico and Olivia aren't here and they're part of the group."

Cage grumbled.

"Cheer up, Cage. You're only here because you live outside of pack lands," Toby joked.

"Shut it, squirt," Cage jeered.

Toby laughed. "Not sure if you've noticed, but I'm as tall as you now."

There was a knock on the door, interrupting the squabbling. "Thank God," Katalina muttered, jumping to her feet. "I'll get it."

A few minutes later, they were all seated in a circle of sorts, various drinks in hands and bellies being filled with treats. Katalina met Bass's eyes across the room, and silence fell.

The group consisted of Katalina, Bass, Nico, Olivia, Cage, Anna, Jackson, Toby, and Dax. These were the people Katalina trusted most within the packs. There were others she considered good friends, but the people with her at that moment were more than friends, they were family.

The group looked to Bass. "This was your idea, Kat. I think you should explain."

"Me?" She felt suddenly nervous.

"Yes." Bass smirked. "You said get the gang together and come up with a plan."

"A plan for what?" Jackson asked.

"To trap Bill, and get rid of him for good," Katalina explained. A few eyes widened, while most of the men in the room looked as if they thought it was about time Bill got what was coming to him.

"Getting rid of him is the easy part. It's the trap that will be hard," Bass said.

"Why a trap at all? Why not just execute him?" Dax asked.

"Because I want solid proof," Bass answered.

"I thought you were certain it was him," Jackson questioned.

"I am," Bass said. "But I want proof for my pack, not just my word of his actions."

"Your word should be enough," Dax added firmly. "It is for me."

Bass smiled. "Thank you, Dax, but we all know it isn't to some others, and I do not want to breed discord," Bass explained.

"Well, if he's reporting to Castor, then he's gathering info that will help him take over Dark Shadow," Toby said.

"Or that will break the alliance," Cage added.

"So, me then," Katalina replied. She didn't like it, but had reluctantly accepted that their enemies saw her as an easy way to damage the packs.

"No," several of them said at once.

Katalina laughed, rolling her eyes. She'd expected their exact reaction. "How many times have I been told I'm what holds the packs together?"

"No" was repeated in unison.

"We can't risk you," Olivia said. "Doesn't matter how good you are at defending yourself. There must be another way."

"I see," Katalina said. "I'm only the glue when it works in your favor, but when it doesn't, we all go on pretending I'm not important." She huffed with frustration.

"It's because you are important that you're not signing up as bait," Jackson shot back. His arms were crossed over the wide expanse of his chest, and the glare he gave her was intended to scare her into obedience.

Not one for being obedient, Katalina sought out the one person she'd need to convince for any kind of plan to work.

"Don't look at me with those puppy-dog eyes," Bass groaned. "I'm with Jackson on this one."

"Look, everyone in this room knows using me as bait will work. You're just too chicken to admit it," Katalina protested.

Bass looked pained. Running his hands through his hair, he gazed at her with tired, worn-out eyes. She instantly felt guilty for causing him more stress. "Why are you so intent on putting yourself in danger?" Bass asked.

"I just want to protect my family. Find me another way and I'll back down," Katalina answered.

Silence stretched on as Katalina finished speaking. It wasn't that she was reckless with her life, or overconfident in her ability to protect herself. It was Bass's worn face, the look of defeat in his eyes, it was the fragile threads that held two packs together that meant more to her than words could explain.

Katalina wasn't so naïve to think this danger would end with Bill, but it could give them all a small window of peace. A window both packs desperately needed and if she had the power to give that to them, she would.

"I'm afraid there doesn't seem to be any other way," Anna said into the quiet. "Not that I can see anyway."

"But does she get through it in one piece?" Jackson asked.

"That I cannot tell you," Anna replied solemnly.

"I'll be fine," Katalina insisted. "It's not like I'll be alone, so if things go wrong, you can all jump in to save me."

"And how do you envision offering yourself up as bait?" Bass asked

Katalina smiled.

"Don't go looking so happy. I haven't said yes," Bass huffed.

But she knew he would. Written all over his face was the

fact he'd relent. He had to use her to protect his pack, and he hated it beyond measure.

An hour's planning turned into an early dinner of pizza, followed by a cake Anna just happened to have brought home from work the day before and instructed Cage not to touch.

It was evenings like these Katalina loved the most. Food, drinks, and family. The chatter flowed easily, and as the sun dipped below the horizon, she wished for these moments to never end. Because they were the times she forgot about shifters and enemies, when she became ordinary, a normal teenage girl surrounded by her family. It was the times she felt her parents' spirits near and was reminded she came from them, not war.

CHAPTER 25

Signing herself up as bait seemed like a good idea until Katalina was on the edge of town supposedly waiting for her aunt to pick her up. Her plans to spend the last few weeks of summer with her aunt and uncle had been canceled, despite Bass telling her she should still go. Katalina knew he only wanted her to go to keep her away from danger. She half expected him to tell her to move there permanently. But she'd called her family and canceled because as much as she missed them and craved "real world" time, the packs came first. When that shift had happened, she couldn't quite pinpoint, and it wasn't a change she liked to dwell on. It was a fact, an instinct as easy as breathing, and it came from both her wolf blood and human heart.

The news of her immediate departure had been told to Bill only—not that he knew that. If all went to plan, Bill would use this opportunity to his advantage, and with it being last minute, the hope was he wouldn't have the time to put a well-oiled plan into action.

Waiting on the road edge, the time she was meant to meet her aunt came and went. Anxiety levels peaked as she wondered what they'd do if Bill didn't show, and what they'd say when she quite clearly hadn't left with her aunt.

Looking at her cell for the fifth time, clocking four minutes past the fake pickup time, Katalina contemplated ringing Bass when the noise of a car engine caught her attention. Sending off a quick text before sliding her phone back into her pocket, Katalina faked a smile when the car came into view, then feigned confusion as Bill smiled at her from inside.

Pulling up, but not killing the engine, Bill got out.

"Bill? I was hoping you were my aunt. She appears to be late," Katalina lied as he approached her. She concentrated on keeping her breathing regular and hopefully her heart rate.

"I'm glad she is. I thought I was going to miss you."

Katalina wanted to growl. "What's up?" She managed a smile.

"Something has come up. Bass sent me to collect you," Bill explained.

"Really?" Katalina frowned, pulling her cell free. "Why hasn't he rang?"

For a split second, nervous anxiety crossed his features. "I-I'm not sure.... You know yourself he's not himself lately."

"No, he isn't," she agreed, her blood boiling. *Because of you.*

"I'll give you a lift back," Bill suggested.

"Okay," she answered, heading slowly toward his car. "I best ring my aunt first."

Not getting in the car, Katalina pretended to dial her aunt. Her nerves were beginning to show; she'd expected Bass to appear by now. The last thing she wanted to do was get into the car with him.

"Do it on the way," Bill urged, a touch of urgency in his tone.

Katalina met his gaze. "It won't take me a second."

His whole demeanor changed, and Katalina felt she was seeing Bill's real personality for the first time. He was a good actor; he'd fooled them all from the very start.

"I'm afraid I can't let you do that, Kat. Put the phone down and get in."

Katalina stared at the gun he pointed at her. She hadn't anticipated him having one, though she wasn't sure why. Indiana's favorite weapon of choice wasn't teeth and claws, but guns. It made sense for Bill to use one if he was working for them.

"Why?" she whispered, looking into his eyes.

"They're my family."

"Family," she ground out. "That's your excuse?"

"I would have thought out of anyone, you'd understand. After all, you cling to your human past even though it has no real connection to who you are."

"My past has everything to do with who I am. My family loves me. Can you say the same?"

He smiled, and it was nothing welcoming. "Get in the car, Kat. That's enough stalling. No one is going to save you this time. As usual, your obsession with humans has put Dark Shadow at risk."

Katalina sensed Bass near. "I don't need anyone to save me," she growled, and ducked.

Bill fired. Katalina moved swiftly enough to avoid a lethal shot but not quick enough to avoid the bullet altogether. Fire ripped through her shoulder as she twisted, sliding to the ground, the car at her back.

Two savage growls echoed around her, stirring the wolf within her to life. More gunfire exploded before Nico's voice rang out, urgent and clear.

"Alive! We need him alive!"

Silence followed, then Bass was kneeling before her. Blood splatted his skin and hair, his jaw ridged with pent-up rage. But as his piercing gaze held hers, all she saw was love.

"Bass?" Jackson boomed from somewhere close.

"She's okay," he answered. "Injured but okay." Bass cupped her face, kissing her gently. "You're never being bait again."

"Agreed," Jackson said, appearing behind Bass, Bill looking half dead in his grip. "Now, when can I kill the peace of shit who put a bullet in my daughter?"

Bass straightened. "Can you stand?" he asked, holding out a hand for her as his gaze roamed over her with worry.

"I think so," Katalina said, smiling through the throbbing in her shoulder. She gritted her teeth as she clasped his hand with her uninjured side, biting her lip to keep the sound of her pain inside.

"Good," Bass said softly, helping her to her feet and steadying her gently before turning to Jackson. "The kill is mine."

Jackson glared.

"You know why, Jackson," Bass added.

"Yeah, yeah," Jackson grumbled. "Doesn't mean I like it."

"None of us like it," Cage answered, approaching. "But right now, Kat needs medical help."

"Can I trust you not to kill him?" Bass asked Jackson.

Though Jackson looked ready to kill, he nodded and dragged Bill up.

"Regroup at Jackson's," Bass instructed to everyone, but looked at Jackson. Only when Jackson nodded his approval did he turn to look at Katalina. "You're with me." Bending, Bass scooped her into his arms.

"I was shot in my shoulder, not leg," she pointed out, begrudgingly.

"I don't care," he replied, walking her to the car Bill had driven, and placing her gently in the passenger seat. "No walking until Karen looks at you."

"I'm still not talking to her. Take me to Oliver," Katalina moaned, as he climbed into the driver seat.

Pulling away, Bass glanced across at her and smiled. "You need to let that go."

"Not yet."

"Cage and Anna are happy. There is no reason to keep punishing her."

"They wouldn't be if she'd had her way."

"Cage has forgiven her."

"Clearly he's more generous than me," she retorted.

"Oh, I'm not sure.... I find you rather generous."

Despite the pain she was in, Katalina couldn't help but smile. Satisfaction filled Bass's gaze, indicating his smooth tone, and the twinkle in his eyes had been intentional.

"Fine, she can treat me, but that's as generous as I'm being. I'm not forgiving her. Not yet anyway." She understood some of the reasons behind Karen's actions toward Anna, but Katalina wasn't ready to accept them. To forgive Karen for going behind her and Cage's back. Not yet. Karen had to know what she'd done was wrong, however justified.

They pulled up outside of Jackson's house as the others appeared from the trees. Jackson had a lifeless Bill over his shoulder. Katalina opened her door to get out when Bass appeared before her and lifted her into his arms without asking.

"I can walk into the house, Bass."

"I know you can. Humor me?" he whispered, planting a kiss on her cheek. She smiled, despite not liking being babied, and allowed Bass to coddle her. Occasionally, she secretly liked it.

Zackary's head appeared between the barn doors, gazing wide-eyed at the scene.

"He's still a kid then," Bass observed, walking past Zakary with Katalina in his arms.

"I told you he wasn't a danger," Katalina answered.

"Debatable," Bass replied, smirking.

"Is… is that blood?" Zackary stammered.

"Out you get, son. You're being upgraded," Jackson answered.

Zackary hesitated for a second before rushing back inside the barn and reappearing with an armful of belongings. Jackson nodded his approval, then threw Bill inside the barn, and bolted the door shut with a satisfied smirk.

Brushing his hands together, Jackson met Cage's gaze. "Organize round-the-clock guards."

"On it," Cage answered with a nod.

"I thought you said I was dangerous?" Zackary asked nervously, trailing after them as they entered the house.

"These days, kid, you're a walk in the park." Jackson patted him on the back. When Zackary's look of fear didn't recede, he continued, "Let me know if you feel out of control. I'll make sure you don't hurt anyone."

"W-what if I hurt you?" Zackary asked.

"I'm tougher than I look." Jackson laughed. "Come on, inside."

And despite being injured and having a traitor in the barn outside, Katalina smiled at the craziness that was her life. At the people around her who she loved. The Indiana pack had used Bill in an attempt to destroy the relationships between both packs, but they'd not succeeded. Instead, they'd all worked together to bring him down. And no matter what Dark Shadow's reaction was, they'd keep working together and bring an end to this war.

CHAPTER 26

It was one of those rare afternoons when they were both free, and they'd snuck away meeting in forest land far away from pack. Arriving in separate cars, Tyler pulled up, grinning as he climbed out of the vehicle.

"Chinese," he said, holding up the bag in his left hand. "Beers," he continued, holding up the right.

"Picnic blanket," she replied, tucking it under her arm, smiling at the sheer joy on his face. "Shall we go, I'm starving?"

They walked at a fast pace, arriving twenty minutes later at their destination. Regan laid the blanket down, taking a seat as Tyler did the same next to her. Looking out over the slight ridge they'd stopped at, she searched the seemingly endless vista of trees and mountains, utterly at peace and relaxed. Tyler opened her food and handed it to her, and as she ate, Regan allowed her mind to wander to a place it often did when they were together on the ridge, stealing moments in time for themselves.

She imagined them never returning, imagined packing up their blanket and food and disappearing into the forest before them. Two wolves free. Free to be together, free from the constraints their packs put on them.

"What are you thinking about?"

Regan glanced at Tyler's handsome face, her chest constricting painfully. "Running away."

From the shock on his face, he hadn't expected her answer. "Regan I… I actually don't know what to say," he admitted.

"Would you?" she asked quietly, fear stealing her breath. Though she wasn't sure if she was afraid of a yes or a no.

"Is that what you really want?" he replied.

"Just answer the question," she pleaded.

"Yes. For you, yes. I love you, Regan. You're everything to me."

She gasped, his answer rolling through her in a wave of mixed emotions. Her cheeks heated, his words whispering through her mind. The three words she'd known but not yet heard from his lips. Her heart expanded, becoming painfully tight with the love she felt in return.

"I love you too," she whispered, a wide smile creasing her cheeks.

Smiling in return, Tyler cupped her cheek then leaned in for a kiss. His lips caressed hers softly. When he pulled away, his gaze studied hers.

"But that's not really what you want is it, Regan?" Tyler didn't look afraid of the answer. It was written in the depths of his eyes that he truly would leave everything behind for her. The knowledge was somewhat scary, yet amazing to know that there was someone in her life who would go to the ends of the earth for her.

"I don't know. Sometimes I think it is.... I guess I just want you. You without all the hiding and stolen moments."

His hand took hers. "Maybe it's time we tell someone."

Regan searched his face, afraid but finding no fear in his gaze. "I'm not sure I'm ready."

"I never told you this because I didn't want to frighten you, but Anna and Cage know about us."

"What?" Her hand flew to her mouth. "How?" she whispered against it.

"I was walking back from meeting you at work when they pulled up beside me to give me a ride. I think Anna had a vision. When I got out, the wind blew your scent to Cage, and Anna stopped me, telling me I should tell someone."

"Tell who?"

"She didn't say who exactly, just someone from Dark Shadow."

"Not yet… I'm not ready yet."

"We'll never be ready, Regan. But you're thinking of running away. I'd say that's a sign it's time."

"Not today," Regan said, putting her food down. She was no longer hungry. "Soon. But not today. I need to figure out how to tell my parents first… I just need… time."

And yet even as the words left her mouth, Regan knew they were empty; she'd had time, and it didn't matter how much of it passed, there'd never be a day that would make risking losing either her parents or Tyler easier. But she wasn't going to waste the precious alone time they had on pondering her empty words and jumbled thoughts. Instead, Regan took his food container from his hands and straddled him, silencing Tyler with her mouth. She wasn't as brave as him, wasn't ready to face the truth like he was, and until that time, Regan would distract him using every weapon in her arsenal to steal a few more moments in time. To fight off the cruel temptress that was fate.

CHAPTER 27

Later that day, when their food had long gone cold and Regan made sure thoughts of spilling their secrets were buried far, far under a mountain of need and desire, Tyler's phone rang.

"It's Bass," he said to Regan, holding his finger to his lips to warn her. "Hey, Bass, what's up?"

"Are you about?"

"Actually…" Tyler's words trailed off as he took in Regan and their surroundings. They'd been walking for a while, getting lost in each other, lost in a wilderness that wasn't their home but looked just like it. "I went on a hike."

"I know it's your day off," Bass replied, regretfully, "but could I be a pain and get you to return? I've a problem I need your help with."

"Sure thing, but it will be an hour or so to get back, depending on how far I push myself." Tyler had said the words convincingly, but as he gazed at Regan, his heart screamed, *No, no, I do not want to return.*

"Don't tire yourself. It's not life or death. Come to Jackson's when you arrive."

"Jackson's?" Tyler questioned, hoping the fear that flooded him wasn't in his tone.

Regan's gaze widened. "What's going on?" she mouthed.

"Yeah, the problem happens to be housed here. I'll explain when you arrive," Bass answered.

"All right. Be as quick as I can," Tyler said, ending the call. His eyes met Regan's. "Sorry, babe, time to get back to reality. Bass needs me."

Her face fell. "It's not about us though?"

"Not that I could tell." Tyler pulled her into a hug. "But if it is, don't be afraid. Never be afraid, Regan. I'll always stand by you."

What neither of them said was that his promise might mean them both leaving behind family and packs they loved.

It won't come to that. His eyes looked to the sky. *Please don't let it come to that.*

Yet Anna's words haunted him. *It ends in pain....* Words he'd never tell Regan. Words he hoped never came to pass. And if they did? He hoped it was his pain and not hers.

They'd returned to their cars after a quick detour to a nearby stream and a wash in icy water, dressing in the clean clothes they'd brought so no one would scent either of them on one another. Tyler had reluctantly said goodbye without kissing Regan and driven away, leaving her to wait in her car for another fifteen minutes before she too would set off for River Run. He watched her car in his rearview mirror before the road twisted to the right and she was lost to the view of the dense forest. An unease sat heavily on his shoulders, the sense that invisible walls were closing in on him. Tyler knew where the invisible walls came from, but not what could be done about them.

Regan's fear was about more than just upsetting her parents; it was a deep-seated issue that had come to life on the day of her sister's death. It had grown and festered year after year as she and her parents allowed themselves to keep living as they were.

A part of Tyler was very angry at Regan's parents for allowing it to go on as long as it had. For allowing Regan to live a lie.

And that lie had nothing to do with his and Regan's relationship. It was every choice that was made that didn't reflect Regan's dominant nature; it was smiling happily when Regan lessened herself to keep her parents happy. For not noticing how truly lost and broken she was by her twin's death even today.

As Jackson's house came into view, Tyler forced himself to concentrate on the present and pushed everything else away to deal with on an unmarked day in the future.

"Hey," Bass greeted, stepping down from Jackson's porch and meeting him near his car. "Sorry to drag you in on your day off. I know you've been working hard lately, and I want you to know I really appreciate it, Ty."

"Thanks, but it's not necessary, Bass. Dark Shadow is my home too."

Bass smiled, though it didn't reach his eyes. His gaze held tiredness and frustration. "Which brings me to why I brought you here. Kat has... well, Katalina has been doing what she does best. Inside, there's a kid I'd like you to meet. His name is Zackary. He was bitten and turned, and is the newest member of Dark Shadow."

"Bitten?" Tyler raised a brow. "Since when do we take on volatile newly turned wolves?"

Bass shrugged as if he really didn't have an explanation. "It's a long story. Anna had a vision. Kat's stubborn and has decided her new hobby is taking in strays, which leaves me with a kid I don't trust to wander alone."

"You want me to watch him?"

"I want you to train him. He's been staying here, but if he's to be Dark Shadow, he must live with us."

"That what the extra guard is for?" Tyler asked, nodding in the direction of William leaning up against the barn doors.

"Hmm. And we also have the issue of lack of housing, so I'm afraid Zac's going to have to bunk with you for a bit. Until we know he's got control over his wolf and can find him and his family somewhere more permanent to live."

"Family? As in humans? Bass, I know you don't like to say no it Katalina, but do we really need the added pressure at the moment? You don't have an obligation to this kid or his family."

"I know that. Believe me, I have thought about the added pressure, but I hope in this case Zackary's family will help ease the burden. You see, his father is a builder, and I hope in exchange for helping his son, he'll help us rebuild."

"I guess that would help. The kid inside?" Tyler asked, indicating with his head toward Jackson's door.

Bass nodded, making his way into the house. Tyler closed the door behind him and followed Bass as he headed for the kitchen. Inside, Jackson was seated at the kitchen bench, a cup of coffee in his hand. He nodded a greeting at Tyler, not moving from his position.

"Zackary?" Bass said, turning away slightly from Jackson and speaking to a young guy who was currently playing video games with Toby.

"Hmm?" he answered, not looking away from the screen as his fingers moved aggressively over the controller.

"I'd like you to meet someone," Bass added, sounding just the slightest bit annoyed.

"He'll be done in a moment," Toby said, glancing over his shoulder for a spilt-second. "I'm going to annihilate him in three, two, one… boom! Dead, sucker!" Toby cheered.

"Ugh! As if," Zackary groaned. "Rematch?"

Toby glanced over at Bass, a hopeful look in his eyes. When he got nothing from Bass, Zackary sighed. "Sorry, another day maybe. Looks like you've got places to be, Zac," Toby said.

Reluctantly, Zackary climbed to his feet, handing the controller back to Toby. "Okay, what is it?"

And while the kid sounded polite enough, Tyler couldn't help but note Zackary held Bass's gaze with the defiant eyes of his wolf.

"Zac, I'd like you to meet Tyler. He's going to be looking out for you for a while."

"Watching me so I don't wolf out on anyone you mean," he grumbled.

"I'm going to help make sure you don't wolf out on anyone unintentionally, actually," Tyler corrected. "I'm guessing you'd like to learn control?"

"Yeah, I guess." Zackary met Tyler's gaze with a little less aggression.

"Great. Well, you'll be staying with Tyler. He trains our dominant teens, so you're in good hands," Bass said.

"So, I'm leaving Jackson's?" Zackary asked.

"Yes, though you're welcome back whenever you'd like," Jackson answered, joining in the conversation.

"Thanks," Zackary answered.

They left together, Bass catching a lift with Tyler. His alpha was quiet for the short journey, Tyler sensing the man had more than a stray kid on his mind. He thought of asking Bass if everything was okay, but the fear of Bass saying no and then confiding in Tyler had him holding his tongue. Tyler wasn't sure he could take his alpha sharing his troubles while knowing he himself kept his troubles a secret.

The worst part was that Tyler knew exactly why matings between two different packs would cause issues, because even though he and Regan weren't mated, the lines between loyalties were becoming blurred. He loved her, would protect her without question, even if that meant protecting her against his own alpha.

Not able to take the silence any longer, Tyler asked a question. "Do you want Zackary training with his fellow peers?"

Bass glanced back at Zackary in the car. "I'll leave that up to you, Ty. Spend a few days getting to know each other, then decide if he has enough control to be able to join in."

"Okay, will do. So, what am I to say if people ask who he is?"

"The truth. He's here to learn, and hopefully in exchange, his father is going to help us rebuild. I'll go tell the necessary people of his arrival now."

They departed a short while later, Zackary quietly following Tyler as Bass went a separate way. Arriving at his cabin, Tyler opened the door, gesturing for Zackary to go in ahead of him. He paused on entering, his eyes quickly scanning the space.

"And I thought the barn was bad," Zackary muttered under his breath.

"Not so keen on my home, then?" Tyler said, a little too loudly, causing the boy to jump. "Step one. No point whispering because wolves will still hear you."

"Not sure if you've noticed but there's a hole in your roof," Zackary replied sarcastically.

"Yeah, I noticed. Some asshole tried to burn it down."

He faced him wide-eyed. "Really? That why this place looks the way it does?"

"Yeah. Dark Shadow has seen better days, that's for sure," Tyler answered. "Let's hope your dad can help."

"Speaking of my dad, do you think I'm safe enough to see him yet?" Zackary asked quietly, seeming younger than his age.

"Let's get today over with, and we'll see, okay. First thing's first, let's go grab dinner and then we'll find you something to sleep on."

The kid did another quick glance of Tyler's cabin. "You don't have a kitchen." His brows lifted.

"No. But there's a pack kitchen. Kinda like a cafeteria at school, but way better. If you're ever hungry, head there and they'll always be something there to eat, or someone willing to cook you something."

"Awesome. I'll live there." He grinned.

And it was the first real expression Tyler had received. His first glimpse into the boy underneath the wolf. At the boy before fate had done a one-eighty on.

CHAPTER 28

Throwing her phone not so gently onto the bed, Regan swiped angrily at the tears that rolled down her face. She'd hoped to see Tyler later, but he'd messaged saying he couldn't make it. It wasn't the news he couldn't make it tonight that upset her, but the news he might struggle to come to her for the foreseeable future.

With a sigh, Regan picked up her phone and read the message again.

Tyler – I can't make it tonight, sorry, babe. I've got a new pack member living with me now. Kid named Zac, and he needs my help controlling his wolf.

Regan had heard about the kid who'd been living in Jackson's barn. The one Anna foresaw; her parents had done nothing but gossip about him the other day. It seemed they didn't agree with Anna's visions either. It made Regan wonder if her parents had always been closed-minded or if it was a side effect of losing a child. She hoped it was the latter, and hoped one day they might heal, as she was doing with Tyler's help. Yet with Zackary to watch and train, Regan knew it would be even more difficult to find time for themselves, and while a part of her was proud of him for being trusted with Zackary's care, the other more selfish part was a little bit annoyed.

The screen on her cell lit up, indicating another text. Her heart leaped, assuming it was Tyler again, but on inspection, she saw it was from someone she'd not expected to contact her, even after their conversation the other month.

Mia – Hey, Regan, I know we've not spoken since… well, you know. But you've been on my mind, and I thought what the

hell, I'll text and see. So here goes…

The phone vibrated with the second message.

Mia – Hey, chick! It's Friday night. The girls and I are heading into town for a few drinks. You should come!

Regan stared at the phone like it might explode. *Go out. Have drinks. Should I? No. Yes. Oh God, what am I thinking…? No, the answer is no.*

Yet ten minutes later, Regan hadn't moved.

"Urgh, you're so stupid, Regan!" she groaned to herself.

Picking up her phone again, Regan dialed the one person who'd have at least a little idea of the turbulent thoughts currently circling her.

"Regan?" Tyler answered in a soft whisper. "I'll be right outside. Gotta take this," he continued. "Sorry, babe, I'm back. Kid's living with me, so…."

"I know I'm sorry, Ty. I —"

"No. Don't ever apologize for needing me, Regan. I'll always make time for you. Always."

She sighed, her tension washing away. "I got a text from Mia," she said.

"Really? What'd she say?"

"If I wanted to go out for a few drinks."

"That's great, babe, you should totally go," Tyler replied with enthusiasm.

"Really? I mean, is it really that great?"

"Come on, Regan. I know things have been hard between you for years, but she reached out to you. That means she wants to rebuild a friendship with you. You need friends, Regan. Everyone needs at least one."

"Oh God, Ty. I want to go, but I'm… I'm terrified. I'm so lame. When did I get so lame? I used to have a backbone. Meg would be horrified I've become this uncool."

Tyler's laugh drifted through the phone, soothing some the turmoil inside of her. "What are you so afraid of?" he asked her gently.

"I've ignored most of these girls since Megan died. What if they hate me? How do I even talk to them after so long?"

"Well, for starters, there's nothing to forgive. Your sister died, Regan, you get a pass, and as far as talking goes… well, I've never known you to have a problem with talking once you've gotten over your nerves, which a shot or two will help with."

It was Regan's turn to laugh. She'd half expected Tyler to tell her to stay in, that it was too dangerous, but here he was suggesting she have a drink or two. *What did I ever do to deserve you?* "So, you're suggesting I get drunk?"

"Tipsy, Regan. I don't want to be sneaking out of here at 1:00 a.m. to rescue you."

"I think those days are well and truly over."

"Seriously though, I really think you should go, Regan, even if it's for a couple hours. It will be good for you."

She sighed heavily. "I just don't know if I'm that brave anymore."

"Do you know what you need?"

"Some of your fierceness?"

He laughed. "No, though if you look hard enough, you'll see there's enough of that inside of you already. What you need is a buffer."

"A buffer?"

"Yeah. Someone who isn't from the old days, someone

new, so it's not like stepping back in time."

"But who?"

"Kat," Tyler suggested. "She'd be so happy to be invited."

"You really think so? I mean we speak but…?"

"I know for a fact she'd love to go out. Plus she's pretty badass so I won't have to worry about you not having protection."

Regan shook her head. "I'm pretty certain you're not supposed to be offering up your alpha's mate as a sacrifice, Ty."

"Ah, come on, she's no lamb. Besides, you'll be fine anyway."

She was quiet for a minute, Tyler's breathing the only sound coming through the phone. "How's Zac?"

"He's a good kid, but stop changing the subject."

"Okay. Okay, I'm going to go."

"You are?"

"Yes. I'm doing it!"

"That's my girl." She could hear the smile in his voice and it lightened some of the unease weighing her down.

"I wish you could come with me." Regan sighed.

"One day, baby, one day."

Gosh, I hope so….

"I better go, Regan, before the kid starts wondering where I've gone. Text me when you get home, okay?"

"I will, and thanks, Ty. Thanks for understanding."

"It's my job, babe. Now go have fun. Love you."

"Love you too," she whispered, then ended the call.

Taking a deep, calming breath, Regan texted Mia back, then dialed Katalina's number, nerves like butterflies flapping in her belly. *I'm really doing this. I'm really goddamned doing this.*

And she hoped that wherever Megan was, she was smiling down on her, probably shouting, *it's about freaking time!*

Chapter 29

Katalina had been surprised by Regan's invite. She considered the woman a friend, but they weren't exactly close. Not invite-out-for-drinks close anyway, though Katalina wasn't about to complain. She needed all the friends she could get, and Regan was a good way to start. A night out with some fellow girls was just the reprieve she needed from Bass's not-so-pleasant mood.

She didn't blame him. Bass was under a lot of stress, and Katalina knew adding Zackary into the mix hadn't helped things, yet she'd be damned if the Indiana pack was going to affect the very core of who she was. It wasn't in her to turn away from someone in need, nor was it in her to stay in just to please a man. Katalina understood why Bass would have rather her turn down Regan's invite, but she couldn't follow through. Where she came from, it was normal to meet with friends and have a few drinks. And as life became more complicated, she needed normal more than ever.

The compromise had been a bodyguard. Logan was currently sitting at the bar chatting to Cage, and for the most part, the men were acting discreetly so Katalina could ignore their presence.

"You know, Jackson has never insisted on a guard before," Mia said, leaning toward her so she could be heard over the music. "I mean, we're all mostly dominant here, and quite capable of protecting ourselves if need be."

"I suspect he's here because of me," Katalina explained, cringing. "Sorry about that. Bass probably rang him the second my back was turned. It would have been the only way he got away with two guards watching me."

"Doesn't bother us," Mia said. "I mean, we don't need to elect a sober driver now." She laughed. "Bet it's frustrating for you though."

"Honestly, I'm just pleased I was allowed out the door." Katalina shrugged. "And that Bass isn't here looming over us all."

Katalina picked up her rum and Coke, draining the last of the drink. Dropping the glass back on the table, she rose to her feet. "Next round is on me." She smiled. "But first, a visit to the ladies' room."

"I'll come with you," Regan said, getting to her feet.

So far Regan had been mostly quiet and looking a little out of place. Katalina linked her arm through Regan's, heading for the bathroom. She squeezed her arm slightly, smiling warmly at her.

Cage and Logan were on their feet the second she stepped away from the table.

"Bathroom," Katalina mouth, eyeing them firmly, indicating there was no need to follow.

They stared back, uncertainty in their gazes, but when Katalina didn't back down, they gave in. Cage shook his head as he sat back on his stool, his eyes followed her all the way across the room.

"Sorry, I didn't think about it being a problem with you coming out," Regan murmured as she glanced at Cage.

"God, no, don't be sorry, Regan. In all honesty, I probably needed this night more than you. Things at home aren't all that great. I feel like Bass and I are on completely different wavelengths at the minute."

Regan let out a long, slow breath. "If we're being honest, I'm not sure I needed this night. I feel totally out of my depth."

Katalina pushed through into the toilets, the door closing behind her and dulling some of the noise. She studied Regan for a moment. "There's a change in you."

Regan's wide gaze met hers, bewilderment and a little fear in them. "Is there?"

Stepping forward, Katalina pulled her into a hug. "Yes, keep going. You're on the right track," she whispered near her ear. "I know a little about feeling lost. Hell, somedays I still am. So I want you to know, Regan, you aren't the only one fumbling around through life without a clue as to what you're doing."

Regan's smile was a little hesitant, but the fear cleared from her eyes. "Thanks, Kat."

"I'm good at listening if you ever want to talk. To be honest, I could do with someone to talk to."

"I'd really like that. My mom wasn't impressed with my plans for tonight. She's been acting like I've turned into some irresponsible teenager. It's really difficult at home right now."

"Well, you're not being irresponsible, Regan. You're being normal. It must be hard for your mom too though, I guess. Maybe she feels like she's losing you, however irrational that is."

Regan turned away and walked to the bathroom mirror, fixing her hair as she stared at herself. Katalina wondered what it must be like to have the same face as the sister she'd lost. Whether she grieved every time she looked at herself. Katalina knew sorrow well, but she couldn't imagine the pain Regan had gone through and still contended with.

"I feel guilty for causing her more pain." Regan sighed. "But I can't stay in the darkness of Megan's death any longer."

Katalina joined her at the mirror, brushed a few strands of her own hair back into place before meeting Regan's gaze in the mirror. "Don't feel guilty for being braver than she is. Lead the way for them, Regan. They'll catch you up eventually."

Regan brushed away a stray tear that rolled down her cheek. "I hope so," she whispered.

"Give it time." Katalina hugged Regan. "Right. That's enough heavy crap for one night. Don't you think?" Katalina smiled, leaning her head on Regan's shoulder as she wrapped her arm around her. "I haven't done this whole 'girls' night' thing in a while, but I'm pretty certain we're supposed to be having fun."

Regan laughed.

"Pee first, then I'm ordering us a round of shots. If we're going to have bodyguards, we might as well let our hair down and make the most of it!" Katalina declared.

The girls finished up, leaving the bathroom a little lighter and with a friendship that had bonded over shared loss. Laughing, the two skipped onto the dance floor, and moved to the beat, their bodies twisting, their hearts pounding. And for a while, Katalina didn't think about Bass and the distance he'd put between them, or how far away she felt from the person she'd once been. For that fraction of time, Katalina was happy. She was free.

CHAPTER 30

Regan – Ty, you were totally right. A few drinks worked wonders.

She smiled down at her phone as the screen glowed, Tyler's replying text coming through seconds later.

Tyler – I'm always right. Remember that. ;)

Regan – Though I totally see through your asking Katalina out suggestion. How convenient that she'd have guards, so you don't need to worry.

Tyler – I've no idea what you mean. ;) :)

"Who's texting you that's causing that smile?" Mia asked, nudging her shoulder.

Regan hid her phone against her chest. "None of your business," she said, trying to hide her happiness.

Mia grinned wickedly. "Like that is it? Well, if he makes you smile like that, he must be doing something right. But enough on that phone. Come dance with me."

"Oh, I'm not—"

Mia didn't give her a chance to answer, Regan found herself dragged to her feet and onto the dance floor seconds later. She only just had the chance to slip her phone back into her jeans pocket before Mia was grabbing her hands and lifting them into the air as she jumped up and down laughing. And as nervous as Regan was a few moments ago, Mia's silliness had her laughing and forgetting all about it. She threw her head back, closing her eyes as she moved her hips to the music. And for just a second, it was as if Megan had never died; she was the Regan from the past. She was her true self.

It was late. Far later than she'd ever expected to stay out, and to her surprise, she wasn't in the least bit ready to go home to an empty bed.

Regan – On our way home. Wish you were waiting for me **:(**

Tyler – One day, baby. One day <3 <3

Dropping her phone into her bag, Regan rested her head on Mia's shoulder, so pleased to have her old friend back. "I don't want to go home," she moaned.

Mia laughed. "One night has you back into a party monster."

"Come on, it's only half past twelve."

"Only. Some of us have patrol in the morning," Mia answered.

Patrol… I'd be doing it too if my life hadn't derailed. Regan sat straight, visibly shaking her head to dislodge the thought. *Now I* really *don't want to go home and be alone.* She pouted and contemplated showing up on Tyler's door, but Zackary put a hole in that plan. *Maybe I should just screw it all and tell everyone?*

Katalina saved her from her crazy thoughts. "Come back to my place. I've no plans for the morning."

"Are you sure? Won't Bass be bothered I'm River Run?"

Katalina grabbed her hand, linking her fingers through hers. "Of course not." She squeezed. "You should totally sleepover. It will be so much fun." Her face turned thoughtful. "Though, we live in kinda a hovel since the fire." Katalina's face screwed up. "I'm so over living like a homeless person."

Several people in the car laughed.

"I don't know why you're all laughing. It's the truth. You know I used to own a house. An actual whole house, with a roof and everything."

"I'm sure you will again," Mia said.

"Sorry, I ruined the mood, huh?" Katalina sighed. "Forget my moans. You should all come back for drinks."

"Kat," Logan warned from the driver seat.

"Oh, shut up, you," Katalina replied, poking out her tongue.

Regan couldn't help but laugh. Katalina's complete lack of concern when it came to the intermingling of the packs made Regan wish she was more like her. That she had just a fraction of Katalina's confidence and faith.

Maybe we should tell Kat…. She almost opened her mouth then and there, but thought better of it. *I'll ask Ty first.*

"No need to panic, Logan. I've got to be up in five hours, and so does Holly. My bed is calling me I'm afraid, ladies, but go drink until dawn. I'll come and laugh at you when I get off shift."

It was Regan's turn to poke her tongue out. "I remember a time when you'd have skipped sleep altogether."

"What can I say? I'm getting old," Mia responded.

"We're here," Logan said as the brake lights lit up from the car in front. He turned around in his seat, his gaze scanning them but lingering on Mia a little longer than her and Katalina. "Don't look very old from where I'm sitting, Mia." He winked.

"It's dark," Mia replied, not reacting to his attempt at charm. Katalina giggled.

Cage climbed out of the car, coming to Logan's window. "It was great hanging with you, dude. See you around, yeah?"

"Bye, Cage," Katalina called from the back seat. "I'm stealing Regan for the night. Let Jackson know please."

Cage saluted her before walking back to his car.

"Bye, Mia," Regan murmured, taking in her old friend. "Thanks for inviting me."

"Anytime," Mia replied, dragging her into a hug. "Don't be a stranger." Mia searched Regan's gaze, hers glistening with unshed tears.

Swallowing the sudden lump in her throat, Regan was unable to answer with words, so she smiled and nodded. Her time of hiding was over. She knew her parents wouldn't be happy with her rekindled social life, but it wasn't a good enough reason to lessen herself anymore. She couldn't do it, and in her heart, Regan knew it wouldn't be what Megan would have wanted either. She just hoped her parents would catch up soon too.

CHAPTER 31

Moaning, Regan brought a hand to her throbbing head, hoping to keep her skull from splitting in two. Opening one eye, she groaned louder, shielding her face as she opened the other. It took her a second or two for her vision to clear and focus on her surroundings. Katalina was sitting opposite her, knees tucked up to her chin, a mug of something hot and steaming in her hands. "Morning," she whimpered, a crease appearing on her brow as if in pain.

"It's nearly noon," Bass said, appearing behind Katalina. "Coffee, Regan?"

"Hmm, please," Regan answered softly, afraid to speak too loudly and cause herself more pain. He returned a moment later and handed her a mug. Without alcohol in her system as a confidence boost, Regan felt suddenly shy and awkward for being there. "Sorry, I'll be out of your hair shortly."

Bass's face softened. "Don't leave on my account. I've got to head out anyway. I'm sure Kat will love to have the company." He leaned down, kissing Katalina on the cheek, then his grin turned wicked, and it was the first time Regan had seen Bass as anything other than an alpha. "You can suffer together."

Katalina pulled a face. "Stop enjoying this so much. This is your fault," she groaned.

"How'd you figure that?" Bass asked.

"Because if you let me out more, I wouldn't be such a lightweight. I'm a wolf. I'm supposed to be immune to alcohol poisoning."

Bass chuckled. "There's an empty bottle of vodka and wine over there. If you were human, you'd be in the hospital."

"Go away," Katalina grumbled. "Leave me to die in peace."

With a grin and a blown kiss, Bass left the cabin.

"I'm so sorry I dragged you here and got you wasted," Katalina said when Bass left. "I tend to go overboard when I've had a few too many drinks."

Regan took a sip of coffee, then smiled. "Don't be sorry, Kat. The truth is I was dreading going home last night. I'm grateful you invited me."

"Your parents?"

"They'd have been none too pleased to find me a little drunk. I turned my phone off after texting them to say I was stopping here."

Katalina raised an eyebrow then winced as if the movement hurt. "Bet your phone's going to blow up when you turn it on."

"Yup, which is exactly why it's staying off until my head doesn't feel like it's going to crack open."

"Wanna watch a movie on my laptop? We don't have a TV anymore. It got blown up." Katalina rolled her eyes.

"Yeah, sure, sounds good."

Hours later after another few cups of coffee, a movie, and some more sleep, Regan and Katalina were alive enough to venture out of the cabin.

"I can't wait to have a real house again and an actual kitchen to cook food in. I mean, it's handy having a pack kitchen nearby, but I'd rather have not got out of bed today," Katalina rambled on.

Regan jumped in quick as Katalina took a spilt-second break to drag in a breath. "Kat, are you sure I shouldn't just go home and get food?"

"Are you ready for an earful from your mom?"

"No." Regan shrugged. "But I don't think I'll ever be ready."

"Probably not," Katalina agreed. "But a full stomach will help. You're with me. No one will say a thing."

"O-kay," Regan replied, still unsure. A part of her was worried she'd run into Tyler and not be able to act like she hardly knew him. She'd thought about texting him that she was with Katalina, but that would require her switching on her phone and seeing what her parents had to say.

If Regan were honest with herself, the promise she'd made not to hide anymore was already being broken. She was just hiding from a different thing.

They entered a building, and Regan had to force herself to keep breathing. It was close to 2:00 p.m., but even though it was between meal times there was still at least eight members of Dark Shadow in the room.

A few waved hi to Katalina as she entered. She waved back half-heartedly, too busy scanning the menu board. "So, we're kinda late for breakfast," Katalina sighed. "I'd kill for a massive stack of pancakes."

"No need to kill me for them," an old lady said, popping her head out from what Regan guessed was the kitchen area.

"Kerry, hi." Katalina smiled.

"I hear you were a little worse for wear this morning."

Katalina smiled sheepishly. "Just a little. Kerry, have you met Regan before?"

Katalina stepped to the side, allowing Kerry full view of

Regan. "Hello, nice to meet you," Regan said.

"You too. So, are you after pancakes too? I'm guessing you were Katalina's partner in crime?"

Regan laughed softly. "I was I'm afraid, and pancakes would be lovely, thank you."

"Take a seat, girls. I'll have them to you shortly."

Katalina led Regan over to a table in the far corner. "I don't know about you, but I've had way too much coffee today. Tea instead?"

"I'd love an herbal tea actually, if they have anything like that?"

"Yup, we'll have something. Do you have a preference?"

"Mint is my favorite, but any will do," Regan replied.

It was a short while later, after their pancakes had arrived and they were happily stuffing their faces and chatting, that Regan's back stiffened as a familiar voice stammered her name. Katalina locked eyes with her. Regan forced what she hoped was a smile on her face before turning away from Katalina and facing Tyler.

"Hey, Tyler," she answered smoothly. "How're things?"

"How're things?" He frowned. "What are you doing here?"

Katalina cut in. "Rude much!" She glared at Tyler.

Tyler seemed to snap back into himself, his eyes roaming over Katalina then Regan. "Sorry, that came out wrong. I just… I didn't expect to see you here."

"We went out for a few drinks last night and decided to continue the party back here," Katalina answered for her.

"Hi, Kat," the boy behind Tyler said.

Tyler glanced back at the boy as if just remembering he was there. Regan wanted the ground to swallow her up. Here she'd been worrying about seeing him and not being able to keep her cool, and she'd never once thought about the possibility of Tyler not being able to keep his cool.

"Hi, Zac, I hope Tyler here is treating you nicely. Come see me if you've got any problems, okay?" Katalina answered.

"Hmm… yeah, 'kay. Ty's cool, don't worry," Zackary reassured.

So, this is the boy who's messed up our secret meetings. Regan looked Tyler in the eyes. *I miss you, Ty.*

He gazed back at her, and she was sure she read his silent message back. *I miss you too.*

Zackary cleared his throat. "Hmm… food, Ty?"

"Yeah, right, food. Zac's not stopped eating all day," Tyler explained.

"I'm a growing boy," he countered.

"Yeah, yeah. Well, it was nice seeing you again, Regan. Later, Kat." Tyler left with a quick smile and headed with Zackary over to the kitchen entrance.

"Well, that was awkward," Katalina observed.

Regan ducked her head, concentrating on her food.

"The two of you had a thing right, at that party I threw months ago? Seems like a lifetime."

Regan felt her cheeks heat. "I didn't know that was common knowledge," she mumbled.

"It's not. Alpha's mate, remember?"

Regan laughed. "I actually forget that fact on occasion."

"It's all right." Katalina shrugged. "I'm not all that alphary."

Regan looked up, studying Katalina's face; while she'd said

the words as if in jest, Regan got the sense the fact bothered her a little, like she thought it was a flaw.

"It's not a bad thing, Kat. It's good you're not like that. We need you to not be like that."

"That's good then, 'cause I'm not planning on changing."

The next few minutes were spent eating with the occasional chitchat. Not long after Tyler had arrived, Regan sensed him leave, though she tried her hardest not to look at the exit as he did. She imagined he'd be blowing up her phone later, which only made her not want to turn it on even more, but it seemed life had other plans because Bass entered a few minutes after Tyler had left.

"Hi," he said as he walked over to their table. "Regan, I've just had Jackson on the phone. Apparently your parents have been trying to call you, and I've got to come and check if you're alive."

"Sorry," Regan replied. "It's dead."

"Anyone would think you were twelve, not nineteen," Katalina added.

Regan smiled. "They worry, after.... Well, I best be going. Thanks for the pancakes, and... everything else, Kat."

"No problem. Anytime." Katalina smiled warmly.

"I can give you a lift back if you like?" Bass offered.

"That's all right. I think the walk will do me good."

"I'll walk you to the border then," he said with a smile.

"Okay." Regan hugged Katalina then got to her feet. With each step away from Katalina and toward home, she became heavier, her feet harder to lift.

"Everything okay?" Bass asked softly as they neared Dark Shadow's boundary.

Regan glanced at him, seeing in his gaze that he meant what he was asking. She'd never spent much time around the Dark

Shadow alpha, but if today's encounters were anything to go by, it seemed Bass was a pretty good guy.

"Yeah, just not looking forward to the argument that's coming."

"I take it they aren't the biggest fans of the alliance?"

"No, no, it's not—"

"It's all right. I know we still have a lot of ground to cover on healing the wounds between our two packs, but I have hope." Bass smiled warmly. "Sleepovers such as last night give me that hope."

"Katalina is the hope."

Bass paused as they came to the boundary. An expression filled his face that could only be described as one thing: pure, unadulterated love. "Yes, she is. She's the hope for many things, but not all are ready for it, so we must tread carefully into this new and uncertain future."

Regan had no answer to Bass's words; they'd hit home more than she guessed Bass realized. She too was treading carefully into a new and uncertain future. At least, she was trying to. Most days it felt like she was crashing through it headfirst, but she too was going to have hope. Hope and faith that somehow, they'd all get through it in one piece.

"Well, see you around, Regan. Get home safe."

Chapter 32

Tyler watched Regan being escorted from Dark Shadow by Bass with an ugly pit of jealousy in his gut. Seeing her in the pack's kitchen had affected him more than he cared to admit. He'd most definitely not kept his cool.

"You got a thing for that chick?" Zackary asked, stepping up behind him and looking over his shoulder. "She's hot. Seems a bit shy though… not that that's a bad thing."

Tyler swallowed the urge to snarl and reminded himself the kid had no idea about pack workings and having a motormouth wasn't a good enough reason to kill him. He'd been quiet the first few hours, but once he'd realized Tyler wasn't planning on growling at him for being there, the kid opened up. But maybe a little too much.

"She's not from this pack," Tyler said.

"What's that matter? She's still hot. You should totally bang her."

Tyler couldn't contain the growl that erupted from him this time. Zackary stumbled back, but when Tyler turned to face him, there was aggression on his face. Aggression it was clear Zackary was struggling to control.

"Not sure where you come from, but where I come from, we don't speak about women that way. My father wouldn't be too pleased to hear me say a thing like that."

The kid clenched his fists as he slowly regained a little control. "Mine wouldn't either. Sorry, I kinda fell in with the wrong crowd back home. Guess their douchebag ways rubbed off on me."

"I'd work on that," Tyler suggested.

Zackary nodded. "So that girl?"

Not going to drop it then. Tyler internally rolled his eyes, then closed his door and turned to face Zackary. "Is from River Run, so therefore it doesn't matter what I think."

"You like her, though, right? I mean you were a stammering mess earlier in the food hall."

"Kitchen. And I was not."

"Pfft. So was." The kid rolled his eyes, and Tyler had the urge to strangle him.

"Fine, I think she's attractive. Happy now?"

"Sure, ecstatic," he answered sarcastically.

"Great. Now give me a bit of peace. I've got a training session to plan."

"Ugh, but I'm bored, and you haven't even got a TV."

"Read a book," Tyler suggested, waving his hand at the collection he had stacked in the corner.

"A book!" Zackary groaned.

"Look, Zac, in an hour, you'll be meeting some of the other kids your age, and I can get a true sense of the control you have, but until that time, I'm afraid you're stuck bored with me."

"Should have stayed at Jackson's," he grumbled under his breath.

Tyler didn't reply. Part of him wished he had.

Cooper leaped out of the way as Zackary shifted without control, snarling at him savagely.

"Shit," the boy swore.

"Zac," Tyler snarled, closing in on him. "Calm yourself."

Zackary growled back, glancing at the kids behind Tyler, not with aggression but embarrassment.

"Session's over," Tyler announced to the group behind him, without taking his focus from Zackary. They didn't need telling twice. A minute later, it was just Tyler and one very confused, pissed-off wolf.

"Okay, Zac, it's just you and me now. Can you shift?"

The wolf looked pained.

"Tell you what, I've got a better idea. Let's wear that wolf of yours out." Stripping his clothes quickly, Tyler shifted, racing past Zackary with a playful nip and bark. It took Zackary all of two seconds to move into action and follow.

Tyler darted through the trees, making sure to lead Zackary away from the more popular areas of Dark Shadow and anyone who may get in the way. Zackary was surprisingly fast, keeping up with Tyler well. Deciding to up the game a little, Tyler began to make sharp changes in direction, leading them across terrain that would require careful thought and not just the brunt of the wolf. This slowed Zackary down, the exercise making the kid have to connect both his human brain and wolf. They ran for miles, only stopping when Tyler's muscles began to ache.

As Tyler came to a stop, Zackary did too, the boy shifting immediately and collapsing on the ground.

"Ugh, I wished clothes stayed with the shift," he gasped between breath.

Tyler shifted. "Gotta get used to the nudity." He chuckled. "Do you think you can shift back for a slow walk home?"

"Not sure."

"Have you ever voluntarily shifted?"

He shook his head.

"Well, now would be a good time to work on that," Tyler suggested.

"Hhh, give us a minute. I'm wiped."

Tyler smiled. "Good job I didn't go at full speed, then."

"That wasn't full speed?" Zackary gasped.

"Not even nearly, little wolf. You've got a long way to go."

He grumbled incoherently, wrapping his arms tightly around himself. "Cooper and the others probably think I'm a total a-hole."

"Nah, they won't. They've all been there."

"So, they've all shifted without control and made a total fool of themselves?" he asked unbelievably.

"You'd be surprised, Zac. I'd say at least 90 percent of them have."

"Still."

"You've got a long road to walk, Zac. I'm not going to lie, but you'll get there. And Cooper and the others will understand, you'll see."

"Okay."

He didn't sound all that convinced, but Tyler knew now wasn't the time to push him. "You good? Ready to try a shift, or are you walking back nude?"

Zackary rolled his eyes. "What do I do?"

"Take a few deep breaths. Let all the tension drain from your body, then think of your wolf. The feel of it, the power and speed that floods you, that feeling of complete freedom, let it all fill you up and then let go."

A few minutes later, Zackary screwed up his face in frustration and glared at Tyler. "It's not working. Can't you just punch me or something?"

Tyler laughed. "No, I can't. Now come on, believe in yourself. You've got this."

The kid closed his eyes and dragged in a deep breath before letting it slowly out. Tyler saw the second he'd cracked it. Zackary's entire body seemed to sigh and then the next moment, it was morphing into a wolf.

Amber eyes set in a tawny wolf face met his with amazement.

"You did it." Tyler smiled. "Told you, you could." He shifted, then indicated with a flick of his head and soft growl for Zackary to follow. Their path through the trees was more sedate on the journey back. Tyler could feel Zackary's wonderment as he wove through the forest. He'd been running at full speed in more ways than one since becoming a wolf shifter, and Tyler suspected he was finally beginning to see that wolf life wasn't all that bad.

CHAPTER 33

It had been four days. Four days without seeing her, four days without tasting her lips. He couldn't take it anymore. Tyler was on the verge of madness with the uncontrollable need inside of him. Just to see her, to hold her, just for a moment.

They'd come back late from a meeting with the kid's dad at Jackson's. Bass had thought the River Run alpha's home was a better setting than the burnt down ruin they currently had at Dark Shadow. The meeting had gone well, with Zackary's dad agreeing to help rebuild Dark Shadow. Bass and he had slipped away later in the evening, and Tyler had filled Bass in on all he'd learned about the kid. He'd informed Bass about the incident with Cooper but noted that it wasn't aggression toward Cooper that had triggered the unwanted shift but at himself. Zackary seemed not to like himself all that much. His lack of skill and control frustrated Zackary to the point of losing himself to the wolf. Yet in four days, Tyler had seen improvement. He wasn't a bad kid, just lost, like so many others had been in Dark Shadow and still were.

The meeting had tired Zackary in more ways than one, and not long after they'd arrived home, he'd fallen asleep on the rollaway bed they'd dragged in for him.

Tyler was currently staring at the kid, contemplating if he'd wake up and if he did, would he be a danger if Tyler was gone? There'd been no talks of Zackary returning to stay with his family at the local bed and breakfast in town. It appeared he'd be a long-term guest in Tyler's home, and normally, it wouldn't have bothered him, but nothing about Tyler's life was normal at the moment.

I'll be quick, he told himself, easing the guilt inside. *Even if he does wake up, would it matter? He'll likely just roll over and go back to sleep.... He won't wonder where I am. I'll leave a note, just to be on the safe side.*

Picking up a pen and note pad, Tyler quickly jotted down a message.

Gone for a run. Stay inside. Won't be long.

Tyler left the note on the floor beside Zackary, gazing at him for a moment longer just to be certain he was in a heavy sleep.

I'm not going to be long. Thirty minutes, tops, I'll run there, kiss her, and run back.

He reassured himself all the way to River Run, telling himself he only needed to hold her, to breath her into his lungs just for a moment. One kiss wouldn't hurt. It would be just enough to see him through.

And it was for the first night, but by the third, one kiss wasn't nearly enough. His thirst for Regan grew with every passing second. But it wasn't just the physical desire he struggled with, but being without her completely—talking with her after a long day at work, hearing her opinion on something that was bothering him. It was falling to sleep with her in his arms and waking up with her beautiful face as his first view. Tyler missed Regan beyond measure, and he knew the stolen moments they were having weren't nearly enough to sustain them into the future. Time had run out. He just had no idea what to do about it.

Chapter 34

It was as if a noose had been hung around her neck and being tightened centimeter by centimeter with each passing day. Her parents had become suffocating since she'd stayed out with Katalina all night. The telling off they'd given her on her arrival back that day had made her feel like she was fourteen all over again and being grounded for climbing out of her window and sneaking off with friends. Only she wasn't fourteen; she was nineteen, a grown woman quite capable of making her own choices. But telling her parents wasn't going so well. She'd tried to break it to them gently as they shouted at her that afternoon Bass had escorted her off Dark Shadow. Tried to make them see that things had changed, that the Dark Shadow who had killed her sister didn't exist anymore, but they were too blind in their grief and anger. Even after three years her parents weren't ready. Regan was beginning to think they may never be.

To make matters worse, she'd hardly seen Tyler. Zackary had made things impossible for them, not that the kid knew anything about it. The truth was, on the fourth day of not seeing Tyler, if he hadn't shown up, she'd have gone to him. Their kiss that night had felt like breathing again after nearly drowning. His touch was like electricity across her skin. Time apart had only served to multiply their need for one another, and it was becoming difficult to cope with.

Regan knew Tyler wanted to tell Katalina, and a part of her did too, but her parents were struggling with simple things like her being friends with Mia again and having a social life. How would they react to the news of Tyler? How could they possibly be okay with it if they weren't okay with her being friends with someone who'd been her friend for most of her childhood and came from the same pack?

Time was all they needed, she told herself daily. Time to adjust. When they welcomed Mia back with open arms, she'd introduce Tyler, and everything would suddenly be all right.

"Keep dreaming," Regan muttered to herself as she headed out of her bedroom. "Keep dreaming." Heading downstairs, Regan entered the kitchen finding her mom by the sink.

"Morning. What are your plans today? You've class, right?" Her mom asked, glancing over her shoulder.

"Yup, morning classes, then an afternoon shift at the café. I'll be home late though as I'm going to see Mia straight from work."

Her mother's jaw clenched. "Not out drinking I hope?" she asked coolly.

"No just hanging at her house."

"Right," her mom answered sharply.

"Mia's a novice soldier now, you know. She's not a kid anymore."

"Yes, I know."

Regan sighed. Turning away from her mom, she grabbed a nutbar out of the pantry, then filled a travel mug with coffee. She was beginning to worry no amount of time was going to prepare her parents for Tyler, and the time instead was to prepare herself for the loss of her parents.

"Hey, your boyfriend's just walked in through the front door. Since when does he use the front door?" Johnny said as he poked his head in through the door to the staff room.

"What?" she gasped.

"Tyler's out front. Took a seat in a booth, got a kid with him too. You guys fallen out or something?" he inquired, sounding far too hopeful then he should.

"Kid's his cousin from out of town," she lied. "And no, we've not fallen out. I'll be right there."

Regan took a few moments to compose herself before walking out front and heading toward Tyler. He'd taken the seat that meant he'd spot her the moment she exited the backroom. His face lit with a brilliant smile before he schooled his expression into a natural face, but he'd slipped up long enough for Zackary to notice and for him to turn around and see who Tyler was smiling at.

Careful, Ty, you'll give us away.

"Hello, Tyler, Zackary, what can I get you guys?" she asked politely.

The kid smirked. "Seriously, you two can give it a rest. I know you have the hots for one another."

Tyler's attention snapped to Zackary's as dread uncoiled inside of Regan.

"What are you talking about?" asked Tyler

"The two of you pretending like you barely know each other. I followed you last night, Ty, saw you guys all over each other, so secret's out, you can stop pretending."

All the energy drained from Regan. She slumped down into the booth Zackary was in, nudging him along, then buried her head in her hands.

"We're doomed," she cried.

"Babe," Tyler whispered, taking her hands and kissing them. "I'll think of something."

"I really don't know what the problem is," Zackary said. "I'm not going to tell anyone. Though honestly, I can't for the life of me figure out why the two of you can't be together."

"I've told you, she's from River Run," Tyler said, glaring at Zackary. "And what were you doing following me?"

"Well, I woke up the first night, saw your note, so went back to sleep. The second night I did the same, but on the third, it was getting a little weird that you were reusing the same note over and over, so I thought I'd see if I could follow you without you noticing. Honestly, I was just doing it for the fun of following you, wasn't actually expecting to see you two sucking each other's face off." He made a gagging face. "But like I said, I'm not telling anyone."

It was Tyler's turn to bury is head in his hands. "Urgh, I'm so stupid," he grumbled.

"You're not," Regan insisted. Tyler met her gaze, and despite everything, butterflies set flight within her.

"I should have sensed him, Regan, and if I didn't sense him, I could not have sensed someone else, someone far more dangerous."

"You weren't on patrol, Tyler."

"Stop freaking out already. I don't see why you can't just tell everyone," Zackary said.

"Because she's from another pack, Zac," Tyler repeated.

"Well, isn't Katalina technically from River Run? And that's not a problem, so why would you two be?"

"It's complicated, Zac," Regan said softly.

"Allegiances would be questioned, Zac, Katalina is different. She didn't grow up here."

"Well, can't you just join River Run instead of Dark Shadow?" Zackary suggested.

"I'm an enforcer, Zac. I can't just abandon my pack."

Zackary began to look a little worried. "I wish I hadn't said anything now. I just thought it would be easier if you knew I knew so, you know, you didn't have to keep waiting until real late for me to be asleep, or trying not to smile when you pretend we're just randomly going out for coffee when I don't even drink coffee, just so you can catch a glimpse of your girl." He let out a huge breath. "I'm not going to breathe a word of this to anyone, promise. All right?"

Regan laid a hand on Zackary's shoulder, her wolf seeking to soothe his. "Okay, Zac, we believe you." She felt for the kid, could sense how overwhelmed and confused he was. It was clear he looked up to Tyler and needed him to know he was loyal.

"So, why does he look like he might throw up?"

"Because you've just reminded Tyler that we've been walking a fine line these last few months, and how easily it can go wrong." Reaching across the table, Regan took Tyler's hand. "I'm going to go make us some drinks and food; then I'll be back, okay?"

Tyler glanced up, he looked broken. "I should have sensed him, Regan."

"I know, Ty, I know." Getting up, she slowly closed the distance between them and bent toward his face, tipping his chin up with her finger and planting a soft kiss on his mouth. "It's going to be okay," she breathed against his lips. It has to be, she added silently. *It has to be.*

Thankfully it was a quiet afternoon at the café, and she only had to serve two other customers while Zackary and Tyler were there. By the time they'd left, they'd almost convinced themselves that Zackary knowing was a good thing. The kid was right; it would mean less sneaking around, and Tyler could see her at work again. But what neither Tyler nor she admitted, even though it was on their minds, was the fact time had run out, and they needed to somehow find a way to tell somebody. It was better her parents found out from her own lips then secondhand gossip. They'd most likely be furious if it was a week or a year from now when she told them anyway. She just had to find the courage to follow through and do it.

CHAPTER 35

Since Bill's capture, Katalina had sensed a rift forming between her and Bass. At first, it hadn't worried her. She'd put it down to stress, which they'd both had a lot of lately. But she'd caught him in a lie; he wasn't where he said he'd be, and the fact he was lying and sneaking around behind her back worried Katalina more than the constant threat they lived under.

It was as if the two of them had taken one too many hits and were now going off in different directions. Bass wore his mask more and more, to a point Katalina didn't always recognize him. It frightened her; she'd always feared losing herself to this life, but never Bass. Bass was her one constant, the one she could always rely on.

Yet he'd lied.

Nico looked confused when she asked him where Bass was, and when she said what Bass had told her; that he was with Nico, he tried to cover, to lie for Bass, but not all that well. It wasn't fair of Bass to bring his friend into the deceit and knowing he hadn't told Nico what he was up to told Katalina whatever it was he didn't want his moral compass to know.

"Where are you going?" Nico called as she stormed off.

"To find him and kill him!" she yelled.

"He might have an explanation," Nico said, running after her. "Why don't you come back and calm down and ask him when he returns?"

Katalina came to an abrupt stop. "Because I need this

anger to face him, because I keep letting things like this slip and it's gotten me nowhere. I won't stand by while he lies to me and pretends it's okay."

"It's not okay, Kat. I'm not saying that. He's just.... There's a lot going on, and he's not coping like he thinks he is."

"Then he should turn to us for help, not shut us out. I'm sorry, Nico, I'm doing this."

It took her a little while to track him down, and where he was surprised Katalina. She'd not expected Jackson to be in on the lie. But there he was as guilty as Bass, and by the looks on their faces, they knew it.

They were in Jackson's barn with Bill tied to a chair his face swollen and covered in red and purple bruises. His eyebrow had split, fresh blood running from the cut, joining the blood that also flowed from his lip. Bill had been beaten bloody, and by the evidence on Bass's knuckles, he's done most of the damage.

"What the hell is going on in here?" she snapped as she dragged the barn door open.

Bill laughed. "Naughty, naughty, boys. Keeping things from the princess."

"Shut it," Jackson snarled, punching Bill in the gut.

Katalina studied them, the two men who weren't supposed to lie to her, who she'd considered good, but at that moment, she saw a darkness in them. She saw how easy it was for a wolf to turn into a monster.

"I don't believe you two."

Turning on her heel, Katalina marched from the barn. She'd wanted an explanation, a valid reason as to why Bass had lied, and she'd found just that. Only in her eyes, it wasn't valid at all.

"Katalina," Bass called.

She didn't wait to see if he followed; she was hoping he

hadn't. But his hand was touching hers, pulling her to a stop, and she had no choice but to face him.

"I'm sorry, okay," he said as she met his eyes.

"For what? What are you sorry for, Bass?"

"For not telling you where I was going."

He said the words, but they were flat; he was wearing a mask, saying what he knew she wanted to hear, but Bass had forgotten one vital thing—she saw through his masks. He'd only ever been one person to her.

"No, you're not. Do you think I don't see? Your masks won't work on me, and you should know that. I'm your mate, and you lied, and then lied to me again. You're not sorry. You're only sorry you got caught."

Katalina couldn't look at him, dragging her hand from his she walked away.

"I had to find out the truth, Kat," he called. "I had to make Bill tell me the truth."

"What truth?" she asked over her shoulder.

"What he told them, and who else is involved. I must know, Katalina, don't you see? I must know who I can trust."

Katalina paused. Turning, she faced him, seeing everything he hid from the world: the hurt, the desperation, the betrayal. His eyes and his tone said it all, but it wasn't enough for Katalina to forgive him, to accept what he was doing in the barn was justified.

"And you think beating a man will have him spilling the truth? What you were doing in there was torture, Bass. That's not who you are. Not the man I fell in love with anyway."

"Please, Katalina," he whispered, full of pain.

"Please, what? What is it you want from me?" Her anger was fading, and as it did, all the energy left her body. Disappointment was a heavy thing, and there was more than just that weighing her down.

"Forgive me," Bass begged, taking a step toward her. "Please forgive me."

"I can't even look at you right now."

Her words hurt him. She could see them like the flick of a whip hitting skin, yet they were the truth.

"You're letting them win," Bass said, angrily.

His words fuel her fire. Hands scrunching into fists, Katalina closed the space between them. "No, it's you who are letting them win. This is what they want, Bass. They're wearing us down bit by bit, planting seeds of distrust and sowing darkness in our very veins. Castor doesn't just want our home; he wants to twist us up and change who we are until our hearts are as black as his. And you're letting him. What you were doing in that barn wasn't right. That's not who you are."

"A message needs to be sent," he insisted.

"And what message were you sending, and who to? Why is Bill even alive? He should have been killed the moment he was captured. Instead, you've held it off so you could beat him while he's tied to a chair."

"To get answers, to find out if he was working with somebody else."

"And did you find any? Did he give you what you wanted?"

"No," Bass answered quietly.

"So, then how long do you plan to do this for? It's been five days, Bass, and people are noticing he's missing, and your lies aren't holding up."

"Today. It's set for later today."

"What is?" she asked, though she already knew she'd not

like the answer.

"His execution."

"An execution?" Katalina shook her head, tears stinging her eyes. "What are you going to do, drag him up in front of the entire pack and slaughter him?"

"Yes, and it will send a message to anyone that's working with him that we will no longer be playing nice. Mercy will not be given."

"Playing nice." Katalina laughed with disbelief. Turning away, she gripped at her hair. It was like Bass hadn't just taken the wrong path, but had gone to another planet. She didn't know how to deal with this version of him. He was alien to her. He frightened her.

"Have you heard yourself? I won't stand by while you do that. While you execute him in front of innocents."

"This world is harsh, Kat, you know that."

"No." Tears ran down her face. "I can't accept that. I don't fit in a world that can accept that, and you know that, Bass, or at least I thought you did."

"I'm sorry, Katalina," he whispered.

"For what?" she sobbed, unable to contain her heartbreak anymore.

"For failing to change this world," he answered, his expression hollow.

"It's not too late. You don't have to do this. You could go in that barn right now and just end it, please."

A mask slipped back onto his face, his gaze hard and empty, and Katalina had never felt so out of place, or Bass so far away. "Part of me wants to do as you ask, but you don't understand this world, Katalina. It must be done; a message must be sent. I can no longer allow myself to be weak."

"That's where you're wrong. I understand this world perfectly, and I have always understood that I didn't want to be a part of it, the way it was. But you promised me it wouldn't be this way, and there's no going back for me now. You're my mate. I love you even as you're breaking my heart. If you do this, there is no changing it. It will only change us."

He didn't answer, but he didn't need to. Katalina could see it written all over his face, in his body language. Bass had decided on this path long before their argument, and nothing she could say would make him change his mind. The fact broke her, and she walked away feeling as cold and empty as Bass looked.

"I must ask one more thing of you, Katalina."

She paused but didn't look back.

"You must be there. We must show a united front."

"I'll be there," she called. "But I don't wear masks, Bass. They'll all know we're not united, and I'm glad of that fact."

Throughout all the attacks Indiana had sprung on them, Katalina hadn't once felt they'd won. Packmates had been injured, homes burned to the ground, but she'd always felt they'd walked out in one piece, together, whole. But Castor had finally had his win. Bill was the ultimate trap and Bass had fallen for it. They were heading down the path to self-destruction, and Katalina only hoped she was enough to drag them back—that it wasn't too late.

Chapter 36

Tyler was connected to his alpha and pack in a way that told him there was something wrong. But he'd never anticipated Bass walking onto Dark Shadow's inner lands, dragging Bill not so gently with him. Bill was clearly injured, and his first instinct was to go to him, but the look on Bass's face had him holding back. Nico, Dax, and Katalina followed not so far behind. They didn't look confused, though Katalina did not look happy. In fact, he'd never seen Katalina look so… empty. Whatever had happened, Bass hadn't told his inner circle, or what should have been his inner circle. It was becoming clear that the dynamics of Dark Shadow were shifting, and his second and enforcers were no longer trusted.

"What's going on?" Zackary murmured, coming to stand beside Tyler. "Hey, that dude's the one who took over my spot in the barn."

"What?" Tyler gasped.

"That guy. Jackson told me to move out of his barn, so they could keep him locked up in there instead. Who is he?"

Tyler didn't answer; instead, he met John's gaze across the way, shaking his head slightly at his silent question, then did the same to Logan, Noah, and Jacob. They all walked forward, meeting in the center before Bass and the others, as stone-cold dread settled heavily in his stomach. *What did you do, Bill? What did you do?*

Katalina stood beside Bass, appearing strong and unaffected. But Tyler detected an uneasiness in the depths of her gaze, a deep sadness that she was trying her best to hide. He'd thought up to that moment that Bass and Katalina trusted him, but it appeared he was wrong.

A sliver of uncertainly wormed its way into his mind. *Do they know? Have Regan and I been caught?*

Bass's gaze roamed over them all, hard and unflinching. "It came to my attention after the Indiana attack that there was a leak in this pack, giving information to our enemy," Bass said into the unsteady silence.

A hushed murmur spread through the crowd as tension increased. Zackary moved closer to Tyler, his shoulder touching his.

"Unfortunately, my suspicions were confirmed," Bass continued gravely.

Tyler studied Bill, his heart a pounding drum in his chest. Not Bill, not their second, a man they'd all trusted without doubt. Who he'd have given his life to defend. *Not him, please not him, not him.*

Yet Bass continued, confirming what Tyler already knew was coming. "Earlier this week, I told only Bill that Katalina had decided she would spend the end of summer with her human family. Bill used this information and attempted to abduct Katalina, with the intention of taking her life and shattering the alliance beyond repair. Katalina was shot in his attempt, and Nico, Dax, and several River Run wolves bore witness. It was also recorded for anyone who does not believe my word, and the word of those here," he finished, sweeping an arm toward Katalina, Dax, and Nico.

He paused, his gaze hard as he took in the crowd. "If he had succeeded, not only would we have lost Katalina, we'd have been left vulnerable to attack as we suffered with grief and betrayal. The alliance and friendships forged because of Katalina could have shattered. Do not doubt the very real threat Bill's actions have bought us. An attack after such a huge loss would have quite possibly been successful, altering all we know and love."

"Why?" John whispered from beside Tyler, gazing at Bill. "Why would you do this to us?"

Bill looked up. One of his eyes was swollen shut, the right side of his face covered in angry bruises and cuts, but his other eye looked at them with rebellion. "Castor is my brother. He should have never been cast out."

"You supported Bass," John responded angrily.

"You've fought beside us," Tyler added.

"I pretended to for as long as I needed to complete our goal. Castor should be alpha, not this exc—"

Bills words died in his throat as Nico's knife grazed his throat. "That's enough bullshit from you I think," Nico said, mouth a hard line.

"Bill is right in some ways," Bass said, surveying them all. "Castor shouldn't have been cast out. He should have followed me or died for the insolence."

Gasps erupted. Tyler couldn't quite believe Bass had said them. It was like they'd all been sucked into an alternate universe, even Katalina was gazing wide-eyed at Bass, not even attempting to hide her thoughts.

"I've been too lenient in my attempts not to be my father," Bass explained. "That was a mistake, one I will not be repeating." In one swift action, Bass moved with the speed of an alpha. One second Bill with standing defiantly even in defeat, the next lying dead, his neck broken, and body sprawled at an odd angle.

Shock rocked through Tyler and the pack members around him. Zackary gasped beside him, turning his face away and gripping Tyler's hand.

"It's okay," Tyler whispered, squeezing the boy's hand, as he moved his body to shield Zackary from the view. Tyler had not seen the resemblance between Bass and his late father before, and it was clear by the atmosphere around them that no one had expected Bass to deliver death as Bill's punishment either. Tyler had never known Bass to kill in cold blood; it seemed war had far worse consequences than death.

Zackary began to tremble behind him. Tyler was torn between wanting to help the boy and needing to see this betrayal through.

"Hang on, Zac," Tyler murmured, turning to look him in the eyes. "Keep control. You're safe."

"To anyone thinking of jeopardizing this pack and the alliance, or if any of you didn't agree with what I did today, or are guilty of the same crimes, I urge you to leave or come forward. You have twenty-four hours to make your crimes known. After that, there is no redemption available to you, and this will be your fate," Bass continued, pointing at Bill's dead body.

Tyler's back faced Bass as he kept his attention on Zackary, but that didn't stop Bass's words from traveling down his spine like sharp icy claws. *This will be your fate.*

Every little mistake Tyler had made because he'd been too caught up with Regan entered his mind. Was this the same? Was he as bad as Bill? *Is this my fate?*

Silence followed. Tyler's shoulders suddenly became heavy; his stomach lurched with unease. Regan appeared in his mind—silk black hair draped over a pillow, her dark-blue eyes full of joy, and her smile like sunshine. *Will she be punished too?*

Urgency gripped him. Pulling out his phone, Tyler text Regan.

Tyler – Babe, I'm sorry I won't be coming tonight. Something came up x

He slid it away, ignoring the vibration that indicated her reply. It didn't matter that Zackary knew and it made meeting easier. Tyler couldn't risk Regan's life. Even if there was the smallest of chances, he couldn't do it.

"Well, shit," John whispered beside him. "I did not see that coming."

"Bill or his death?" Tyler's voice sounded empty even to his own ears.

"Both. I trusted that man. Fuck, I even let the bastard

babysit my kids." John shook his head, bewildered. "How could he do this to us?"

"I don't know," Tyler whispered.

Bass continued talking, but Tyler couldn't concentrate on his words. It was as if the blood in his veins had frozen. The crowd started to disperse, and Zackary tugged on his hand, not letting him go. Tyler studied him, the fear on his face, the need for escape. He was only fourteen, and he'd been a wolf for no time at all. But nothing Tyler could have done would have prepared Zackary for seeing a man executed.

"Please," Zackary begged.

Tyler glanced around; everyone was leaving but the inner circle and those who'd arrived with Bill. Yet it was his job as an enforcer to protect his pack, and right now, that meant taking Zackary far away from here.

"Come on," he murmured, guiding him away.

"Ty? Tyler?"

"Yeah?" Tyler forced his focus on John.

"Where are you going?" John asked.

"To help Zac. Fill me in later okay?"

John glanced at Zackary. "Go, go help him," he agreed with a nod.

And as Tyler led Zackary away, his mind struggled with the reality Bill's death and Bass's words had given him. He had no choice but to tell someone about Regan, someone he trusted to be rational, someone who'd make sure Regan wasn't harmed even if he was.

Katalina. He decided. *It has to be Katalina.*

CHAPTER 37

She hadn't been able to stop herself from flinching when Bass had delivered the killing blow. As it was, it was a miracle she hadn't closed her eyes. A part of her understood his actions; the hardened, primal part, but her soft heart? It couldn't take this side of Bass, the side born from the casualties of war.

Katalina could feel the pack's emotions as if they were a living beast inside of her—hurt, shock, and betrayal. Bill's actions were going to affect some more than others, but for all, it was another chip at an already worn-out armor.

Glancing at Bill's still form, Katalina wondered what they'd do with his body. Burying him with the other members of the pack wasn't an option; she'd settled on burning him when her ears tuned into Bass's conversation with his enforcers.

"Deliver him to Castor," Bass said.

"What?" Katalina gasped, certain she'd heard wrong.

Bass's gaze swept toward her, his mask securely in place. This man was a stranger to her. He wasn't the soft, loving man who curled up with her on a night or the hard protector who'd strike down anyone attempting to hurt her. This side of him came from his father and what he'd been wrongly taught was strength. A chill ran down her spine.

"I'm going to deliver Bill's body to Castor as a message," he repeated.

Her blood ran cold. "Will that not just cause him to retaliate? I think enough messages have been delivered today."

"Possibly, but Castor is going to attack at some point either way. He cannot be allowed to continue thinking he has the upper hand. I need to send a message."

"When?" John asked.

"Now. You, Logan, and I will take him. That leaves Tyler, Noah, Jacob, and Dax in charge of the pack's defense, and Nic, you'll be with Kat," Bass instructed.

Katalina didn't bother saying she didn't need a babysitter; he wouldn't listen to her. He was beyond reasoning. Bass was out of her reach and she feared he might always be.

The group broke up, Noah reassuring Bass he'd fill Tyler in when he came back from dealing with Zackary. Katalina didn't voice her opinion on that. She didn't say that Tyler shouldn't have needed to help Zackary because a fourteen-year-old boy shouldn't have ever seen a man executed. She didn't say a word when he said goodbye as he left to deliver Bill's body. She didn't tell him to be careful, or that she thought what he was doing was a bad idea. Instead, Katalina forced a smile and watched as he walked away, wondering at what point in this war Bass had become so lost that she couldn't stand the sight of him. And how had she not noticed? Why had she not done something when he'd first turned down the wrong path?

"So, shall I bring Livy over for a movie?" Nico asked her when she turned away from watching Bass's departure.

Katalina focused on Nico's face.

"Kat?" he said, warily.

"I'm sorry, Nic, but I'm not staying here. I can't stay here."

"What do you mean?" he asked, reaching for her.

She stepped out of his reach. "I'm sorry, Nic," she repeated. "But I can't stay here. I need to be with my family."

"But, Kat?"

Katalina shook her head. “Don’t follow, Nico. I can’t stay here. I’m going to my family. I’m going to River Run.”

She ran from the cabin, Arne giving chase after her as Nico shouted her name. There was an emptiness spreading throughout her body, a hollow ache in her heart. She was in shock, so much so that she’d not realized the significance of her words. *My family. River Run.* Not Bass, not her aunt and uncle, but River Run. Jackson.

He was already waiting for her when she tore from the trees as if an invisible ghost was chasing her. His arms opened for her as she neared, and as Katalina fell into Jackson’s arms, she felt she could breathe for the first time since Bill had fallen dead.

“It’s all right, Kat,” Jackson soothed. “It will be all right.”

Tears fell from her eyes as she shook her head. “I should have done more. I should have stopped him.”

“You’ve done all you can, Kat.”

“Then why didn’t you say anything when he was coming here?”

“It wasn’t my place, Katalina. He’s an alpha. It’s not my place to question him. It will be okay, you’ll see.”

“You didn’t see him. It was as if he wasn’t Bass at all.”

“Shush, Katalina, I’ve got you, shush.”

Gripping Jackson tightly, his hold safe and comforting and with Arne pressed against her legs, Katalina cried. She cried for Bass and the hard choices he’d been given. She cried for the simple, human life she missed, and most of all, she cried for the realization that there was nothing she could do, no choice she could wish to take back and change. She cried because Bill had to be made an example of. His death had to mean something. It had to be the message that would say they would not roll over like dogs. Dark Shadow was their home, and they’d kill to protect it.

Chapter 38

Bass stumbled, dropping Bill as he did. His lungs had seized up, a sharp pain cutting into his heart.

"Bass? Bass, what is it?"

He clawed at his chest as if he could get the invisible shard that was cutting into him out of his heart. Logan and John held him up, their concerned voices all around him, but Bass couldn't focus. All he saw was Katalina. His love, his heart.

What have I done?

He'd felt the first niggling sign when she'd found him beating Bill, but he'd ignored it. He'd already prepared himself for the fact Katalina wouldn't agree with or like what he'd planned to do. He'd made up his excuses, justified the means.

He'd been given too many hard choices lately, and made mistakes. He was stumbling down a road he wasn't sure he could walk anymore.

We'll make the world fit you. That was his vow, his promise. And he'd failed her.

The pain subsided as he felt Katalina's pain through the mating bond freeze and turn to ice. She was in pain and he wasn't there.

A message came through on his phone, already telling him what he knew in his heart.

Nico – Bass, Kat's gone. She's gone to River Run, to Jackson.

His mate had been breaking, and he'd been so caught up in his own mess to realize. She'd run to someone else, to Jackson, because it wasn't the war causing her pain this time. It was him.

Bass wondered if she'd come back to him or if she had gone to River Run for good. He wanted to turn around, to race until his lungs were on fire, and his muscles screamed, until she was in his arms being comforted by him, her mate.

But instead, Bass stood tall, squashing down any last trace of pain through their bond. He smiled and nodded to his packmates, reassuring them everything was okay. Picking Bill up, Bass carried on toward Indiana's land to deliver his message, and with each step he took, he knew he walked farther away from a world that fit Katalina, the Katalina he'd once known.

CHAPTER 39

Mia – Hey, have you heard from Katalina?

Regan – No why?

Mia – I was on patrol this afternoon, and Kat shows up crying. She ran right into Jackson's arms….

Regan – Oh no, poor Kat. I wonder what's wrong?

Mia – Go find out! Duh.

Regan – I'm sure she doesn't want me bothering her.

Mia – You guys had a sleepover like a week ago! I bet she could use a friend right now that isn't male.

Regan – I guess you're right. I'll let you know if she's okay.

Mia – Tell her I send love and tequila xo

Regan – XOXO

Closing the study book she'd been reading, Regan moved her notes to the side and climbed from her bed. She checked out her reflection in the mirror, then groaned at the mess that was her hair. Pulling a hairband from her wrist, she gathered up the long locks and twisted it into a messy pile on her head, securing it with the band.

"Hmm." She bit her lip studying herself. "It'll do."

She headed downstairs and passed her mom in the kitchen calling out as she went, "I'm heading out. See you later."

The front door opened seconds after Regan had shut it. "Where're you going? Shouldn't you be studying?"

Regan rolled her eyes, then schooled her face into a smile before turning to face her mother. *I need to move out.* "I can do accounting in my sleep, Mom, I'm just heading to Jackson's, nowhere dangerous."

"To see Katalina?" her mom said, raising her brows and crossing her arms at the same time. "That girl is trouble, Regan."

Regan gritted her teeth. "Is that because she mated a Dark Shadow, or because she stopped a war?"

Her mother tutted. "I don't know what's gotten into you lately. It's like you've suddenly decided you're fifteen again."

"Really, Mom? Fifteen? I remember myself at fifteen, and I can assure you I'm nowhere near as bad as that."

"Just..." Her mom's face softened, and for a spilt second, Regan saw the pain and fear beneath. "Just be safe okay?"

Regan sighed sadly. "I will, Mom, okay? I love you."

"Love you too, honey."

Walking away, Regan picked up her pace, falling into a steady jog when she turned the corner and was no longer in view of her house. It wasn't a long walk to Jackson's and with jogging, it took her seven minutes tops.

Anna was sitting on the porch swing when Regan arrived. "Oh good, I've been waiting for you."

"You have?" Regan said, a little taken back.

"Yes. Katalina needs a friend."

Regan frowned. "Aren't the two of you friends?"

"Yes. But I'm not the friend who has a Dark Shadow wolf as a mate."

"Shush!" Regan gasped, whipping her head around wildly. "One, he's not my mate, and two, it's a secret," she hissed.

"Oh, yes," Anna replied cheerfully. "I forgot."

"Anna who are you chatting— Oh, hey, Regan, here to see Kat?" Cage asked.

"Yeah."

"She's in the front room. Come on in," Cage said. He held the door open for her, then walked out of it himself, folding Anna into his arms. Regan glanced at them for a second, slightly jealous of the two being able to show public affection. She wanted that herself… with Tyler.

In the front room, Regan found Katalina curled up at the end of the sofa, Arne at her feet, and Toby next to her. Jackson was in the far corner like a silent watcher, guarding over her.

"Hey, Regan," Katalina said as she entered. "Word gets around fast here, huh? Who told you?"

"Mia was on patrol earlier. She was worried about you."

"Well, you're in good company. Come join the 'let's worry about Kat because she had a nervous breakdown' club. Shift up, Toby," Katalina instructed, nudging him with her foot. "Come sit." She patted the spot near her feet that Toby had just vacated.

"I'll go find some more ice cream," Toby said, picking up the empty carton, and leaving the room.

Regan sat next to Katalina and took her hand. "So what are you watching?"

"Some chick flick. He's in love with his lifelong friend. She doesn't know she feels the same way so is marrying some ass who's all wrong for her…. He'll stop the wedding, she'll realize her mistake, and boom, they'll get married instead and live happily ever after." Katalina made a gagging face. "If only life was that simple. Stupid idiots. They make me sick."

Regan glanced at Toby as he reentered, following him were Cage and Anna. They all looked at her as if she was supposed to know the magic words to say, but Regan felt kind of lost.

"That bad, huh?" she said in the end.

Katalina laughed darkly. "Pass me the ice cream, Toby."

"She'll be okay once Bass gets back," Jackson piped up from the corner.

Katalina rolled her eyes at him before stuffing a huge spoonful of ice cream into her mouth. "He's not coming," Katalina said around the spoon.

"Sure, he is. Don't be silly, Kat. As soon as he's done with what he's doing, he'll be here," Jackson reassured her.

"No, he's not. He's afraid. I can feel it. He's afraid because he's broken me, and he doesn't know how to fix it," Katalina replied matter-of-factly.

Her tone frightened Regan a little. She'd never heard her sound so…pessimistic. She squeezed Katalina's hand gently. "He loves you, Kat, of course he'll come for you. You're his mate."

Katalina met her gaze. "I know he loves me, nothing will ever change that, but this world, it's changed me. It's changed him."

An ominous silence settled over the room. Everyone looked at one another, everyone except Katalina, who'd gone back to watching TV. Regan searched her mind for the right thing to say, for anything to say, but she didn't even know what had happened, if Katalina and Bass had fought, or if something else had happened, and frankly, Regan was too afraid to find out. Instead, she squeezed Katalina's hand a second time and turned her head toward the TV. If she couldn't make it better, she'd sit there with Katalina for as long as it was bad. It was the one thing that she'd longed for when Megan had been killed; someone to weather the storm with her, someone to hold her hand in the dark.

Nico and Olivia arrived after dark. Jackson met them in the hallway, where they were currently having an angry but hushed conversation.

"Told you he wasn't coming," Katalina whispered, glancing at her briefly.

"Bass never struck me as someone who's afraid of much," Regan whispered back.

"He's not. He's only afraid of one thing."

"What's that?" Regan asked quietly, glancing at the door to make sure they weren't coming yet.

"Losing me."

Regan touched Katalina's cheek. "And has he lost you, Kat?"

"I'm not sure," she admitted, facing her with large eyes full of unshed tears. "I think I lost myself in this world, the me I thought I was anyway. The madness and bloodshed swallowed me whole and now I'm just…."

"Just what, Kat?"

"Changed. I don't feel like me anymore. Not the hopeful me who thought we could all get through this craziness with our humanity intact anyway."

"Oh, Kat," Regan whispered, brushing away the one tear that Katalina couldn't hold back. "I don't know what to say."

But the worst part was, as Katalina's words left her mouth, they hurt Regan as much as they were hurting her, because if Bass and Katalina couldn't get out of the fight with Indiana untouched, then how were she and Tyler going to find a happy ending?

"It ends in pain," Anna said out of nowhere, turning to

look at them both, and placing a hand on both her and Katalina's knee. "But sometimes we need it to. We need it to push us in the right direction, to help us make the choice we might have not necessarily taken."

Katalina dragged in a harsh, jagged breath, as dread uncoiled in the pit of Regan's stomach. *What does she mean? Does she mean Ty?*

Nico, Oliva, and Jackson choose that moment to walk into the room.

"I'm fed up of hard choices," Katalina spat. She straightened up, her feet falling to the floor as she glared at Anna. "You tell the universe I've had enough of pain, and I've had enough of this goddamned war."

Cage growled. "Kat, don't speak to her like that."

Katalina snarled back. Getting to her feet, she glared at Cage. "I'm not talking to her, stupid. I'm talking to whoever speaks to her." Her angry, hurt-filled eyes studied them all. "Ugh. Will you all just stop looking at me like that?" She swiped at the tears that spilled down her cheeks. "I'm not made of glass!"

Storming from the room, the front door rattled through the house as Katalina closed it. No one said a word for several long moments as they looked at one another. Even Arne sat upright and looked as stumped as the rest of them.

It was Jackson who broke the silence. "You better go after her," he said, addressing Katalina's dog. "Come on." Jackson ventured back out into the hall, opening the front door. "Go bring her home, boy," he said, ruffling the dog on the head as he passed. "And gods help us if you can't."

Regan watched out of the window as the dog bounded off in the direction Katalina had gone. Her body was a hum of emotion—shock from Katalina's reaction, but understanding as Regan herself often felt as overwhelmed and angry at the world. She hurt for Katalina and for herself and Tyler. Life wasn't easy or fair, and Regan had to somehow hold onto the belief that it would be okay in the end. She couldn't allow events to knock her from this new forward path, no matter how difficult it was. Regan had to keep looking forward.

CHAPTER 40

After a long afternoon with Zackary, trying to explain that what he'd seen was normal, but not a frequent occasion, they'd both returned tired, mentally and physically, to Tyler's cabin.

Tyler had acquired a laptop from another pack member, so Zackary had something to keep his mind off things, and they'd decided to eat in, Tyler popping out briefly to collect the chips and burgers he'd ordered from the pack kitchen earlier.

He'd just finished stuffing the last of the chips into his mouth when his phone rang. It was the ringtone he'd set for Regan, so he'd know only to look at his phone alone, but seeing as Zackary knew, nothing stopped him from pulling his phone from his pocket and smiling at Regan's face flashing on his screen.

"It's Regan," he said, as Zackary glanced back at him.

"I know." Zackary rolled his eyes. "You've got that lovey-dovey face again."

Poking his tongue out at the kid, Tyler answered as he climbed to his feet. "Hey, babe, sorry I cancelled on you earlier."

"It's okay. I think I know why.... I need you to do me a favor, Ty."

"Okay?" Tyler agreed, wondering what was going on.

"I'm not exactly sure what happened at Dark Shadow today, but I know it must have been something bad because Kat is here and she's in a bad way."

"Wait, what?"

"Didn't you know?"

"No, I've kinda—" Tyler glanced at the kid engrossed in the movie, but still walked as far as possible away from him before continuing. "—been dealing with Zac. He… he didn't take today well either."

"What happened?"

"I probably shouldn't be telling you." Tyler sighed. *This right here is why people won't want us together.*

"Don't tell me if you think it will compromise Dark Shadow, but I think the fact your alpha pair seem to be living in separate packs… I should know."

"Separate? You mean Katalina's left for good? Bass should be back by now. Hasn't he come to get her?"

"No. And honestly, Ty, I'm not sure what's going through Kat's head. I just know she's feeling rather lost at this moment and for some reason, they've pulled apart, not together."

"Bass marched Bill up in front of the pack and executed him today."

Regan's breathing hitched but she said nothing.

"Bill was leaking information to Indiana. That's how they knew where our kids would be, how they knew where patrols would be and who'd be there. He was a mole from the beginning."

"Gosh, Ty… I'm so sorry. I think I understand what's bothering Kat a little better now though. I'm going to try and help her, but I need you to help Bass. Convince him to get his ass over here and bring Kat home, and obviously, do it all while making out you've no idea what's going on." She laughed nervously. "Easy, right?"

Tyler rubbed his hand over his face, sighing deeply. "I'll do my best." He shook his head. "What a mess. At times like these, we need our alpha pair strong not apart. What is Bass thinking?"

"Hopefully you can find out. Hey, I've gotta go. She's just turned back up. Good luck. I love you," she whispered at the end before putting the phone down.

Tyler turned to take in Zackary. *What am I going to do with the kid?*

"What?" Zackary asked, glancing over his shoulder. "Regan all right?"

"Yeah, she's fine, but there's something else I've gotta go deal with."

"Can't you do it later?" he whined. "The movies just getting good."

"You can't come, but I don't like the idea of leaving you alone. How do you feel about a few of the boys from training coming over?"

"Great, I'll be the epitome of cool, needing a babysitter," he grumbled.

"How about you go over to Coop's? He's got all the video games you could ask for."

"He does? I didn't think you had things like that in this caveman town."

Tyler laughed. "Some of us are less caveman than others."

With the kid dropped off with Cooper and his parents, Tyler headed over to find Bass. While he walked, he searched for the right thing to say, something that would get his alpha talking but not give away he already knew what was going on.

By the time he reached Bass's door, he'd thought of absolutely nothing, other than *Hi, how's it going?* Fortunately for him, maybe not so fortunate for Bass, as the door opened to let Tyler in, Nico appeared behind him, and barged his way inside first. Anger radiated off Nico as he marched toward Bass, and Bass backed up wide-eyed and confused.

"Just so you know," Nico said as he closed in on Bass, "you're my friend at this moment and not my alpha, which means I'm quite entitled to do this!"

Nico's hand balled into a fist, his face going rigid, and as he brought his arm back, ready to swing at Bass. Bass did nothing. Nico's fist swung, hitting Bass square in the face, the force whipping Bass's head back.

"Are you done?" Bass asked calmly, touching his fingers to his bleeding nose,

"Oh, not even nearly," Nico growled.

"Whoa, whoa, whoa," Tyler yelled, leaping forward and restraining Nico. "What the hell's going on?"

"It's all right, Ty," Bass said. "I deserved it and many more."

Nico struggled in his arms. "You can let me go now. If he wants to be punched, I'm not obliging."

Tyler released Nico though stayed close to him in case he changed his mind on the violence front.

"Can someone please explain to me what's going on? First you execute Bill, and now the two of you are fighting. And where is Kat?"

"Yeah, come on, tell us, Bass, where's Kat?" Nico ground out.

"She was supposed to be with you," Bass replied to Nico. "You were supposed to be looking after her."

"It's not my job to look after her, Bass. That's yours," Nico shouted, jabbing Bass in the shoulder.

Bass didn't react at all; it was like the man had shut down.

"So where is she now?" Tyler asked, even though he knew

the answer.

"River Run," Nico confirmed, glancing at Tyler, then zeroing in on Bass. "She was crying. Did you know that? I've never seen her look so…."

"Broken?" Bass filled in for him, sounding just as broken himself, staring at the floor.

"Then why are you here?" Nico asked, exasperated. "Why is she surrounded by River Run when she's Dark Shadow, when she's ours, yours?"

Bass looked up, his gaze haunted. "Because I broke her, Nic. I brought a rose into a place full of death and she withered and died like the rest of us."

Tyler had no words. He'd grown up in a pack with a cruel, sadistic alpha, grown up with bloodshed and fear, and a lifelong war that had everything to do with greed and hate. The day Bass had taken over, the day he'd brought Katalina home, Tyler had thought that day was the start of a new beginning. Bass and Katalina had brought with them a new dawn, a brighter, happier, love-filled future, and his alpha was telling him it was over. That the new light had been extinguished.

Regan's face filled his mind. She was his happy future, his light, but without his alpha pair, they'd have no chance, and he couldn't let that happen. "Then fix it!" Tyler growled. "Stop hiding here and go to her. Fix it."

Bass straightened a little. "I trusted Bill. He was my second, my packmate. I'd have died for him, and he betrayed me."

"And he lost his life for it," Tyler replied.

"I think he won in the end though. We captured him nearly a week ago, and instead of killing him right away. I kept him locked up for questioning. I let him weave his lies into my mind until I reached a point that I was no better than my father. Kat tried to tell me I was losing myself. She warned me an execution like I did was wrong, and I told her this was our way, that her human upbringing stopped her from being able to see what needed to be done. I wanted to make a statement, to show them all that Bill hadn't won. That we were stronger than them, but I played right into their hands. They won."

"They will if you stand by and do nothing," Nico warned. "You made a mistake, Bass, everyone makes mistakes, but what separates us from those like your father is owning up to them and fixing what went wrong."

"It's too late, Nico. I can feel Katalina inside of me. I can feel how she's hardened, how she's realized she's too soft for this world."

Tyler thought of Regan, how instead of hardening herself, she'd lessened herself. He thought of how he wished he'd have been there for her when her sister had died. How if maybe she'd had someone to hold her and walk with her into her new, darker, painful world, then she might not have spent three years hiding from her true self. Tyler couldn't have made her sister's absence any less painful, but sometimes all a person needed was someone to walk beside them in the dark as they searched for the light.

"Then go to her. Don't leave her alone in this harsh reality. You're her mate. Hold her hand in the darkness, be her shield against it," Tyler urged.

"I'm afraid," Bass whispered.

The anger in Nico seemed to drain out of him. The two of them fell forward together, holding each other upright. "We all are, Bass. So at least you're not alone."

Bass and Nico walked from the cabin side by side, Tyler following. As the three of them exited the cabin, Bass turned around, his expression looking more like that of his alpha's. "The kid?" he said.

"He's okay. I took care of him," Tyler reassured.

Bass nodded grimly. "He shouldn't have seen that. I shouldn't have let him see that. I failed that kid today too."

"I looked after Zac, now all you need to do is bring Katalina home."

"I will," Bass replied. "Nic, I need to do this alone. Go, go be with Liv."

Tyler and Nico watched Bass as he walked away, the darkness beneath the tree canopy swallowing him into their shadows, and as Nico patted him of the shoulder, leaving to go be with his mate, Tyler's every cell longed to be with Regan.

A raw, hollow hole carved itself into his heart as he denied himself his desire. Regan and he walked in the darkness alone, and it could go on no longer.

"Tomorrow," he whispered upward at the sky. "Tomorrow I tell Katalina."

He'd gone too long promising he'd tell someone and not following through. It couldn't go on. They'd reached the end of the road. A line in the sand had been drawn. It was time, no matter the fear it brought or the anxiety it produced. Tyler had to follow through; he'd not allow himself to do anything different.

CHAPTER 41

She'd sensed his decision to come to her before he appeared out of the trees like a living shadow, elegant and sleek in his approach.

"Is that?"

"Yeah," Katalina replied to Regan. They were sitting together out on Jackson's porch, Arne at her feet after he'd brought her back. She could hear and scent others in Jackson's house, though none had been brave enough to see her since she'd departed in a fit of rage and tears. Nico and Olivia had returned to Dark Shadow, and Katalina couldn't help but wonder if Bass had come on his own wishes or been forced by Nico.

"Do you want to see him?" Regan asked her gently. It had been good to talk to her, to have her beside her as a friend; sometime over the last few weeks, they'd crossed a line in their friendship, growing closer.

"What would you do if I said no?"

Regan glanced at her nervously, pulling her bottom lip into her mouth. "Go tell him to stay away I guess."

A smile tugged at Katalina's lips. "You'd really do that for me?"

Her gaze filled with determination. "Of course, I would."

Placing a hand over hers, Katalina squeezed it briefly before climbing to her feet. "Today's not the day you face down an alpha, Regan. Though I must say courage is a good look on you."

"I'll be inside. If you need anything at all, shout. I'm sure Jackson, Cage, and Toby will come running to defend you."

With a nod and a deep, steady breath, Katalina stepped forward and down the steps of the porch.

"Are you afraid?" Regan whispered.

Katalina paused. She glanced over her shoulder at Regan then studied Bass who'd halted a good twenty feet from the house. "Does it sound weird that I'm not afraid of seeing him but looking him in the eyes. I'm afraid that when we look at each other, we won't see us anymore, and if we can't find each other, what hope do we have?"

"I understand," Regan murmured. "But remember, it takes time. It's taken me three years to even realize I was lost. Be kind to yourself, Kat, be kind to him."

Time. It was the one thing that was always against them. There was no wonder she and Bass had come to a head. They'd both been ignoring the niggling issues because there were more pressing matters at hand. Both hurtling forward, toward the future they wished and hoped for.

Be kind to yourself, Kat, be kind to him. Regan's words stuck with her. She wasn't sure if they'd been kind to each other. Whether she'd been kind to Bass. Did they both expect too much from this world too soon? The time had come she guessed. She had to face him, and he her. They'd become the pressing matter.

The walk to Bass seemed to take forever. Each step increased the nerves buzzing through her veins. She felt silly for being apprehensive; he was her mate, her heart. Walking to him shouldn't have been hard at all. As his features came into view, her heart increased its speed, pulsing through her head like music, the buzzing of her chaotic thoughts adding to the melody.

Thoughts, emotions, and expectations pushed at her mind, her skin, her bones. It was as if she might burst from the anticipation. She was angry at him for leaving and then staying away. She was frustrated and hurt that he hadn't listened to her, that instead of talking to her, he'd pulled away. But most of all, she was saddened and defeated by the simple realization that this world could never have fit her, no matter how many promises and hopes they made. As irrational as it was, she was cross Bass had ever promised her otherwise. She was mad he'd allowed it to change them.

Katalina couldn't bring herself to look at him. Instead, she stared at his chest, his taut muscles currently rigid with tension. They stood for a moment, neither moving or saying a word, not daring to connect gazes. His finger was gentle as it caressed the side of her face, sliding its way down until it reached her chin to tip her head up.

"Look at me, Katalina," he whispered. "Please, look at me."

His tone broke her, as if he were just as afraid as she was, as if he really thought there was a chance they'd not be able to move past this. Maybe there wasn't, not as the same people anyway, not unchanged.

Her eyes stung from the tears she refused to let fall and as Katalina lifted her head to meet the eyes of her shadow wolf, her heart froze, her breath stalled. Bass's eyes studied her—the sorrowful, lost gaze of her wild wolf.

"I'm so sorry," Bass breathed. "I'm so so sorry."

And the dam Katalina had been holding back burst. But it was Bass who went to his knees, Bass who clung to her hands as he buried his head into her thighs and begged for forgiveness.

"My winter wolf, my winter wolf, my winter wolf," he rasped between jagged breaths.

She'd been right to be afraid, to avoid this moment for as long as possible. Looking down at the man she loved—broken and on his knees—hurt her very soul. He wanted her forgiveness, but Katalina wasn't sure what she was forgiving him for. Yes, he'd not listened to her, he'd ignored her warnings, her begs to change course, but was it really his fault?

Anna's voice entered her head. *It ends in pain, but sometimes we need it to. We need it to push us in the right direction, to help us make the choice we might have not necessarily taken.*

Was this the same? If it hadn't been this time, would it have been another? They lived in a hard world, with hard choices. Had they been young and idealistic in thinking they could change their world and not change themselves? Bass's actions had been too gruesome for her, too savage, but maybe it was time she accepted they weren't human. At their core, they were wild, primal wolves. And in the end, maybe that's why she'd run, and he'd stayed away, because admitting that to themselves was too hard, too painful. Accepting that the idealist image in their heads wouldn't ever quite come to be was heartbreaking. Life was cruel, full of dark, dark lows and so much disappointment, but then without it, would they ever truly savor the highs and be able to see the light? Without grief, there wouldn't be joy. Without emotions, they'd not be human at all.

Katalina fell to her knees with him, and together they clung to each other, their tears hitting the earth and taking with them their pain.

"Please forgive me," he murmured. "Please, Kat, forgive me for not coming to you when I should have, for not listening when you spoke the truth. Bill was a mistake. It needed to be done, but I did it wrong.... I should have—"

"Shh," Katalina whispered. "It's okay, Bass. It's okay."

He lifted his head, taking hers in his hands. "I promise you, I will make this right."

"It's okay."

"No. No, it's not. I can feel that you think it is." His hands fell away, sliding down and covering her heart. "But please don't let my mistakes be the reason you harden your greatest gift."

"I'm not human, Bass. I never was."

He shook his head, expression filling with desperation.

"It's you who taught me being human had nothing to do with one's blood and everything to do with their heart. And yours, Katalina, is human. It is big and generous and beautiful, and human."

"And too soft," she added. "I can't walk this road as I am. It hurts too much."

"It's going to get better," Bass promised. "Bill's gone. It's over. We'll rebuild. You'll see. I'll make it better."

Katalina smiled sadly and leant forward, resting her forehead on his. "It's only just begun, and you know it." She sighed. "There will be consequences to Bill's death. They were playing this game from the start by being willing to kill their own people with their own hands. We can't win with unrealistic dreams. We can't protect those we love without being willing to cross any line. I've accepted that, even if I don't like it."

"I can't accept that."

"You already have. You've accepted it from the beginning, even if you didn't want to admit it. And it's okay. There was nothing you could have done. I was in this war from the very beginning. Jackson didn't spare me from it. He just gave me time, time enough to know what to aim for. I didn't end the war. I changed it. I drove out those who reveled in death and fear, and now together, we must end it. You and me, Jackson, Cage, Nic, Ty. Everyone. Everyone who wishes and dreams for a better life. Dark Shadow and River Run. Together, we must end this fight."

He was quiet for so very long—torn, grieving, full of regret and pain, but in the end, his face hardened, his eyes changing back to those of the man within. Bass took her hands and stood, pulling her with him. Staring at her with eyes full of determination, he whispered, "We'll end it. Dark Shadow and River Run. Together, we'll end it."

Chapter 42

They were far enough away that they couldn't hear Bass and Katalina, but close enough to see when two souls were breaking. It was heart wrenching to watch as the tears flowed, the anger drained, and realization and acceptance sank in.

"I shouldn't have ever brought her back here. I should have hidden her better, or taken her away the day they found her," Jackson whispered from besides Regan.

"Don't say that," Cage said. He stood with them at the window, unable to tear his eyes away. "She's brought us so much, brought River Run and Dark Shadow together."

"But what have we brought her?" Jackson asked, his tone tight.

"We're her family, her blood," Karen replied from the sofa. She'd only entered the house when Katalina had left it, waiting out back, knowing her granddaughter still hadn't forgiven her for her mistakes, yet unable to stay away when Katalina was in pain.

"She was never prepared for this life," Jackson continued, his jaw stiff, arms crossed tight.

"None of us were. I've seen and done shit no one my age should have, and the fact I grew up here hasn't made it any easier," Toby said.

Anna stood abruptly from the sofa, causing the people in the room to look at her. She stared at them all for a moment, her eyes eerily otherworld, then smiled sadly.

"There was nothing you or anyone else could have done to

prevent this. Kat was always meant to be here. All you gave her was time, Jackson, and that was enough. She is the key that binds us all together, and she'll realize that when the time is right. Whether she likes it or not, whether it's fair or not, nothing can change it. It is her destiny." She blinked rapidly, shaking her head slightly as if settling back into herself.

"Anna?" Cage murmured, tone one of love and concern.

"Take me home, Cage. I'm tired," Anna asked.

"Of course." He took her into his arms.

"You should all go home," Anna suggested. "It's over now. There is nothing more we can do."

Regan smiled goodbye to the pair as they left the room, exiting the house out the back. Returning her gaze to the window, she realized Anna had been right. Katalina and Bass were on their feet, hand in hand, walking away from the house and into the forest beyond.

"Come on, Arne, you can come home with me," Toby said, leaving. "Holler if you need me," he added with a salute.

"Well, I guess I should go as well," Regan said.

But Jackson stopped her as she reached the threshold of the room. "Regan, I've been meaning to talk to you. I think it's time for you to resume your training."

Regan dragged in a breath, leaning back a little, not at all expecting the words that had left her alpha's mouth. "My parents," she answered, unable to put properly into words the thoughts that his statement had spun.

"Need to accept they had one submissive daughter and one dominant. Your wolf will wither and die if I set you the tasks the maternal wolves are set. It's been three years, Regan, and I'm not telling you that's enough time to grieve. I'm telling you that's enough time not living."

"I know," she said quietly. "I just don't know how to tell

them."

"I can talk to them," he offered.

"No. I just need time."

"Time's running out, Regan," he replied sadly.

In more ways than one….

With a grim nod, she left, slowly walking back home. Only it didn't feel like home; it never had. Megan had been her home and when she'd died, it had too. Then Tyler had come along and relit something inside of her, driving her forward again when she'd been trapped in time. Tyler was her home now, only just like Megan, it was a home she couldn't quite reach.

CHAPTER 43

"I was just coming to track you down," Noah said, approaching Tyler as he appeared from the trees in wolf form. "Meet at Nico and Dax's in five?"

Tyler gave a nod of his wolf head, then padded past Noah and toward his cabin. He'd woken early to take a morning run and clear his head for ready the day. Knocking his head on the door lightly, it opened seconds later.

"Dude, I don't think I'll ever get used to opening the door for a wolf," Zackary said, as Tyler walked in.

Shifting as he reached his bed, Tyler picked up the nearest clothes he could find to get ready for the pack meeting.

"Won't get used to the nudity either," Zackary grumbled. "It'd be so much better if your clothes just reappeared."

Tyler smiled but didn't comment. The kid was back on form this morning and as annoying as ever. Spending some time with Cooper had done him good.

"How are you feeling this morning? Think you'll be all right alone for a short while?"

"Yeah, I'm good. Why, where you off to?" Zackary replied, flopping down onto his bed.

"There's a pack meeting happening. I need to be there and it's only for the inner circle."

Zackary sat up. "Hey, Ty?"

Tyler pulled his T-Shirt over his head and turned to face him. "Hmm?"

"My dad and sis are coming to go over those plans this afternoon. It's safe for them to, right?"

"We've tightened up our defenses. Indiana aren't likely to get through. Try not to worry, Zac."

Zackary rubbed at his neck, awkwardness filling his gaze. "I actually meant safe from Bass."

"I think you've gotten the wrong idea of Bass, Zac. He's a good alpha. It's just this world, being a shifter… it's not all black and white. There are lots of shades of gray. Bass would never hurt your family unless they tried to hurt his, and, Zac, your part of that family now, part of that pack. That means Bass would give his life to protect yours."

"He doesn't even know me," Zackary mumbled.

"It doesn't matter. He's alpha. He's responsible for every member of this pack. He has help of course, from us, his enforcers and his sec—" Tyler's words died in his throat. *His second,* he'd been about to say, the man who'd betrayed them. Zackary frowned at Tyler's sudden silence. "Well, what I'm saying is, your part of this pack now, which means we protect what's yours. Your dad and sister will be fine."

"Okay. Am I allowed to come to this meeting later? To see them I mean?"

"Can't see why not. I'll be back soon, after this morning meeting, okay?"

Zackary nodded, falling back onto the bed with a dismissive wave of his hand.

Tyler exited his cabin and crossed the clearing toward the cabin Dax, Oliva, and Nico lived in. It was one of the few cabins not to have been damaged in the fire, and currently had two more occupants camping out on the sofas while the pack's current housing crisis was fixed.

The door was already open when Tyler arrived. He knocked once as he entered. Oliva glanced over her shoulder, smiling.

"They're all in the front room. Go on in. I'm just laying out some food for you all," she said, placing a plate of pastries down.

Tyler's stomach grumbled. "Mind if I snag one now?" he asked, approaching her and taking a danish from the serving plate. He kissed her on the cheek. "I should eat here more often."

"Quit flirting with my mate, and get your butt in here," Nico grumbled from behind.

Tyler laughed as he winked at Olivia and faced Nico. "Feeling insecure are we, Nic?"

Nico shook his head with a smile. "Go find your own girl."

He raised one eyebrow. "I might just do that." Tyler scanned the room and noted what he'd suspected. Bass and Katalina weren't present.

"They've not returned then?" Tyler stated, glancing at Nico. "Has this pack lost its alpha pair as well as its second?"

"I heard from Bass this morning. They'll be returning soon," Nico answered, addressing the whole room.

"They're good then?" Tyler asked.

"As far as I know, yeah," Nico said.

"I called this meeting," Jacob said into the lull. "Because I thought with recent events the pack would benefit from seeing a united front from us all. I think security needs to be tightened against the possible payback from Bill's death, and we all need to be listening out for fears and discord. So far no one has come forward and answered Bass's ultimatum, and the twenty-four-hour deadline is nearly up."

"Let's pray no one does. What are we saying to soothe fears?" John asked.

"That times are unstable, but we'll get through it together as we always have. That Dark Shadow is strong and will face whatever comes," Jacob answered.

"There's also the issue of electing another second," Nico added. "Bass would like us all to think on who'd we think is suitable and put it to a vote on his return later."

"I'd have thought he'd have just elected you," Noah said a little bitterly. "After all, it's you who has the alpha's confidence."

"What are you accusing my son of?" Dax growled.

"It's all right, Dad," Nico answered, holding up his hand.

"I get that some of you may be angry or hurt that some of us knew about Bill before the rest of the pack did, and I can't speak for Bass, but I do know he's just as wounded from Bill's betrayal as the rest of us. He did what he did to keep Katalina and this pack safe. I won't be electing myself as second. One, I'm far too young for the role, and two, Bass is my friend, and he'll always be my friend before my alpha, which makes me unsuitable for the role."

"Nico's right," Tyler said, patting the man on the back. "I think we need to give both Bass and Katalina a break. I mean, Bass hasn't exactly inherited a well-functioning pack, has he? Most of the dominant seniors left with Castor, which I think speaks volumes for the type of pack Dark Shadow has been for decades. Bass is trying to change that, and it's not going to be easy. We're a young pack trying to find our way in a hard world. There are going to be mistakes, but as long as we stick together, we'll get through this."

"Well said, Ty," Jacob murmured. "I trust and respect Bass. I'd like to think everyone in this room does, which means while he's not here, we should rally together and show others we're not like Bill."

Tyler knew the next few months were going to be a difficult time for the pack; they'd all feel Bill's betrayal and mourn the man they thought he'd been. For Tyler, though, he had more than Bill on his mind. Recent events had highlighted what Tyler was doing was wrong. Secrets were not meant to be kept from his alpha.

He had to trust Bass would do the right thing. Yet Tyler was also cautious. Regan had already suffered enough losses in her life via Dark Shadow's hands, and Tyler couldn't allow their relationship to be another.

As the group finished up, with orders given out and plans on security checked over, Tyler stepped out of the cabin and off to the side where he pulled out his phone and typed a message that could quite possibly be his doom.

Tyler – Katalina, I know you're dealing with something right now and I hope you're okay, but I really need to speak with you alone. Today if possible. I wouldn't bother you if it wasn't urgent. Ty

It was thirty minutes later while Tyler was watching his young dominants sparing that her response came through.

Katalina – Hey, Ty, I'm doing okay. I can meet you today, 4 p.m., just over the pack border, east of the car park.

Tyler – Thanks, Kat.

He blew out a breath, reading the message twice. *Today, today our fates are decided.*

"Hey, Ty! What's so interesting? You just missed me throwing Cody on his ass in epic style!" Max exclaimed with a grin.

"Sorry, Max. Please perform this epic stunt again."

Max rolled his eyes. "Ain't going to happen a second time. Cody will have cottoned on to my moves."

Tyler chuckled. "Let's call it a day, guys. You've done well, and my mind is elsewhere."

"On a lady by any chance?" Cooper cooed.

"Yeah, let's see." Cody laughed, trying to snatch the phone from Tyler's hand.

Tyler shook his head, smacking Cody playfully on the

back of his head. "Today is not the day you'll get my phone from me, Cody."

"Hiding love letters on there?" Max teased.

"He's blushing!" Cooper laughed, pointing at Tyler.

"Go on, scram the lot of you!" Tyler mock growled. "Before I make you run laps."

They ran off, laughing and shouting teasing songs as they wound through the trees. Tyler followed more slowly, pleased to see the younger members of the pack weren't as affected by Bill's betrayal as he'd feared. He had hopes that if he and the others of similar age could grow up under Alistair's rule with their humanity and morals intact, then the next generation should have a far better chance.

Zackary was waiting for him outside of their cabin, having ran off with the group.

"Regan okay?" he asked as Tyler approached.

"Yeah, why?"

"You looked at little ill while reading your message," Zackary observed.

"It's nothing, Zac. Don't worry."

"'kay. Coops invited me over to play video games. Can I go?" he asked, a hopeful spark in his gaze.

"Go on. I've got somewhere to be anyway. I'll come get you before the meeting with your dad."

"With Regan?" he asked quietly, glancing around.

Tyler smiled. It was nice having someone who didn't get the ramifications of their relationship. "Yeah."

"Say hi for me," he said, waving as he ran off for Cooper's cabin.

Zackary was very quickly adjusting to pack life, and while he still had anger issues and struggled for control, Tyler had had him doing a few basic moves with the group his age today without incident. He'd need extra training and lessons for a while yet, but Tyler didn't see there being any issues long-term. Deep down, Zackary was a good kid with a kind heart that had been bruised too much by life's hard truths. The teenager would find himself in good company. Dark Shadow and River Run were full of many who knew the harsh reality of life's truths. Regan being one of them. Tyler hadn't seen Regan since Bill's execution. They'd texted a few times after the phone call about Katalina, but both had been busy since. They'd made plans to meet that night by the river they'd once run daily, but Tyler couldn't ignore the urgent voice inside of him that said he needed to see her now. One last time before he revealed the truth and everything changed, before she may be taken away from him forever.

Tyler – I know you're studying, but I really need to see you. Meet me by the river?

Regan – Everything all right? Should I be worried?

Tyler wrote and rewrote his text message several times, torn between telling her the truth or not. They hadn't discussed telling anyone since Regan had asked for more time, and while it felt wrong to be keeping secrets from her, he also didn't want to worry her when there might not be any need.

Tyler – I just need to kiss you xoxo

Regan - :) I'll be there in 5 xo

She ran into his arms like they'd been parted for months, the breath that rushed out of her deep and audible. "God, you've no idea how much I needed to be in your arms."

"Everything okay?" he murmured against her hair, planting kisses on her head as he ran a hand up and down her back.

"You'll never believe this, but Jackson wants me back in training."

"When did he say that?"

"While I was there staying with Kat."

He pulled back slightly, running his hands through her hair then cupping her face. "And how do you feel about that?"

Regan's first reaction was a nervous smile, before it dropped away, and she chewed on her bottom lip. "Terrified, excited, worried like hell what my parents are going to say. But it's time, I think."

Tyler closed the space between them, claiming her lips as his own. "It is. I agree," he breathed as they broke for air.

"I know. I've asked my parents to meet me this afternoon. Dad's finishing work early so we can have a family talk. I've no idea what I'm going to say to them. I wish you could be there holding my hand."

He caressed a thumb over her cheekbone, marveling at the smoothness of her skin. "You'll find the words I'm sure."

"My plan is to break all of the changes to them a bit at a time. Once they get used to the idea of me training again, I think we'll be ready for the next bombshell."

"That could be months away, Regan." Tyler closed his eyes, leaning forward and resting his head on hers.

"I know, Ty."

"Regan, after everything that's happened with Bill, I just don't think it's a good idea that I'm keeping secrets from my alpha."

"Ty, please. I know its really hard for you, but I'm so afraid I'll lose what I have left of my family."

Letting out a long, sad sigh, Tyler brushed his lips gently over Regan's, losing himself in the way she made his body and heart feel. How a simple touch could reach him in so many places, how she seemed to have a direct link to his soul. He wanted more than anything to tell her about his rendezvous with Katalina, but he knew she couldn't handle it right at that moment. It was taking all her courage to meet with her parents, to fight the fear he could taste in her scent and break the news. Regan didn't need anymore pressure. She'd been standing still for three years and life had hurtled forward suddenly, but it was going far too fast; she was barely keeping up.

"You can do this, Regan. Concentrate on your parents. We'll be okay."

"I know it's killing you to wait. It's killing me too. I just can only handle one change at a time. I'm sorry, Ty."

"You've nothing to be sorry for. Don't ever doubt how strong you are, Regan. I believe in you."

No more words were spoken between them. Instead, the pair silently talked, using their mouths and bodies to say how much they loved one another. There was no urgency, no whispers of the ticking clock above them. They parted with a promise to meet each other later that night as originally planned, and he murmured good luck for Regan's family meeting.

Tyler left more determined than ever to meet with Katalina and convince her to help. Anna's prediction couldn't come to pass. He'd do anything to make sure it wouldn't.

CHAPTER 44

"These are really good, Katalina. I can see what you're thinking. More luxury ski lodge than rustic cabin," Tim said, looking up from the sketchpad she'd drawn her visions of a new pack on.

"Thanks." She smiled, happy to have at last found someone who appreciated her vision.

"Do you have builders' plans?" he asked, glancing between her and Bass.

It was weird to be discussing building plans when less than twenty-four hours earlier she'd felt as if her entire world had shifted. Things between her and Bass were tense; he'd moved to touch her several times, then paused as if unsure she'd welcome it. She didn't like how they'd gone from being as in tune as two people could be, to being off-kilter, as if they'd suddenly started spinning on an opposite axis.

They'd spent the time since leaving Jackson's alone together, running as wolves, being as one as two people could get, but coming back to pack land had reminded them not everything had gone back to normal. And she knew they'd have been a time not so long ago that she'd have dreamed of running away, of taking Bass and leaving all things pack behind, but that wasn't her dream anymore. They were her people as much as Bass's and while the responsibility frightened her, Katalina couldn't walk away.

"No. That's where I am hoping you can help us," Bass answered. "We have the manpower but not the expertise."

"It's a big project. I have men I could bring—"

"No," Bass cut him off, making Tim flinch.

"What Bass means is we can't risk having strangers on site and knowing our secret. I'm sure you can understand how dangerous that could be for us and them."

"Yes… well, I guess if you have the manpower, and we kept it relatively simple. Building shouldn't be too hard with my guidance."

"You'll be paid of course, and Zackary has already been welcomed into the pack. Tyler tells me he's doing well."

Katalina watched as Bass and Zackary's gazes met. She thought it was possibly the first time they'd looked at each other without aggression.

"Yes, Zac tells me he's been welcomed, and it's helping to be here." Tim looked back down at Katalina's sketchpad, frowning as he flipped through the drawings and then looked at the area around him. "But this current space, Katalina, it doesn't match your vision. There's no light here, the trees are too thick. Are you planning on cutting down some trees and opening up this area?"

"No. I'd picked out another site to rebuild on," Katalina said, glancing at Bass as she did, knowing the subject had been one they'd argued over frequently.

His eyes met hers, and he smiled. "I've been told many times by Katalina that our current site is more like a prison camp than a home."

Tim looked a little nervous. "Well, I didn't like to say." He laughed cautiously.

"And I've come to realize that if we are ever going to leave the past and its ways behind, we must truly leave and start again. If you're up for a trek, Tim, we can head there now."

"Oh, yes, sure. It will be good for me to get a feel of the land before drawing up plans," Tim answered.

Shock rolled through her as well as a pulse of love through

the mating bond between them. Bass reached out, taking her hand into his, and pulled it to his mouth to kiss.

"I told you," he murmured softly, "I will make this right, even if that includes dragging everyone in this pack kicking and screaming into a brighter future."

And she believed him. For the first time in a long time, Katalina felt the future she dreamed of within reach. Maybe Anna had been right. Maybe they'd needed to go in the wrong direction to truly see which was the right way. They needed the pain to push them, and while Katalina knew it would take more than this to fix what had gone wrong between them, she had hope they would with time.

CHAPTER 45

Katalina was late for their meeting. Tyler glanced at his phone, nervously watching as the minutes ticked by. He paced the small clearing, debating whether to ring her when it vibrated in his hand. Glancing at the screen, his heart leapt as he saw Regan's face smiling back at him. "Regan?" he answered quietly.

Instantly he knew something was wrong. The catch in her breath before she spoke told him she was crying and the words that poured from her were desperate and broken.

"I'm going to lose them, Ty. They'll never forgive me. I don't see any future that allows me to keep you and them."

"Wow, wow, slow down, baby. What's happened?"

"I told them, Ty, and they freaked out. I've never seen my dad so angry. He's stormed off to have it out with Jackson. My mom's sobbing in her room. It's such a mess, Tyler. I don't know what to do."

"About starting training?"

"Yes," she whispered, dragging in a ragged breath.

"I'm sure they'll come around," Tyler reassured her, hating that every instinct told him to go to her and he couldn't.

"I don't think they will, Tyler. You didn't see them, my dad especially. He said, he said—" Her voice broke as she sobbed. "He said wasn't it enough that I'd killed my sister, now I wanted to kill myself."

Anger licked through him like a flame. "Listen to me,

Regan, what he said was wrong and cruel, and not at all true. Do you hear me? Megan's death was not your fault and being true to yourself is not trying to get yourself killed." The sounds of her crying softly through the phone killed him.

"I know, Ty. I know he said it in anger and it's not true, but I can't help how it makes me feel."

"I'm coming to get you. Meet me by the stream."

"No, Ty, I'll be okay, and it's probably best I stay in right now. God, I hope Jackson doesn't kill my dad."

He'll deserve all he gets. Tyler growled silently in his head, wanting to get his hands on the man himself.

"It's killing me that I can't comfort you when you're upset, Regan."

"Just hearing your voice is enough." She let out a deep, steady breath, then another. "I've gotta go. I can hear my mom coming."

"Ring me when she's gone. I love you."

The call ended without a reply. "Fuck!" Tyler kicked at the ground, gripping his hands into his hair behind his neck. "Goddamn it, why?" he yelled.

"Tyler?"

Tyler whirled around. "How long have you been standing there?" he asked Katalina quietly.

"Long enough to know something is really bothering you. What's going on, Ty? Why'd you bring me here?"

Tyler dropped his hands away from his neck and pulled in a breath. Looking at his phone, he brought up a picture he'd snapped of Regan as he'd kissed her cheek and studied it. There was a gleam in her eyes that wasn't always present and should be, a lift to her lips that spoke of true happiness. He made her happy after she'd spent so long sad; he couldn't see what they had as a bad thing.

"Ty?"

He met Katalina's cautious stare. She'd not approached him yet, as if fearful of what he was about to say, but Tyler was having second thoughts. Regan's phone call had made him question his reasoning, made him question everything. *Maybe we should just leave. Maybe it will be easier that way....*

"Talk to me, Tyler. Does this have something to do with Regan?"

Shock rolled through him. "What do you know?"

"Honestly, I'm guessing a little. After you asked after Megan, and well, Regan's grown so much over the last few months.... Let me help you."

"I'm not sure you can, Kat. I thought you could, but Regan's just called after telling her parents she's going to start training again and... well, let's just say they took it badly. Even if we could make it work with the alliance, they'd never accept us."

"Is she your mate?"

Mate. The word resonated through him like a curse and miracle all at once. He opened his mouth to answer but as he did the foliage behind Katalina rustled. "Kat!" Tyler gasped, racing forward.

Her eyes widened in fear as she whipped around. But it was too late; they hadn't sensed the danger in time and Tyler wasn't close enough to attack and push the intruder back. Sliding across the ground, he twisted around Katalina, shielding her body with his as the knife that was swung hit flesh.

A silent scream left his lips as pain burst through his back, blackening his vision. He fell to the ground, bringing Katalina down with him, a cry leaving her mouth.

Chapter 46

Zackary

He'd been bored, and Tyler had been buzzing with a nervous kind of energy that he's never sensed on the man before. Curiosity had gotten the better of him, so he'd snuck out after him, suspecting Tyler was having a secret rendezvous with Regan but instead, the man hadn't headed toward River Run at all.

What Zackary hadn't been expecting was Katalina. Nerves rolled through him, and he was about to turn around when something inside of him said to wait, a voice of sorts that came from the new half of himself that he really didn't know all that much.

Seconds later, noise came for the right of him and then before Zackary's eyes, the world turned to hell. A man appeared from the trees wielding a knife. Zackary watched wide-eyed with icy dread crawling over his skin as Tyler ran to protect Katalina but didn't get there in time to fight off the attacker. His only option was to shield her from the blow. Blood seemed to fly in slow motion through the air as the nasty-looking blade met Tyler's muscled back. Katalina screamed as Tyler slumped forward, collapsing to the ground and trapping her beneath him.

The man laughed as he hovered over them, drawing a gun from the holster at his back.

"This is for my brother, bitch."

Zackary felt a wave of fear and rage rush through him. His vision blurred as his body cracked and twisted, pain shooting through him. A half scream, half growl erupted from him as the wolf within took control. Zackary watched as if a passenger within his own body as the wolf he'd shifted into leapt on the man aiming the gun. Blood filled his mouth, coppery and warm, making the boy inside gag as the wolf reveled. Muscle and bone were exposed as the life left the man's eyes. Zackary screamed silently as his wolf controlled his mind, ripping and tearing at the man below him.

"Zac, stop. Zackary, stop!"

The voice was familiar, and it had power behind it. A power that made him want to obey, made him want to submit. The wolf snarled, shaking of the compulsion as his focus turned on her. Fear scented the air as her eyes widened.

"No, Zac, it's me, it's Kat." She struggled out from under the mangled mess of her attacker and Tyler, scrambling backward on her butt as he approached.

"Zackary, stop. Gain control, you can do this. You're the master not him."

His steps faltered, the boy within yelling for the wolf to listen, to stop. But the wolf was powerful, far more powerful than the scared, lost boy.

CHAPTER 47

A silent warning had gone to every phone within Dark Shadow, alerting them all to an intruder but not alerting the intruder to the fact they knew. He'd been spotted on the outskirts of Dark Shadow's grounds, hesitating as if debating which point to try to enter their home.

Fear was in the back of his mind, threatening to derail his cool as he raced across his home ready to kill anyone who dared harm his pack, his family. Katalina had been unreachable. She'd left not that long ago, telling him she was going to visit Jackson, but a call to Jackson had confirmed she'd never made it.

Nico ran beside him, as did John. The others on patrol were at their stations, alert and ready. Bass moved half on instinct, half on the knowledge the man had last been spotted near the pack's car park.

Bass missed a step as fear burst inside of him coming from the mating bond, from Katalina. His hand pressed against his chest as he whispered her name.

"Bass?" Nico questioned from beside him.

"She's afraid." He picked up her scent the next second, altering direction to take the route she'd taken. Nico and John followed without question and as a cold, killing calm entered his mind, all Bass's emotions dropped away, his mind, his body on one thing, and one thing only—reach Katalina.

They broke through the trees to find a scene of blood and devastation. It took Bass a split second to access the scene, then he was hurtling for Zackary, landing on the boy in wolf form and pinning him down.

Rage raced through him at the unruly boy that had been about to attack his mate. Zackary didn't submit. The wolf beneath him snarled and twisted, his teeth trying to tear at Bass's flesh.

"Bass, no," Katalina called, running to his side. "He saved me. Zac saved me."

Bass flung Zackary away, leaping to his feet and positioning himself in front of Katalina as her words sank in. The wolf scrambled up on all fours, turning with a snarl toward them.

"It's okay, Zac." Katalina soothed. "You're safe now. You can come back."

Relief washed through him as Bass heard Katalina safe and unhurt. Glancing at her briefly, he smiled before returning his attention to Zackary. Holding out an arm, Bass backed Katalina up as the wolf prowled toward them.

"Bass, do something," Katalina hissed. "You're his alpha. Help him."

He studied the wolf. So much rage was contained in one person, but in the wolf's eyes were the pleas of a lost boy, desperate for control. Bass stopped backing away and took a step forward, softening his shoulders, facing his palms out.

"You're okay," he said, lowing his voice. Bass submitted in all the ways he could, showing Zackary he meant no harm. "It's okay, Zac, you did good. You protected Katalina when I couldn't."

The wolf paused.

"Do you hear me, Zac? You did nothing wrong, you protected your alpha's mate, but your job's done now. The danger's gone. I'm here. The danger's gone."

"Come back to us," Katalina whispered, stepping up beside him. "Come back to us."

Zackary shifted, the boy sinking to his knees and crying

out. Bass rushed forward at the same as Katalina, catching the boy in his arms.

"I… I… I killed him."

"You did what you had to do," Bass answered.

Katalina brought her hands to his face, cupping it gently. "Listen to me," she whispered, searching his face. "That man would have killed me and you and Tyler. He'd have then gone into our home and took out as many innocents as possible. This world is harsh, Zac, but it doesn't mean you have to be, and it doesn't mean that what you did was wrong."

"Do you understand, Zac?" Bass asked a little firmer. "You've done nothing wrong."

He nodded.

"Bass, Tyler's hurt really bad," Nico yelled from across the clearing.

Bass met Katalina's gaze. "Go," she urged. "I've got Zac."

Leaving Katalina and Zackary, Bass rushed toward Tyler. He was on his front, his white T-shirt coated in blood.

"He's breathing… just," John said as Bass dropped to his knees. "Blade's cut deep."

Hesitantly, Bass placed a hand on Tyler's shoulder. His pain hit Bass like a punch to the gut, causing him to gasp as he absorbed the pain and gave Tyler the lifeforce of his alpha blood.

"Hold on, Ty," he whispered, as his energy drained away, feeding Tyler life. *I need you to hold on. I can't lose anyone else.* "We need to get him to Oliver, now," Bass instructed, meeting John's gaze. "He's in a lot of pain."

"Karen. Take him to Karen," Katalina said, appearing above them.

"Kat, he's Dark Shadow," Bass replied.

"Trust me, Bass. Take him to Karen, and we need Regan too, I think… I think she's his mate," she urged.

"What?" John and Nico gasped together.

Shock was Bass's first emotion. Then everything clicked into place, the late days to patrol, how he'd felt Tyler pulling away from him after the day he and Nico had found him frozen in the forest. As a friend, Bass was nothing but happy for them, but as an alpha, he worried of the complications this union would bring, but all of that could wait because if Regan was his mate, then she may be the only way to save Tyler's life.

An alpha's bond was strong and able to hold a packmate to life for a short while if needed, but Bass could already feel Tyler fading, already feel himself reaching the point where he could give Tyler no more. Yet a mate, a mate was the one bond stronger than an alpha. Regan, Bass hoped, might just be able to keep Tyler with them in the living, long enough for Karen to fix his wounds.

Bass nodded his okay to John, and he and Nico helped pick Tyler up and carry him.

"I've got the keys to my truck in my pocket. It'll be quicker to drive to River Run," John instructed.

"Stay alert," Bass warned everyone, but his gaze locked with Katalina. "The danger may yet remain."

Zackary might have killed Tyler's attacker, but the Indiana pack might have sent more than one wolf. They couldn't afford to let their guard down. Racing toward River Run, Bass focused on keeping his emotions in check. On being a strong, grounding presence. An alpha.

Chapter 48

Regan sat opposite her mother as she again tried to explain her reasoning behind beginning her training again. Her mom said nothing as she spoke, the expression on her face grim and worried, but at least her mom was listening. It was more than her father had done. Jackson had informed them he'd been instructed to "run off some steam." Their alpha had said nothing more about her father's anger toward him and for that, Regan was grateful.

"But I'd thought you were happy," her mom said finally after a long silence.

"Did you really think that?" Regan asked, disappointed in her mother's delusions.

Her mom sighed heavily. "Well, no, but recently you've seemed to be."

She spoke the truth, but Regan couldn't tell her the reason behind her happiness. Wouldn't dare whisper Tyler's name after the reaction they'd had today. "Yes, because I've finally started to get back to the person I was before everything went wrong." *Because Tyler made me want to live again.*

Her mom began to speak, but Regan heard none of it. Doubling over in pain, Regan cried out as pain sharp pulsed through her heart. Her phone began to ring at the same time realization hit. *Tyler!* Regan answered the call, bringing the phone to her ear.

"Where is he?" she rasped, shutting out the pain that was Tyler's not hers.

"We're on our way to Jackson's. Karen's meeting us there.

Be quick, Regan," Katalina implored.

Regan was on her feet before Katalina finished speaking. Running to the front door, she paused, only to slam her feet into her shoes.

"Regan, what is it?" her mom yelled, clasping her arm and preventing her from exiting the house.

"Tyler's hurt. I need to go," Regan explained, pulling from her grasp.

"Tyler? But we don't have a—"

"He's Dark Shadow, Mom," Regan answered, racing from the house, not bothering to wait for a reaction or reply.

A truck skidded to a stop as Jackson's house came into view. Regan saw Katalina and Zackary jump from the cab and dash into the house. She reached Tyler as Bass and Nico were lifting him down from the truck bed. "Oh, God," she gasped, taking in the sight of him covered with blood. "Oh my God."

"What's going on?" Jackson asked, running from the house, Karen behind him. "Where's Oliver? Why bring him here?"

Bass didn't answer or look at Jackson. Instead, his piercing dark eyes met hers. *He knows.*

"Ask questions later," Karen ordered, barging past Jackson. "Quickly, inside."

Regan followed the group inside, her mind a jumbled daze. Her feet carried her upstairs and into the medical room they'd carried Tyler into. She walked to his side, not daring to touch him as tears burst from her eyes. He was so pale. If it wasn't for the slight movement of his back indicating he was breathing, she'd have thought he was already dead.

"Everyone out," Karen snapped, and then gentler, "Bass you've given him enough. It's up to him now."

Bass had a hand on Tyler's shoulder as he slumped against

the bed, struggling to keep himself upright. Nico stepped forward, hooking an arm around his back, helping him stand. "Come on, Bass."

But Regan couldn't move. Her feet were frozen in place as if cemented to the floor. Terror coursed through her blood as she watched him take each far too shallow breath. *Don't leave me, Ty. Please don't leave me.*

"You too, Regan," Karen ordered as she began to cut away the material surrounding Tyler's wound.

Her head snapped upright. "B-but I can't," she stammered.

"She can help," Bass said.

Karen glanced up between Bass and Regan. "How?"

Regan's gaze met Bass's, willing her to keep Tyler with them. There was no contempt or hate that she'd feared for so long, just understanding and a shared pain.

"I'm his mate," Regan whispered. And as she said the word, she felt the bond snap into place. Tyler's pain surged into her, his fading lifeforce connecting with hers.

"She's his what?" Karen and Jackson asked together.

"I'm his mate," Regan repeated firmer. "And I cannot lose him."

The bond had been there waiting. Giving her the time she needed, waiting until she was ready to accept it. For her to be brave enough to face their uncertain future together. Taking his hand, Regan willed Tyler to live. She threw all that she had into anchoring him in the land of the living right beside her.

"Okay then, well, someone get this girl a chair and then give me space so I can make sure these two get a future together," Karen said into the quiet.

Regan took the seat, keeping her hand firmly in Tyler's as she repeated a mantra in her head. *Stay with me, Ty. Stay with me.*

Please stay.

CHAPTER 49

"How long have you been keeping this a secret for?" Jackson and Bass snapped almost at the same time.

"This is the type of thing you're supposed to tell alphas," Jackson added with a pointed glare.

"Hey!" Katalina's hands landed on her hips. "I just found out, and that's rich, coming from the two of you when you've been doing the same. Tyler asked me to meet him, and when I arrived, I caught the tail end of a conversation that upset him. He was so upset, I had to take a wild guess to get the truth from him."

"Who was the conversation with? He asked you to meet him alone and then you were attacked," Bass replied.

"No, no, Bass." Katalina placed a hand on his arm. "Don't let yourself go there. Tyler's not Bill. Ty protected me. He didn't lure me there."

"I suspect the conversation was with Regan. She'd had a big argument with her parents before you rang for Karen," Jackson explained.

"They've been keeping it secret for a while," Zackary added quietly, not looking at anyone in particular.

Katalina sensed a deep hurt in the boy that worried her, as if killing had damaged him on a fundamental level.

"You knew?" Bass asked, shocked.

"I'm good at sneaking about." Zackary shrugged. "I followed him one night, so he didn't have much choice but to tell me."

"And you said nothing?" Jackson said in disbelief.

Zackary looked up for the first time, meeting Jackson's then Bass's gaze briefly. "Why should I have? Don't see what's so wrong with them being together."

Katalina touched Zackary's arm gently. "There isn't anything wrong with it."

"Kat," Bass warned.

"Don't Kat me. You should know out of everyone that we don't have control over who we fall in love with."

Cage entered the room at that moment a little out of breath. "I heard what happened and came right over. Are they all right?" He glanced through the small window in the door. "Poor Regan."

"You don't sound all that confused over Regan being in there with Tyler," Jackson observed.

Cage froze, then turned to face the room, wincing. "I'mmm not." He dragged the words out, his expression saying, "don't kill me."

"Cage!" Jackson growled.

"I'm sorry, okay. Anna had a vision a while ago and made me promise not to say anything.... She's my mate. What was I to do?"

"What did Anna see?" Katalina asked.

"It was more of a message than a picture, I think. She warned Tyler he had to tell someone. Otherwise, it would end in pain."

"Pain?" Katalina glanced at the door as if she could see Tyler through the wood laid bleeding out on the bed. "As in he dies?"

"You know Anna's visions are subjective. *It* could be a number of things. It could be the secret. I mean, that's ended and they are both in a lot of pain."

"I hope that's all it is," Katalina whispered. Tyler had been injured defending her, which was hard enough for her conscience to take. She wouldn't handle his death.

"How are we going to handle this?" Bass asked, running his hands through his hair in an unusual display of emotion.

"Tyler will be welcomed into River Run with open arms," Jackson reassured him.

Bass growled. "You think you're having one of my most gifted enforcers?"

"Oh, so I'm supposed to just give up Regan? Her parents have already lost one daughter," Jackson countered, raising his voice.

The tension in the room skyrocketed. Zackary shrank back in his seat.

Jumping to her feet, Katalina placed herself between the two alphas. "Stop it, the both of you. Now is not the time or place for this conversation, and Regan and Tyler's future are their own to choose, and who says they must choose. I'm of both packs. What's the difference?"

"You're Dark Shadow," Bass answered.

Katalina sighed with a shake of her head. "If you truly believe that, then we're in more trouble than I thought. We might say I'm Dark Shadow, but in my heart, I'm both."

Bass turned from Jackson and pressed a hand to her cheek. "I know that you are, but this situation is a little different."

"Only if we treat it as such," Katalina insisted.

Toby burst into the room. "Sorry to interrupt guys, but Regan's father's here and he's looking more pissed off than he did earlier, Jackson. William is trying to calm him down but...."

Jackson groaned. "I'm coming, Toby. Bass, Katalina is right. At this moment it's not important. What's important now is them both pulling through this whole."

"Agreed," Bass said.

"Do you need help with Noah?" Katalina asked.

Jackson met her gaze. "I'm afraid right now, Kat, Noah probably likes you about as much as he does Tyler. I suggest both you and Bass stay up here out of the way."

"I actually need to get back to my pack. Nico will stay behind with Katalina," Bass said.

Jackson nodded. "Well, slip out of the back unseen then. We'll talk later."

Bass left after Jackson, promising to return as soon as he could. There'd been no further sightings from the Indiana pack, but that didn't mean Dark Shadow didn't need Bass. This attack had stirred fears that hadn't quite left them since the last time. They needed their alpha strong and present. But most of all, they needed the fresh start Katalina hoped building new homes on a new site would bring them.

She sat back down next to Zackary. "How you are doing?" she whispered, bumping his shoulder with hers softly.

His desolate eyes met hers. "Do you want the truth?" he asked her quietly.

"Always." She nodded.

"Every time I close my eyes, I see that guy's face, mangled and blank with death."

Katalina wrapped an arm around his shoulder. "You'll get through this, Zac. I know it might not feel like it now, but you will, I promise."

He shrugged off her hold. "Oh yeah, how many guys have you killed?" he asked sarcastically.

"I've lost count," Katalina replied honestly. "But I'll never forget my first. I think it will always haunt me."

Zackary blinked twice at her, searching her face as if he wasn't sure she told the truth. "How do you live like this, after being… normal?"

"I guess we don't really have a choice, do we? We can't go back. We're not normal. We're shifters."

Zackary nodded sadly, sinking down in his chair. "I hope Ty makes it."

"Me too, Zac," she sighed. "Me too."

CHAPTER 50

Unable to watch Karen as she operated on Tyler, Regan kept her gaze fixed firmly on Tyler's face. Her free hand stroked his mop of dark hair from his forehead, her thumb brushing over his too pale skin. She studied him, tattooing every detail of his face to her memory, each freckle across his nose, the sweep of his eyelashes, and slight dip in his cheek even when asleep. She imagined he was sleeping, imagined they were alone in bed, and as he pulled the energy from her body, she gave it willingly.

At one-point, Clare—Karen's trainee—came and checked her pulse. She spoke but Regan was struggling to stay focused. Her eyes were becoming heavy, her breaths harder to pull in and out of her lungs. With each passing minute, her body became numb, but still, she willed her life into Tyler, chanting silently, *Stay with me. Stay.*

I'm just going to close my eyes. She rested her head on the bed beside Tyler, leaning her weight against the table. *Just for a moment, only a moment….*

"Regan… Regan, baby, wake up."

"Ty?" She blinked, trying to focus her vision. Tyler's face was above hers, his smile like sunshine after a storm.

"Hey, beautiful girl," he whispered, pressing his lips to hers.

His kiss breathed life back into her but only for a moment. "I'm so tired, Ty."

"I know, baby. It's time to let go."

His hand tried to leave hers. Regan's gaze fell to their linked hands as urgency and fear flooded her blood. "No. Stay with me!" she gasped, holding him tighter.

His free hand caressed her face. "You've given enough, Regan. It's time to let go."

His hand was slipping from her grip. "Tyler, no!" she screamed as his face dissolved above her. "No, stay with me!"

"I love you," his voice echoed around her.

"Tyler!" Regan shot upright, her heart in her throat, terror in her veins. "Tyler?"

"Regan, shh, it's okay."

She whipped her head around, staring at Katalina next to the bed she'd lain in. Beyond her was Tyler, on his stomach, his face tilted her away from her. Her heart stalled, stone-cold terror racing through her. Regan swung her legs from the bed, dropping to the floor to go to Tyler, but as she stood upright, her head swam.

"Wow," Katalina soothed, reaching out and steadying her. "Take it slow. You've been out for a while." She helped her over to a chair seated next to his bed. Regan still couldn't see Tyler's face and with her blurry vision, she was unable to make out if he was breathing or not. "Here, take my seat."

"W-What happened?" Regan stammered as she sat. Her heart pounded through her skull, her gaze unable to look away from Tyler's too still form.

"You passed out about halfway through. Karen said you gave all you had to keep Tyler here."

Please let it have been enough. "Is he… is he going to be okay? Is… Is he alive?"

Terrified of Katalina's answer, Regan almost didn't want to hear it. Her fear was like a living thing inside of her. Icy cold as it crawled through her veins, freezing her mind, her rational thoughts. *Please, I can't live without him.*

"He should make a full recovery." Relief flooded her, thawing her mind into living once more. "The muscle damage was severe. Karen thinks it might be months of physical therapy, even with his shifter healing. The knife cut deepest into his shoulder. He'll struggle to use his left arm for a while."

Regan lifted an unsteady hand, placing it gently on his uninjured shoulder. Pleased to feel some heat back in his skin, Regan took her first deep breath since she'd awoke and allowed a few moments to be grateful they were both breathing before asking, "When will he wake?"

"That's all on him. You've been out for four hours. Karen finished operating about three hours ago. It's the middle of the night."

Regan glanced out the window, seeing nothing but darkness beyond. "I had a dream," Regan whispered. "He was telling me to let go."

Katalina's hand landed on her shoulder, the touch one of comfort and support. "Tyler's going to pull through. He's a fighter, and he loves you, Regan. He won't leave you."

"Sometimes the people who love us have no choice but to go." Regan dragged in an unsteady breath, swiping at the hot tears rolling down her face. "Everybody knows."

"It's going to be all right, Regan," Katalina promised.

Regan turned in her seat, staring at Katalina. "How? How are we ever going to work? The packs, my parents.... Oh God, my parents. I bet they hate me.... We'll have to leave."

"No one is leaving," Bass said as he entered the room.

"I agree," Jackson added, entering behind him. "And as for your parents, give them time."

Bass pulled Katalina into his arms, kissing her forehead as he did. "I'm heading back now. Dark Shadow needs its alpha present. Are you staying with Ty, or shall I send someone to take over?"

"I'll stay." She kissed him. "I'll ring when he wakes."

Nodding, Bass released Katalina and walked to Tyler's bedside. He placed his hand over Regan's resting on Tyler's shoulder, then touched gentle fingers to her cheek. Regan sucked in a breath as the eyes of Bass's wolf met hers, his smile soft and reassuring.

"Welcome to Dark Shadow," he murmured.

Regan had no words. Her wolf stirred deep within her as she gazed back at the alpha who had just accepted her as his own. A tear slipped down her cheek as the heavy weight lifted from her shoulders. She didn't know the right words to say to him, to explain what Bass had done for her, for Tyler. Instead, she smiled back and cupped her hand over his on her cheek, leaning into his touch in acceptance.

"Get that idea out of your head, Bass. You're not stealing my girl," Jackson grumbled.

Bass's smile turned mischievous as he rolled his eyes, and Regan had the sense she was meeting the real Bass for the first time. He released her and stepped back. "I'm just letting her know I'm here for her if she needs me. That Dark Shadow welcomes her."

"I'm onto you, son. If anyone's stealing anyone, I'm having Tyler. I'd say Dark Shadow owes me a few good fighters after all these years."

The two alphas eyed each other, and Regan tensed. She'd been afraid of this, afraid her and Tyler's relationship blurred too many lines.

Bass laughed. "I dare you to try. Tyler's loyal to me."

"Squabble later," Katalina scolded, shooing them with her arms. "Out, the both of you." Silence descended when Katalina closed the door, shutting the two alphas out. She turned toward Regan, leaning her back against the door.

In some ways, Regan was relieved and touched from Bass's gesture. To have his acceptance eased many of her fears and she knew many of Tyler's, but while Jackson and Bass had appeared playful in their banter, it didn't silence her concerns of where she and Tyler now belonged.

As if reading her mind, Katalina walked to her and pulled her up out of the chair and into her arms. "Please don't worry about them. Yes, your mating complicates things, but we'll find a way to make it work."

"Our loyalties are blurred, Kat. How will that ever work?"

"Don't you think my loyalties are blurred? I know I didn't grow up here, but that doesn't change the fact River Run is my family as much as Dark Shadow. Hell, it was like five minutes ago that my world was falling apart, and I didn't stay with Dark Shadow. I ran to Jackson, my father, the other alpha. It's complicated and messy, but we all make it work because that's what you do for those you love."

"I guess you're right, but I can't see it being that simple. How are you anyway?"

"We don't have to discuss me and my emotions right now."

"Actually, it would be quite nice to think about something else other than Ty."

Katalina smiled. "I tell you what, I'll go fetch us some drinks and food, and I'll tell you all about my messed-up life."

She smiled at Katalina's retreating figure and turned to face Tyler. Standing slowly, Regan leaned over the bed and brushed his hair from his face, getting her first real look at him. Many emotions churned inside of her, but mostly Regan was grateful Tyler was alive, and thankful for the extra time they'd been given.

CHAPTER 51

He was on fire. His back, his arm, it was like the blade had been molten lava melting his flesh. The pain consumed him, blackening his vision. He had a distant thought of Katalina, an urge to get up and defend her, but the agony of his wounds was too much. His body betrayed him. His body gave up.

A numbness beckoned him, an endless, eternal silence. It promised the pain would stop, promised him peace. And oh, how Tyler begged for it to stop. With each shift of his body, his wound protested, raw and angry. His mind was slipping, his body ready for the fight to be over, yet there was another voice calling him. One far more powerful than death. It started as a whisper, a distant memory he couldn't quite reach, and then it was there, a face in his mind, a voice in his ear, a plea. *Regan…*

Stay with me. Stay, she begged.

Always, always, he wanted to scream, but his mouth wouldn't work. His body was shutting down. Tyler felt the whisper of her touch, the softness of her lips, the cool dampness as her tears fell onto his skin.

Please don't cry, baby.

He was fading, slipping away into nothingness. *No!* His wolf snarled in defiance. *I will not leave her. I will not leave my mate. My heart.*

Mate….

The word hit him like a shock to the heart. The darkness was blinded by a living sun. Regan, his mate, she surrounded him, her scent, her very essence. It flowed through his veins like the sweetest of drugs. She was everywhere, flowing through and anchoring him to life.

The pain faded away, yet it wasn't the darkness that called to him. Instead, Tyler slipped into a peaceful sleep, cocooned by Regan, wrapped in the arms of her love.

He first became aware of the dull ache across his back and then the absence of Regan through his veins. Yet she'd not left him completely. There, connected to his heart, his soul, was the bond that tied him to Regan for all eternity.

Happiness flowed from his chest, momentarily blocking out his pain, but memories invaded his mind—Regan's distraught voice as she told him about her parents, her cries as she'd said they'd never accept him, and they'd have to leave.

Urgency rushed through him. He had to get to her, protect her from the consequences of their mating. Tyler pried open his eyes, his vison too blurred to take in his surroundings. He didn't wait for his eyesight to clear; instead, Tyler moved his arms to push himself up when agony rippled through his back and down his left arm, a thousand tiny needles digging into him at once. He hated the pained cry that left his lips, cursed his body when it collapsed back onto the bed, and refused to try moving a second time.

"Ty! Stay still. Don't move."

"R-Re-gan?" Tyler rasped, his throat like sandpaper. Her blurry face appeared before him. He blinked rapidly, his vison clearing at last. "Regan."

"Hey." She smiled, tears pooling in her eyes. "I thought I was going to lose you."

"Never," he promised.

A tear rolled down her cheek. Tyler went to wipe it away,

but again, his arm protested. He stopped himself from crying out but couldn't control his face as it crumpled in pain.

"Stop moving," Regan scolded. "You're badly hurt, Ty. Please keep still. I'm going to go fetch Karen."

"Karen?"

"Yeah, you're at Jackson's, at River Run."

"Bass? Did he… did he…." But Tyler couldn't finish the sentence, couldn't say his fear aloud. That he'd worried Bass would reject him, that in gaining a mate, he'd lose his family, his pack.

Regan smiled softly, her eyes filling with sympathy. "Our mating hasn't happened without consequence, but Bass hasn't left you, Ty. Dark Shadow stands with you. You're here because Kat knew you needed me."

"I could feel you, willing me to live," he whispered.

She caressed his face, her fingers sliding into his hair, each tiny touch sending warmth through his skin. "I'll always fight for you. You're my mate."

Tyler smiled at the word, his chest filling almost painfully with joy. "I like the sound of that word."

"Me too. Now I'll be right back. Don't move, okay?"

He nodded, and even that tiny movement hurt.

She was back in minutes, Karen with her.

"Hi," Karen said, coming up beside him and taking his wrist. "Let's check your vitals." She peered at her watch as she silently counted his beats, then returned her attention to him. "How's the pain levels?"

"Okay."

She rolled her eyes slightly. "It's just Regan and me. No need to be all macho for us."

"Fine," Tyler grumbled. "Hurts like hell. Even moving my arm does, but I could have sworn the blade hit my back. God, I didn't even asked how Kat is. She wasn't hurt was she?"

"Katalina is fine," Karen reassured him. "And you've been through a lot. I think you can be forgiven for not asking right away. Now, as for your arm, the knife hit your shoulder and cut deep at an angle across your back. The lower half wasn't so bad, but the initial contact cut deep into your muscle and caused a lot of damage, which is why you're having trouble with your left arm. The ligaments and tendons that help your arm move are damaged, and recovery is going to be slow I'm afraid."

"But I will regain use?" Tyler asked. His stomach flipped with unease. He needed to be fully functioning. To be strong. His pack needed him. His mate needed him.

"If I did my job right, which I did, you will. We'll give it a few days, then try some simple tests to gauge the amount of movement you've lost. In the meantime, let's get some painkillers into you and try getting you onto your back. Though I suspect it's going to be painful, I'm guessing you'd rather not meet two alphas laid on your front."

"No, I wouldn't." Tyler met Regan's gaze. "How much trouble are we in?"

Regan winced.

"That bad huh?"

"I've not actually seen my parents, but Jackson told me he had to throw my father out the house when Karen was operating. Bass actually welcomed me to Dark Shadow, which pissed Jackson off a little. To be honest, I've been holed up in here with you, and Kat kept me company for a while. She left not long before you woke up."

"Problems that can all wait," Karen added. "Right now, I want you to concentrate on healing."

Tyler smiled. "Thanks, Karen."

A few minutes later, with morphine running through his veins, Tyler managed to sit up without his body exploding in agony. Both Karen and Regan helped him as he slowly, step by step, swung his legs up onto the bed and leant back onto the raised bed.

"I've put the softest pillows I could find behind you," Karen said as Tyler gritted his teeth against the pain of leaning back on the wound.

"Be… fine," he puffed between breaths.

The simple act of sitting up and moving around to lean back on the bed felt like a marathon to him. He was breathless, with beads of sweat appearing on his forehead. The morphine might have helped but it didn't nearly kill the pain of moving.

"Kat's just messaged to say she and Bass are heading over," Regan said.

Karen touch his hand briefly. "I'll leave you to catch your breath. I suggest spending as much time as possible on your front. I can come help you once your company leaves. If at anytime the pain becomes too much, or you start to feel hot and shaky, call me right away. I've got you hooked up to antibiotics to prevent infection, but it's always a risk."

"I'll keep a close eye on him," Regan assured her. Hearing Regan say such things was both weird and wonderful. He was so used to keeping the feelings between each other a secret, every time a declaration was made it sent a tiny skip through him.

Karen nodded, pausing in front of Regan as she passed, gripping her shoulders. "And you don't let your parents trouble you. Give them time. Grief can make us do terrible things, even years after."

Regan smiled tightly, nodding, and when they were alone in the room once more, she turned her beautiful face toward him and let the true extent of her pain show.

His heart broke. How he wanted to take all her troubles and make them okay. Protect her from every bit of sorrow she'd feel in her life. But even he as her mate couldn't do that. All he could was be there to weather the storms with her. "Oh, baby, come here," Tyler said, opening his one good arm for her.

"I don't want to hurt you," she said between sobs.

"Holding you will never hurt, Regan. Come here."

Carefully, Regan climbed onto the edge of the bed and moved gently into his arms. "I was explaining to my mom about the training, and I think she was trying to understand, but then you were hurt, and I could feel your pain.... Kat called and..." Regan dragged in a breath, sitting up slightly to meet his eyes. "I didn't even try to hide it, Ty. I could feel your pain as if it were my own, and I knew there was no point trying to lie. You're the most important part of my life, Tyler."

"Like Karen said, they'll come around. We're going to make this work, Regan. Just give it time." It was still surreal to him that people knew, and not only that they'd not turned them away. Tyler had to keep reminding himself that he was awake and this wasn't a dream.

"You weren't there when Jackson told me about my father. He didn't say what he said, but he didn't have to; it was written on his face and everyone else's in the room. He's disowned me, Ty, the only daughter he has left, all because I fell in love."

It was hard to contain his anger toward Regan's father. To speak soothingly to her, when his first instinct was to march up to her parents and snarl until they became reasonable. "He'll see reason. I'll make him see reason."

"I don't think you're quite up to taking on my dad right now, even if he's not dominant."

Depends how angry he gets me.

"I'll be out of here before you know it," he promised, forcing himself to lean forward and kiss her.

There was a knock at the door. Regan sat up and pulled away, climbing from his arms and to the floor, wiping her face quickly as she forced a smile and turned to great their guests. Tyler forced his own smile. He wanted nothing more than to get out of the bed and go hunt down the man who'd put tears on his mate's face. Be damned if he was her father or not. No one had the right to do that to his girl.

For a second, Tyler was afraid to meet Bass's eyes, afraid to see an expression that said what he and Regan had was wrong when it felt so right. But Tyler was a firm believer in looking danger in the eye as it came for him. He hadn't made enforcer at twenty-one by being a coward. So Tyler met Bass's gaze, ready to snarl at his alpha if he had to, because no one on the earth was going to tell him he couldn't have her. She was his, always, and forever.

"Ty!" Katalina rushed forward, greeting him with a smile before Bass could get out a word. "Congratulations," she continued, taking his hand and squeezing. "But I warn you, you'd better take good care of my friend."

Letting out a heavy breath, Tyler smiled back. "Thank you, Kat. That means a lot, and I will."

"Hmm… same goes from me," Jackson said, a little more sternly than Katalina. "Though I understand now who's been helping Regan heal these last few months."

Nodding in acknowledgement, Tyler at last returned his gaze back to his alpha. "Bass."

"You should have told me. That night in the forest, you should have said something," Bass said.

"I was afraid you'd tell me to give her up, that our relationship would compromise the alliance," Tyler admitted.

"I hardly have the right to tell you that, Ty, when I went ahead and fell for a River Run wolf myself. But I'm not got to lie. Regan's parents are a complication. Jackson has told me of the bad blood between Dark Shadow and your family, Regan. I didn't know of her death and if Richard was still a member of this pack, the kill would be yours, but he's not and all I can do is apologize on behalf of my pack."

"There's no need to apologize, Bass. Megan's death wasn't your fault, and Dark Shadow isn't the same anymore."

"Have you thought on where you'd plan to live? Which pack?" Jackson asked.

Tyler's heart stuttered. He hadn't. He'd not thought beyond someone finding out, and he'd never imagined choosing a side.

"I've told you, Jackson, you're not stealing my enforcer," Bass grumbled.

Tyler felt Regan's gaze on him and focused on her. He could sense the same distress he felt inside of himself, as well as read it on her face.

"And I told you, you're not having my girl," Jackson counted.

"Oh, for God's sake you two," Katalina said, glaring at them both. "It's so annoying when you're both acting like 'I'm the biggest alpha,' aka two-year-old toddlers. Why exactly do they have to choose?"

"Because a mate's bond comes above an alpha's, which is going to cause issues on whose allegiance they have," Bass explained.

"So why doesn't my allegiance come into question?" Katalina asked, raising an eyebrow.

"You're different, Kat, you didn't grow up here," Jackson replied.

"I don't see why that makes a difference," she argued. "I'm not special and shouldn't be treated that way."

Tyler watched it all play out with dread building within him. *Choose? How can I choose?* He was Dark Shadow. It ran though his blood, sunk right down to his very bones. His family was Dark Shadow. If he left, would that mean he'd need permission to enter the inner lands and see his family?

"I think," Karen said, appearing in the doorway, her voice

carrying over everyone else, "this conversation would be better on a different day, when everyone is well."

Silence enveloped the room.

"So, could someone please tell me what happened after I blacked out? Please tell me you killed the asshole, Kat," Tyler said into the quiet.

"No, I didn't. We fell to the ground together and I couldn't get you off me in time. You weigh a ton by the way." She grinned. "Zac saved us."

"Zac?" Tyler gasped, shock hitting him. He was too young, not equipped to deal with the emotional implications that came with taking a life. Yet he couldn't be sorry. If he hadn't been there, he'd potentially not be here, and Katalina could have died also.

"He'd decided to follow you. Good job he did really," Bass explained.

"Is he all right, though?" Tyler asked. He'd come to care for the kid during their time together. Zackary was like a little brother to him; he'd hate for him to have more emotional baggage. He'd been through enough.

"He's getting there," Katalina said softly. "He wants to see you, but I said to wait until you were up for it."

"Maybe tomorrow," Tyler confirmed. "Tell him I hope he's okay. And thank you. Were there other attacks?"

"No," Bass answered.

"Strange for Castor to send just one person, and his brother to boot. Surely he didn't think one man could get through patrol lines?"

"I think this was Braxton's rash decision made on emotions over the loss of his half-brother," Bass said. "Obviously got a little more heart than Castor."

"He did seem to be the only one to care for Bill when they

were all here. Castor acted as if he didn't exist," Tyler added.

"Yes." Bass turned serious. "Which is why we never saw Bill coming I guess."

Silence filled the room as their thoughts turned to Bill's betrayal.

Jackson took a small step closer. "Karen's said your recovery is going to be long, and I want you to know, Tyler, that whether you choose River Run or not, you're welcome here in my home. And of course, your family is also until you are well enough to move."

Tyler met the other alpha's gaze, his wolf coming into his eyes as he nodded in submission and thanks. "I appreciate that. Thank you."

"Well, we should leave you to rest. I suspect your mother will be here shortly. I think your dad had a hard time stopping her from setting up a vigil at the door. But I thought it would be best for you to both be present when she met Regan," Bass said.

"Do they know?" Tyler asked, fear relighting in his gut; though he'd always feared his alpha's reaction more than his family's.

"No," Bass answered. "At this moment, only a select few in Dark Shadow know, the inner circle, Zac, and I suspect Nico will have told Olivia. There is no need to keep it a secret of course. It just wasn't ours to tell."

"Thanks, all of you," Tyler answered.

"All of River Run know. It was a little hard to keep it quiet with Noah kicking down my door, but I don't want you worrying, Regan," Jackson added.

"We'll come and visit tomorrow with Zac," Katalina said, coming forward and placing a kiss on Tyler's cheek. "And thank you," she whispered, "for protecting me."

Tyler saw the guilt in Katalina's eyes and couldn't ignore the compulsion to soothe his alpha's mate. Even though it hurt him to do so, he lifted an unsteady hand, and clasped hers, rubbing his thumb over her skin. "We're pack. We protect our own. Do not feel guilty, okay?"

She nodded, blinking hard, then turned to give Regan a hug. "Text if you need me, 'kay."

"I will," Regan promised. "See you tomorrow."

Bass came forward and took his hand. For a moment, the pain humming through Tyler's body subsided, and he couldn't help but sigh from the relief. When he looked into Bass's face, it was to see the man's jaw clench against the pain he was drawing from Tyler's body. "I'd take all of your pain if I could for protecting Katalina. Thank you."

"The fact you didn't turn Regan away is more than enough. I was doing my job, Bass. You've nothing to pay back." They bowed heads, touching foreheads briefly.

"Heal fast," Bass murmured. "Dark Shadow needs you."

Minutes later, Tyler was left alone with Regan. "How do we choose?" she asked, her gaze empty.

"I don't know, and honestly, right now, I'm in too much pain to even consider it. Please help me lay down on my front."

Regan rushed to his side. "Poor baby. I hate seeing you in pain."

With great effort and what felt like another marathon, Tyler made it back on his front with the bed laid flat. "I'm going to close my eyes just for a moment," Tyler panted. "Make sure I'm awake before my parents arrive."

Whether she answered or not, Tyler wasn't sure. The last memory he had was of Regan's beautiful face creased with concern. Then sleep claimed him and he welcomed it, glad for the numbness it brought.

Chapter 52

She watched him sleep as the world passed by, happily hiding, not caring at all that life carried on while she was paused in time. It was a skill Regan had perfected after Megan had been killed, and while she'd begun to move forward again recently, current events had her falling back on old habits.

If it wasn't for the pack members slipping almost unseen into the room and leaving her drinks and food, she'd not even bother feeding herself. Tyler was her dream come true, her knight in shining armor who'd rescued her from the dark when she'd not been aware of being lost. Yet he brought with him a consequence she'd feared more than anything—the loss of the rest of her family.

Regan didn't regret him and would never want to go back and change her choice because the truth of the matter was Tyler's loss would be greater, or maybe it was that her true parents had died the day Megan had. Because her mom from before would have noticed Regan had stopped living and only barely survived. She hoped everyone was right in saying they just needed time, yet she feared all the time in the world wouldn't be enough. That her parents, like she had been, were frozen in time, doing all they could to survive, no matter the cost, never realizing death would be a kinder option. That it was Megan who received the easier deal while the three of them served life behind impenetrable bars.

"Regan."

She looked up, sitting straighter, not sure if she'd imagined the whisper from his lips.

"Ty?" she whispered back.

His eyes didn't open, yet he replied. "I can feel your pain, baby. I can sense you're shutting down, locking yourself away."

Smiling, Regan got to her feet and crossed the room to his bed. "I'm sorry. Go back to sleep. Your parents are coming in a few hours. Katalina texted me."

One of his eyes cracked open. "I can't sleep if you're hurting."

"I'll be okay. I have you."

He smiled, and Regan reached out and brushed his dark hair from his face as his blue eye closed. She repeated the movement, stroking him gently.

"Mmm… that's nice," he murmured, a smile creasing one side of his mouth.

"Go to sleep," she breathed, placing a kiss on his cheek.

His smile grew a little wider, revealing the dimple in his cheek, before fading away and as she caressed his face, teasing his hair, and then Tyler relaxed, drifting to sleep.

There was a soft knock, then the door creaked open enough for a head to pop inside.

"Hey," Mia said. "Talk outside?"

Regan nodded before smiling back down at Tyler and then heading out of the door. Before she had a chance to say a word, Mia attacked her with a hug.

"I can't believe you've found your mate at nineteen. I was hoping to have a few years partying with you at least."

Regan laughed softly. "Pretty sure I can still party."

"Hmm… you never know, he might be the possessive kind."

"We were together the last time we went out. In fact, he was the one who said I should go."

Mia grinned. "I love him already. But I've gotta tell you, Regan, I kinda don't love your stench at the moment. Girl, you need a shower and change of clothes."

Regan sniffed at herself, then shrugged. "I've been a bit busy, plus I've got no spare clothes here."

"Do you want me to go to your house and collect you a few things?"

"Actually." Regan glanced back at the door, wondering if he'd wake if she left for a little while. She was sure he wouldn't mind if she did. "I need some fresh air. I'll come with you."

Leaving Jackson's with Mia, Regan swallowed her apprehension and fear. *Dad will be at work at least, only mom to face.* And she realized as she went step by step toward her house, that maybe the bars she'd been locked behind weren't impenetrable after all. Tyler had broken through them, and because it hurt him if she became withdrawn, the only option she had was to keep living, even if it meant facing her demons head-on.

"Nervous?" Mia asked as the house came into view.

"Terrified," Regan replied. "Did you hear what my dad did?"

Mia winced. "Afraid the entire pack is talking about it. On your side of course."

"I don't think there is a side in all of this really. They're still hurting over Megan."

"Doesn't make what they've done right, Regan. You're hurting over your sister too."

"I suppose—" Her words died. "Are they… are they boxes?"

Mia took hold of her hand. "I'll go, you stay here."

Rage tore through her. She'd forgiven her parents for many things but packing up her stuff and leaving it outside like she no longer mattered was something she couldn't even comprehend. "No!" Regan ripped her hand from Mia's. "I'm not hiding like I did something wrong."

Marching up to the door, Regan ignored her stuff and grasped the handle, ready to rip it open, but it didn't give. It was locked. Rattling the handle, she banged on the door, her pent-up anger from years of being alone and repressed surfacing.

"Mother, open this door!" She banged again, the glass rattling underneath her strength. "I know you're in there. Open the door. Come face me!"

"Regan," Mia tried to soothe, her hand landing on her shoulder.

"OPEN THE DOOR!" Regan screamed. "Face me, you coward."

There was a shuffle across the floor, the Regan caught movement up ahead—her mother's shadow as she hid down the hall. "Please, Regan, just go."

All the rage drained out of her, and Regan placed her palm flat against the door. "Please, Mom," she begged. No answer came and Regan sucked in a breath, and let her hand fall away, whispering her parting words just loud enough so her mom would hear, "Wherever Megan is right now, she'd be ashamed of you. I'm ashamed of you."

Turning away, Regan picked up the nearest box, then stacked another on top, turning her back on her childhood home, on her mom, on the past. She was walking into the future, and if her parents chose to not be beside her, then that was their loss not hers.

Mia fell into step beside her, after she two collected a couple of boxes. "Are you okay?"

Regan swallowed the lump in her throat, forced herself to not cry and held her head up high. "Not even nearly," she answered. "But I will be." *And I'll keep telling myself that until I believe it.*

"What are you doing?"

With a frustrated sighed, Regan threw the clothes she held back into the opened box and pulled herself together enough to face Tyler. "I didn't mean to wake you, I'm sorry."

"You didn't wake me, Regan. What's wrong?"

"Nothing, I'm fine."

His mouth lifted into a half smile, as he moved his head from the bed just a little. "You do realize you literally can't lie to me anymore."

Regan smiled, despite herself. "Well, that sucks. Now lay back down before you hurt yourself."

"I will when you tell me what's wrong."

Her hands landed on her hips. "I'm trying to find an old T-shirt that was Megan's so I can go shower. Mia says I stink."

"Okay… but that's not all that is wrong, is it?"

Regan let her hands fall to her sides then turned to pick up a random pair of jeans and top without really paying much mind whether they matched or not.

"Regan," Tyler growled softly.

"Fine. The boxes you see here were left outside my house, along with a load more all containing my belongings. Mia and a few others have gone to collect them for me."

"Your parents chucked out your stuff?" he asked in a tone that was far too controlled.

She met his gaze. "Yes, Ty, my parents have chucked me out."

Out of all the scenarios that had run through Regan's head, she'd never anticipated Tyler's next move. Pain and rage surged through the mating bond as Tyler pushed himself upright and swung his legs off the bed.

"What are you doing?!" Regan cried, running toward him and stopping him from stepping onto the floor. "You, stupid man, you'll injure yourself further."

"I'm going to kill them," he ground out. "How dare they treat you like this? Their own daughter."

"They're blinded by hatred and grief, Ty. Now lay back down. Here, I'll adjust the bed upright."

"I don't care, Regan. That's not a good enough excuse to hurt you like they are."

She took hold of his face in her hands. "I know." She kissed his mouth, dipping her tongue inside, tasting him, washing away all the bitterness she felt. "But they are not worth injuring yourself over. Please, lay back down."

There was a knock at the door, Toby's voice drifting through it, "Ty's parents have just appeared in the distance. Erm, shall I stall them?"

Regan's eyes widened. "I can't meet your parents smelling, Ty!" she whispered, horrified, then said louder to Toby, "Yes, please, long enough for me to shower."

Despite everything, Tyler laughed. "Then go shower, gorgeous girl. I'll still be here when you get back."

Regan wrung her hands together unable to keep still. Her heart was trying to jump out of her chest, and nerves bounced through her body making her fidget. She'd envisioned meeting Tyler's family one day, and in all those visions, she'd been nervous but there hadn't been the fear she held inside of her now, a fear she knew came from her parents' reactions.

Standing beside Tyler's bed, his right hand gripped hers tightly as they both stared at the door. He caressed his thumb over her hand. "Stop fidgeting."

"I can't help it. How are you so calm right now?"

"Because I know my family and I've never feared introducing you to them."

"Still."

Tyler twisted his head and looked up at her. "It'll be okay, I promise."

She had no time to answer him. To tell him even if his parents were thrilled to meet her, life would never be 100 percent okay again because she'd lost her parents, but the door was opening and people were piling in, and the words died in her throat.

Regan tensed as Tyler's mother rushed forward and straight into his arms.

"Ugh!" Tyler cried out. "Jeez, Mom, take it easy."

"Oh gosh, I'm so sorry. I was just so worried." She took hold of his left hand, lifting it slightly.

Tyler gasped in pain again.

"Lauran, come here before you break the poor man even more," Tyler's father instructed.

His mom took a step back, lifting her hands up. "Sorry, Tyler."

Tyler shook his head and chuckled softly. "It's all right, Mom. I'll survive."

"Babe, just move the pillow up a bit more, will you?" Tyler asked her in a pained tone.

Regan moved without thought, not even registering what

he'd called her in front of his parents. She didn't think Tyler had realized either until his little brother spoke up.

"Babe?" his little brother mumbled.

Tyler and Regan froze.

"Wow, dude, busted." His brother laughed.

Regan took a deep breath, readjusted Tyler's pillow, then braced herself to face them. Tyler took her hand and smiled up at her, then at his family.

"Mom, Dad, Lockie, I'd like you to meet Regan, my mate."

Regan held her breath, staring at Tyler's family, waiting for their reaction. His mom's gaze flickered from hers to Tyler's before finally landing on their linked hands.

"When?" she whispered.

"We met a few months ago, but the bond snapped into place when I was injured. I wouldn't be here if for not for her," Tyler answered.

His mother gasped, her hands covering her mouth as tears pooled in her eyes, and then Lauran was hurtling toward her. Regan wasn't sure whether to run or cower. In the end, Regan did nothing, and Tyler's mother crashed into her, wrapping her arms so tightly around Regan, there was no wonder Tyler had cried out in pain when she'd hugged him.

"Oh, my dear girl. Thank you, thank you," Lauran wept.

Patting her back, Regan looked at Tyler for help, but he only laughed. "Told you it would be fine, didn't I?"

"Congratulations, son. Though I'm a little worried what this will mean for your standing within Dark Shadow. I presume Bass knows?" his father asked.

"Yes," Tyler answered. "He does."

"Oh, never mind that right now, Kevin. What's important

is that Tyler is still with us, and that he's happy," Lauran said, releasing Regan from the hug but not letting go of her completely. "Look at you, honey, so beautiful."

"She is. Mind giving her back?" Tyler laughed.

"Oh sorry," Lauran said, taking a step back, and patting Tyler's knee gently. "I'm so happy for you, Ty."

"Thanks, Mom." Tyler's gaze landed on his brother. "Awfully quiet there, Lachlan."

"I'm just stunned you've actually broken a rule." Lachlan's cheeky gaze landed on Regan. "You realize he's the boring brother, right?"

"Dude, you're eleven," Tyler said.

"So, I'm still more exciting than you." Lachlan laughed.

"Be quiet, Lachlan, you should behave a little more like your brother," his mom scolded.

Lachlan answered with a roll of his eyes, and a wink at Regan.

"Well, I'm gonna have to kick you out guys. Hate to admit this but I'm exhausted and in pain," Tyler said.

"Of course," his mom answered, patting his knee again. "We just needed to see you with our own eyes."

The next few minutes passed in a whirl of hugs and goodbyes, Regan was shell-shocked as she shut the door on Tyler's family and leaned against it, staring at him. "I was not expecting that reaction."

"I told you."

"Yes, but I thought you were just trying to protect me."

"Come here. I need to kiss you."

Joy sparked at her core, making its way through her body

as she crossed the space between them smiling widely. “I think it’s only just sinking in that I get to kiss you whenever I want to now. No more hiding or waking up alone. Do you know how long I’ve dreamed of that?”

“Probably as long as me,” he breathed, tugging her forward with his one good arm and locking his lips with hers. “I love you, Regan.”

“I love you too.”

CHAPTER 53

Sitting by the lake her arm around Arne at her side, Katalina watched the hub of activity before her with equal amounts of joy and disbelief. She'd never quite believed this day would come about, that her niggling and pushing would not only convince Bass to take the plunge, but also the rest of Dark Shadow as well. Admittedly, Katalina thought it wasn't only her who had brought about today. Ironically, Indiana had a huge hand in it, which she felt was the best kind of revenge.

Castor wanted to destroy them, break them apart piece by piece so that their home and the remnants of their pack were easy pickings, yet it hadn't worked. He'd sowed fear, spilt blood, then burned their homes to ashes. And while mistakes had been made, and fear lingered with the potential danger hidden around the corner, they'd risen out of the ashes despite it all. Dark Shadow hadn't let him win.

With a hesitant step and cautious hope in their eyes, the Dark Shadow pack had listened to Bass's speech, heard her added encouragement, and looked over the new plans for the pack with curious gazes. And then, surprising Katalina, almost all had voted in agreement.

She wasn't naïve; Katalina knew it was going to take a lot more than some shiny new cabins on a new patch of land to solve all their problems, but for now, it was enough. For now, she'd watch the first markers go down, and the first trees being felled, and soak up the happiness as one dream finally came to life.

"So, Katalina, why exactly did you make me gain permission to come here?" Jackson asked as he paused in front of her, looming above her with his arms cross. "I'm not all that fond of asking Bass for favors."

"Shut up whining and move out of the way," she answered, batting at his legs. "You're blocking my view."

With a huff, Jackson moved and sat down beside her. "Did you really bring me out here so I could watch some pegs being hammered into the ground and trees cut down?"

Katalina laughed, bumping her shoulder with his. "I worked hard for this. You'd think a father would be proud."

The grumpy expression from his face dropped a little, and he wrapped his arm around her, pulling her into his side. "I'm sorry, Kat. I'm being an old grouch, aren't I?"

"You are, but I'm used to it," she teased.

"I am proud of you," he added.

"Good." She smiled. "But I didn't bring you here for praise. I brought you here to hopefully cure a bit of your grumpiness… if that's even possible." Katalina jumped to her feet, Arne also getting up.

"What are you talking about?" Jackson grumbled.

"Get up and come see."

With a roll of his eyes, Jackson obeyed and they walked across the wide clearing together, passed the workers setting out the markers for where the new homes would be built and beyond the area where trees where currently being chopped down for wood.

"All this area is being cleared," Katalina said as she wove through the trees, turning in circles, spreading her arms wide and smiling. "A clear run from Dark Shadow to River Run."

"I know this, Kat. I had to approve it remember."

"Hang on, I'm getting there. Indulge me, will you?" Arne barked and jumped around in circles. "See, Arne gets it."

Jackson laughed. "Your craziness is infectious. I'll give you that."

"It's important to me to have a path from both packs because both have a place in my heart."

Jackson smiled and made an unexpected leap forward, pulling her into a hug. "You have a big heart, my girl," he murmured, placing a kiss on her head.

"When I was young," Katalina continued after he released her, and they began walking again, "I never felt like I belonged. I wandered around with a hole inside of me I never understood, feeling like I was searching for something. For a long time, I didn't tell my parents because I was afraid they'd think I didn't love them, that because they weren't my birth parents, they didn't mean as much, but they were the best parents—supportive, loving—and they also knew me. I had no choice but to tell them."

"And what did they say?" Jackson asked quietly.

"My mom said that there were some people in this world who didn't belong anywhere or to anyone, that they only belonged to themselves, and that for those people, it was okay to not feel like their house was their home, but that maybe one day, I might find a person who would. And she was right. Bass is my home, not Dark Shadow. Bass." Katalina paused and turned to face Jackson. "We're here."

He frowned and scanned the area, his gaze noting the markers she'd had Tim lay out earlier. When he focused on her again, his frown had deepened. "I'm not sure what that has to do with me being here? Though it's nice to know I chose the right people."

Katalina took a breath and prepared to deliver the speech she'd rehearsed a few times in her head. "Regan is one of those people. We've been talking and she told me how Megan had been her home and when she died, it felt like her home did too and she was wandering lost. But Tyler has filled that hole."

"Are you telling me to let her go. To let Bass have her?"

"No, because she couldn't give up River Run if she wanted to. Like me, River Run holds a special place in her heart. You're her alpha, not Bass."

"So then what are you telling me?" Jackson sighed.

Katalina laughed softly at his perplexed expression. "Did you know this spot right here was where they meet?"

"Kat," he groaned.

"Bear with me. Every night for weeks they'd meet as wolves, not speaking at all, and run the border. This spot means something to them, and it should mean something to the packs. I was the catalyst to change, but Regan and Tyler are our hope for the future. I spoke with Tim and we've come up with a house on stilts with a large deck that sweeps over the water, putting this home on both River Run and Dark Shadow."

"And what's Bass think to this idea?" he asked with a raised brow.

"Oh, I haven't told him yet." She shrugged. "I find the two of you band together when it's convenient to you both, and that can be rather annoying."

"So, what are you asking, Kat? For them to have a house here on both lands or for them to belong to both packs?"

"You already know the answer to that. And it isn't just me asking, though they'd probably never dare say. Tyler and Regan should be a symbol, not a problem."

"And the fact I let Dark Shadow have my daughter isn't symbol enough?" Jackson ground out.

"I've already told you, I belong to myself. You haven't let anybody have anything, where as Ty and Regan would be a true symbol. A true start to a future I think we all want."

"I don't know, Katalina. What you're asking…" He shook his head. "So many lines will be blurred. Do you think Bass will agree?"

She sighed sadly, turning away and walking to the edge of the small stream. "I honestly don't know. There was a time not so long ago that I'd have said yes. That I thought I knew him inside and out but… I don't know anymore. After everything that's happened… I just don't know. But what I do know is this gesture will get us all back on track."

"On track for what?"

"Peace? I don't know, Jackson," she answered, feeling a little frustrated. "I just know they are hurting, and they need this."

He came up beside her and put an arm around her shoulder. "And you need this too, don't you?"

Katalina looked up at him, at her father who at times was a stranger but then they'd connect, click, and she'd see an alternative reality of what could have been, and she'd feel for just a moment not like the girl with no parents. "I guess I do. I've accepted I've got to change, but I can't change the very fabric of who I am."

"And we wouldn't want you to." Jackson released her, and Katalina turned and smiled as Bass approached. "Sorry I'm late," Bass continued.

"That's okay. You're not actually. I'm still waiting on Jackson's answer."

"On what?" Bass asked, looking between them both.

She smiled. "You'll see."

Jackson laughed, shaking his head as he rolled his eyes. "My head says no, but my heart… my heart looks at my amazing daughter and says yes, because why wouldn't I want a world she sees through her eyes?"

Katalina chest tightened, emotions threatening to spill from her. "Head or heart, Dad?"

Jackson reached out and cupped her cheek, and Katalina closed her eyes as she leaned into the touch. "Heart, Katalina, always go with your heart."

A tear leaked out through her closed eyes and when she opened them again, Jackson was no longer in front of her but a shadow of a wolf disappearing into the distance.

"What webs have you weaved this time, my winter wolf?" Bass whispered, closing his arms around her from behind and kissing her cheek.

"The best kind. The kind that will make your head hurt and your heart sing."

"I'm guessing it has something to do with these markers right here?" he asked, waving an arm.

Katalina grinned. "Welcome to Ty and Regan's new home."

Bass froze for a second, his arms turning to deadly locks around her. "Do they know?" he finally asked softly.

"No. I thought it would be a nice present to give them at the party to celebrate all the recent matings within our packs."

"Our?"

"Dark Shadow and River Run, silly."

"I don't remember approving a party."

"It's happening whether you like it or not," she said, turning in his arms and kissing him. "I think the packs have suffered enough, and it's time we acknowledge the love that's flourished despite that."

"I think you're right," Bass agreed.

Katalina let out a heavy breath, relief washing through her.

"You were afraid I'd say no?"

"I was, yeah."

He took her face in his hands, staring into her eyes until she felt like he was reaching her very soul. "I know things have been difficult lately, but don't ever doubt that you know me, Katalina.

Don't ever doubt that you have all of me, heart and soul."

Katalina's next words weren't said aloud. She spoke them with each kiss, each touch, a silent language only the two of them knew—the language of their hearts.

Chapter 54

Two days after Tyler's parents had visited, Regan walked into the room they were staying in at Jackson's and avoided looking at Tyler. She'd spent the last hour sparing and received a black eye for her efforts. Turned out she was a little rusty after three years off. Exhausted and sweaty, Regan wanted nothing more than to grab her things and jump into the shower without Tyler noticing the bruise and holding her up.

"How was training?" he asked as she went past his bed.

"Brutal," she replied, groaning.

"You'll soon catch up," he reassured.

I'm not so sure about that. Collecting a change of clothes and her toiletries bag, Regan headed for the door. "I'm just going to shower." She reached the door, twisted the handle.

"Regan?"

"I won't be long," she replied quickly, pulling the door open.

"Regan," he growled.

Damn it…. Turning, Regan faced him and braced for his reaction.

"What happened?"

She met his gaze. "What happened is I'm way, way behind and can't keep up with anyone."

"So, they beat you up for it?"

"It's a swollen eye, Ty. And it was an accident. I didn't react quickly enough."

"And how long were you planning on avoiding me for?" He raised an eyebrow.

"Long enough to shower." She sighed. "I'm exhausted and sweaty, and frankly, I'd like to sleep for a week."

Tyler shook his head and smiled. "Go shower then."

Blowing him a kiss, Regan turned, and made her way to the bathroom. In the end, Regan's shower didn't turn out quick at all. Once under the hot water, she didn't want to leave. It was only when the water began to run cold and she cringed as she imagined Jackson grumbling that Regan hopped out.

"If that's a quick shower, we need to discuss who's paying our water bills," Tyler teased as she reentered the room.

"Sorry, the water felt so lovely. I didn't want to leave." Regan padded across the room and lifted herself up onto the bed, shuffling beside him and resting her head on his uninjured shoulder.

"William suggested I train with the youngsters until I catch up."

"What you need are some one-on-one lessons. Ugh, I feel so useless stuck in this bed when I could be helping you."

"It's all right. William is probably right. I wasn't exactly top of my class before. I was more of the 'cause mischief and have fun' kinda student."

Tyler grinned. "I really wish I'd gotten to meet the rebel you."

"Well, I'd tell the rebel me to start paying attention."

"So what did you say to William?"

"Not much really, but I'm sure he knew I was humiliated as in his next breath, he said I just needed to build up my stamina and then volunteered Mia to run with me daily."

"She's your friend. I'm sure she won't mind."

"I know... I just feel like a charity case who everyone pities."

"That's not how they view you, Regan."

Regan sighed and let her eyes slide shut. "Maybe. Mia's coming over in an hour, and I need to find my running shoes before then."

"What did you have on this morning?"

"Borrowed some, but they were too small and have rubbed my feet." Regan pulled up her foot to show him the blisters. "I need Band-Aids too."

Tyler kissed her on the side of her face. "No one said you had to start training right away, babe. I'm sure everyone would understand if you waited a week or two."

"I need the distraction," she admitted.

"Well, normally I'd be up for a little distracting, but instead, I'm stuck in this bed feeling like I'm no good to anyone."

Regan took his hand. "We're a sorry pair, aren't we?"

"Yeah, I guess we are." He laughed. "Want to have a pity party with me?"

Regan laughed. "Sure. There's no one I'd like to pity party with more."

Closing the lid on the last box, Regan slid to the floor of the barn and buried her head into her hands. In her heart, she'd known it was coming but she'd held off until she'd searched every one of the boxes that had been placed in Jackson's barn.

"Regan, what's the matter?"

Dropping her hands, Regan looked up at Jackson, knowing how pitiful she must look surrounded by half-open boxes and on her knees crying. "I can't find my running shoes," she cried, unable to pull herself together.

Jackson joined her on the floor and lifted her into his arms. "We'll get you new ones."

"No, you don't understand. These were Megan's and I had some of her clothes too and they're all missing. My mom purposely left them out," she explained between sobs.

Jackson went very still, then sitting back slightly, he met her gaze. "I've left the situation alone because I'd hoped your parents would see sense, but this can't go on."

"There's nothing you can do, Jackson. This is my fault."

A growl left his throat. "It most certainly is not. Finding your mate is not a reason to be thrown from your house, Regan."

Dragging in a few deep breathes to gather herself, Regan stopped crying. "I know." She sighed. "I just don't think you going over there and telling them that is going to help."

"I'm their alpha, Regan. They'll damn well listen to me."

"All you'll do is fuel their hate further."

"Well, I can't just sit here doing nothing when one of my pack is hurting."

"Well, you could go ask for my things for me." She smiled, hopeful.

He brushed the tears that clung to her skin away and nodded. "I can do that."

"Thanks, Jackson."

Climbing to his feet, he pulled Regan with him. "Come on. I think you need another shower, though you've already used up all my hot water."

Regan laughed. "Sorry."

"How's Tyler today?"

"Well enough that sitting in bed all day is killing him."

"I think Karen is coming over later to check on him. Maybe she'll grant him permission to venture to the sofa."

"With any luck. I've been meaning to thank you for allowing him to stay here."

"He's your mate, Regan," Jackson answered, briefly touching her arm. "I know yours isn't going to be the simplest mating, but I'll treat him as my own because to not do so would hurt you."

Regan didn't reply for fear she'd cry again; instead, she wrapped her arms around Jackson's waist and hugged tightly.

"I'll go get your things now. So, there's running shoes and…?"

"Mom will know what they are, but the most important are the shoes and a blue T-shirt."

"Okay. Now I want you to go fix yourself and Ty a coffee, and stop fretting over this training, and that's an order, Regan." A calmness settled over her, his support giving her the strength to think past the pain her parents' rejection brought.

With a smile and a salute, Regan left Jackson and followed out his request. She'd obey it for that day but come morning, she'd be up with the sun and training, because while she understood everyone's advice to not worry and take it slowly. Regan couldn't ignore the urgency in her veins, nor the feeling that she'd been sleeping her life away. She felt as though she had to make up for lost time before another three years passed and she was still in the same spot. Still taking it easy and still waiting for life to be simpler. When the reality was, life was never simple. Not in their world, or any other.

CHAPTER 55

Two weeks had gone by and Tyler had healed enough to make it down the stairs and out onto the porch where he was currently watching Regan spar with Mia. She'd been relentless with her training—running every morning, sparring in the afternoon, weight training with Cage. Fitting it all in between work and him. In some ways Tyler was in awe of her determination and proud she wasn't giving up, yet he also knew the almost obsessive approach she was taking wasn't all about wanting to catch up. Inside, Regan was hurting. Tyler could feel her pain inside of himself and see it in her eyes, see it in each punch and clench of her jaw. In the rigid, controlled anger that hummed below the surface waiting to escape.

She was hurtling toward a point of no return, a point where she'd snap and all the pent-up emotions would burst free. Tyler wasn't worried she'd hurt anyone innocent. When the time came, she'd snap, and her parents would be on the receiving end. He was inclined to let it unfold, for Regan's parents to get what was coming to them. But the more rational part of his brain said doing that would ultimately hurt Regan.

He knew all of this yet had no clue how to prevent it. He'd like to march over to her parents himself, but despite all the wishing he'd done, his healing hadn't sped up, and making it to Jackson's porch felt like a marathon.

"Babe, you're letting your guard down." Tyler forced himself to his feet and ambled over to the two women who'd paused on his words. They were both a little breathless, Regan more so. "Like this," he said, coming up behind her and using his good arm to guide hers. "You're collapsing in on the right," he whispered in her ear. His hand slid up the curve of her hip, caressing her waist.

"Stay strong here when you swing, and keep your elbow up and in."

"Thanks," she breathed, breathless for totally different reasons.

Tyler gave into his need and closed his mouth over hers as she tilted her head toward him. Within seconds, the world had dropped away, and his pain dulled to a distant memory. His hand skimmed down her body as she moaned into his mouth.

Mia coughed loudly. "This a make-out session or sparring session?" she grumbled. "I mean, jeez, guys, get a room."

Regan smiled against his lips. "Thanks for the pointer. I'll give it a try."

Reluctantly, Tyler released Regan from his grasp and made his way slowly back to the porch. When they started back up, Regan did just as he'd instructed. Her body was strong, her swing correct, and as the hit connected, Mia stumbled back.

With a huge smile, Regan turned to him. "I did it!" she cheered.

"That hurt," Mia grumbled, smiling. "Training's over."

Running toward him, Tyler braced himself as she collided into his arms. He stumbled back a step, grimacing but kept the sound of his pain inside.

"Oh my gosh!" Regan stepped back, covering her mouth with her hands. "I'm so sorry, Ty. I don't know what I was thinking."

"I'm okay."

"I was just so excited. God, I wish you could train me."

"Believe me, I do too. It's killing me sitting here useless when I could be helping you."

"You did just help her," Mia pointed out, joining them on the step, "and besides, you'd spend the whole time making out and teach her nothing."

"Mia," Regan groaned. "We're not that bad."

"You totally are. It's kinda gross."

Regan stuck out her tongue. "Whatever." A car pulled up to the house. "Karen's here. Time for your training, Ty."

"I'd much rather be sparring," Tyler complained.

"How are you expecting to spar if you can't lift your arm?" Karen called as she climbed out of her car.

"Yeah, yeah, I know, doesn't mean I have to like it though."

"You'll be grateful when I have you out of here in a couple of days," Karen counted.

"Really?" Tyler asked.

"Yeah, I reckon so. Let's do some exercises, and then I'll look at taking your stitches out," she explained.

Regan squeezed his arm. "See, you'll be sparring in no time." She kissed him on the cheek. "I'm gonna go change. See you in a bit."

"I'll see you later, Regan?" Mia asked.

Tyler caught Regan's eyes, speaking to her silently.

"Sorry, I forgot to tell you," she replied. "Mia and I are going to Tom's later for a BBQ. He lives in town."

Tyler's stomach sank, but he refused to allow Regan to see. "That's nice, babe."

She faltered for a moment but didn't question him, instead smiling and heading off inside to shower and change.

Karen touched his hand briefly. "It's good for her to get out, keep her mind off her parents."

Tyler sat down on the porch swing, glancing at Karen. "I know. I've never minded her going out. It's that I wish I was going with her. I guess it was a reminder that our relationship isn't simple, and I won't always be able to go where she goes because I'm Dark Shadow, and not everyone is going to like that."

"That won't be the reason you weren't invited, Tyler. She'll be worried you're not up to it. None of Regan's friends care where you're from. They only care that you're the man who brought the friend they lost back to them. When Megan was murdered, River Run lost far more than one person. It lost an entire family. But you've come along and healed some of that wound. Regan has returned to us, and for that, we can never repay you."

"I don't need repaying. I didn't do anything."

"Ah, but you did. You gave her a reason to live again."

Karen's words stayed with Tyler long after she'd left. Waiting for Regan to return from her friends, the words circled around him like a crown that felt a little too heavy to wear. It wasn't that he didn't appreciate Karen's words; she'd said them as a reassurance, as a reminder of how strong the love between him and Regan was. Yet it also served as a reminder that Regan was missing two very important people in her life. The bond between Regan and her parents needed healing, but he wasn't sure how. So far, everyone's plan had been to ignore the problem and hope with time they'd come around, but Megan died three years ago, and in those three years, a family hadn't healed or moved on. Hoping the problem would go away hadn't worked then and it wouldn't work now.

Gritting his teeth as he slipped down from the bed, Tyler stood, decision made. No more ignoring the problem. He was facing it head-on.

CHAPTER 56

She'd had the best of times out with Mia, reconnecting with pack members, reconnecting with herself, but she'd missed Tyler and decided next time she'd be taking him along with her. When she opened the door to the room they were staying in, it was empty.

Confused, Regan headed back down the stairs, a crease on her forehead the only outward sign of anxiety forming in her gut. Checking the front room, she found it empty, and the same for the kitchen. Switching the lights back off, Regan headed upstairs again and checked the bathroom, even though she knew it would be empty.

He's gone….

Crossing the landing to Jackson's door, she knocked softly, hoping he wasn't asleep. If he had been, he'd jumped out of bed quickly.

"Regan, what's wrong?"

"Tyler's gone," she said numbly.

"Gone?" he repeated, the same crease appearing on his forehead. "Where would he have gone? He's not exactly in shape for taking a stroll."

"You didn't hear him leave, or anyone come by? Bass maybe? His parents?"

"No, Regan. There's been no one here. Wherever he is, Tyler didn't want me to know. Damn well snuck past an alpha, injured no less. No wonder Bass doesn't want to let him go."

"But where's he gone? I need to find him. He's supposed to be resting." Regan squeezed her trembling hands into fists, and dragged in a deep breath. Now wasn't the time to let her fear control her.

"Don't panic, Regan. He can't have gotten far. I'll track him. Come on."

Regan followed Jackson from the house, and as her alpha picked up Tyler's scent and followed, her panic increased. They didn't need Jackson's nose to tell them where Tyler had headed; she'd walked this route many times. The pathway home.

CHAPTER 57

Tyler was very aware he had limited time to complete what he planned. The fact he's snuck out past Jackson was a miracle in itself considering he wasn't nearly at full health. Tyler took it as a sign that the universe was on his side tonight. That what he had to say would sink in, would make a difference.

Once at the front door, Tyler took a minute to catch his breath, to push down the pain coursing through his body so he may concentrate on the task. Taking a final breath and throwing a quick prayer to the sky, Tyler knocked.

It was late, but there was the soft glow of a light further into the house and seconds later, light filled the darkened hall as a door opened. It was Regan's mother; they shared the same dark, straight hair, same tone of skin, but when Regan's mother opened the door and stared at him with questioning eyes, Tyler saw none of Regan's light. None of the spirit he'd fallen in love with. It was as if her mother was an empty shell.

"How can I— It's you...." Her eyes widened, then she glanced behind her anxiously. "What are you doing here?" she hissed. "Go away, before—" But her words died in her throat as the entranceway light flicked on, highlighting Tyler in stark clarity.

"Who's—" Rage filled Regan's fathers gaze. The same dark blue eyes Regan had, only hers would never be so bitter, so full of hatred.

Tyler hadn't known how they'd react to seeing him. He'd only known he'd needed to speak to them and try to make them understand what they were doing to their daughter. Her father hurtling toward him like a deranged wolf wasn't at all what he'd imagined. The man wasn't a dominant wolf, but it seemed even submissive wolves could turn aggressive from grief.

Shock froze his body for a second too long, Tyler twisted out of the way but not before Regan's father collided into him, bringing them both to the ground. Regan's mother's screams filled the air, but Tyler's ears were full of the ringing of his pain. The impact rocked through him, feeling like it shattered his very bones. Injured or not, Tyler was an enforcer, highly trained in several forms of martial arts. Even in agony, he wasn't about to take a beating lying down.

A cool calm spread through his mind, shutting off all pain receptors as he shoved the man off him and twisted and flipped to his feet. Tyler wobbled briefly, a bolt of fire flaring from his wound, but he'd pushed it away by the time Regan's father scrambled up, a wolf's snarl leaving his human lips.

"I came here to talk," Tyler pleaded, holding his hands up, palms out. "Please."

"I'm not interested in anything you or any of your kind has to say," he growled, his voice tight and rough.

"My kind? Dark Shadow you mean?" Tyler answered as they circled each other.

"Savages, the lot of you. Wasn't it enough that you killed one of my daughters, had to claim the other for your own? Had to steal her from me," he yelled, visibly shaking.

"I didn't steal your daughter. I love her."

"Lies! You've turned her head, turned her into the same people who murdered her sister," he screamed, launching forward, his face twisted in rage, fists clenched and ready to hit.

Tyler dodged to the side, avoiding him, but the move cost him. His knees shuddered, his breath catching in his throat as Tyler's wounds protested loudly.

"Noah, stop this madness," Regan's mother pleaded.

He came at Tyler again, throwing a punch. Tyler deflected the hit, retaliating with a defensive move that would only knock Noah back. He refused to fight the man. A fight was not his intention, and he'd be damned if he turned into the monster Regan's father made him out to be.

"Dark shadow isn't the same. The man who killed your daughter isn't among us, and if he had been, I'd have killed him myself. Don't you understand what you're doing to Regan, how much you are hurting her?"

"She chose her path when she chose you as her mate, when she became Dark Shadow," Noah ground out. Noah yelled as he leapt forward. Tyler dodged his first hit, deflected the second but his body was injured, and his energy was failing him. When the man surprised Tyler with a roundhouse kick, there was nothing he could do to avoid it. His breath left him on a pained cry as Tyler fell backward, meeting the hard ground. Noah towered above him, crazed with his hate and grief.

"It's only a name," Tyler replied, breathless. "I'll give it up for her if that's what you want. I'll leave Dark Shadow behind if it means you'll stop hurting your daughter."

"My daughter died the day you tainted her with your blood," Noah spat.

And in that moment, Tyler knew nothing he could say would convince Noah otherwise. The man was lost beyond reach. Twisted and changed by the grief he'd kept inside and allowed to fester. All Tyler could do was pray that the loss of her father wouldn't do the same to Regan.

Noah landed on top of him, slamming a fist into his face, then another and another. Tyler didn't try to fight him. He wasn't sure he could if he'd wanted to anyway. Regan's mother screamed, attempting to drag Noah off him only to be knocked back herself.

"Is this what you want?" Tyler gasped between painful breaths. "Dark Shadow blood?" Tyler met Noah's half crazed eyes. "Go on then, have mine. Take it all."

CHAPTER 56

Regan

At some point, they'd begun to increase their steps, but when Regan felt a burst of pain through the mating bond, she ran. Her heart was in her throat, adrenaline and worry coursing through her veins like a dizzying cocktail.

Her childhood home came into view, the front door open and spilling light onto the lawn. The last of her father's words met her on the wind before he threw himself on top of Tyler, unleashing his fists.

"My daughter died the day you tainted her with your blood."

Her mother was screaming as she tried and failed to pull her father off Tyler. Regan's emotions died away, worry becoming nothing but a dull beat in the back of her mind. Her mate was in danger, his pain flowing through her urging her on.

She didn't slow her pace or call out as she approached. Instead, Regan shot at her father like a bullet, releasing fists of her own. His face was bloody by the time Jackson dragged her off him, but hitting him had done nothing to ease her rage.

"Died!" she screamed. "I'm not dead, Father. I'm right here. If anyone's dead, it's the two of you."

"Regan," her mother cried.

Regan zeroed in on her mother. "Save it. I'm not interested in anything the two of you have to say. The truth is I haven't had parents since the day Megan died."

Her father tried to interrupt but Regan talked over him,

glaring him into silence. “If I had, they’d have noticed how lost I was. They’d have said something when I shut out all my friends and shunned the very nature of my wolf. They’d have encouraged me to take risks and live life to the fullest, not hide and live the half life I was doing. They’d have noticed the pain I lived with daily and done something, even if they were in pain themselves.”

“Regan, please,” her mother begged.

A tear slipped down Regan’s face, but she refused to allow any more to fall, to acknowledge the heartbreaking sorrow inside of her. “They’d have helped me heal, but instead, I stayed frozen in time, trapped in the cage you put me in. Until Tyler came along and reminded what it felt like to live again. Until he made me see I didn’t die with Megan, I lived. But the life I was living wasn’t a life at all, and if Megan could talk to me right now, she’d tell me so. She’d congratulate me for finding my mate, and she’d love me despite everything, even if she didn’t quite agree.”

Regan struggled from Jackson’s grip and went to Tyler. Helping him up, she looked back one last time at the parents she’d accepted as lost, and said sadly, “That’s what family does, but I’m not sure you’ll ever remember that.”

Walking away, her arm around Tyler keeping him upright, Regan felt a shard of her heart break off and fall to the ground. There it would stay, broken and bleeding with the parents she knew where doing the same, but Regan could no longer stay with them. She couldn’t live in a cage anymore. Tyler had set her free, and it was time she spread her wings and flew.

CHAPTER 57

"What was that about?" Katalina asked, sitting up in bed as Bass hung up the phone.

"Tyler tried to reason with Regan's parents and received a beating for his troubles. Jackson says he's handled the situation, and Karen is seeing to Tyler's wounds, but I think I should go over there. He's my wolf too."

"I'm coming with you," Katalina replied, getting out of bed and pulling on some jeans and a sweater over her pajama top. "What was Tyler thinking?"

"I imagine he was thinking how much his mate was hurting and he needed to do something to make it stop."

"But still… he could hardly get down the stairs two days ago."

"Powerful thing a mate's hurt."

Katalina nodded sadly. The two had far too much experience on the subject.

When they arrived at Jackson's, it was to find Tyler's face bloodied and swollen.

"Did you fight back at all?" Bass asked.

Tyler looked up through half-swollen eyes. "He wanted blood, so I gave him mine."

"And I've told him"—Regan glared crossly— "his blood isn't responsible for the death of my sister, and he was an idiot to try reason with my father in his state."

"I don't think reasoning with him in any state would have helped," Katalina said. "I hope you haven't injured yourself further."

Karen looked up. "By some miracle, his back wounds haven't opened up. It's just his pretty face that took the damage." She shook her head at Tyler. "What were you thinking, boy?"

"I was thinking that Regan wasn't okay, and I needed to do something," Tyler snapped.

"I'm fine," she insisted, and even to Katalina's ears, the statement sounded like a lie.

"You are not, babe. You've been obsessively training since I was attacked, spending every spare minute running, sparing, and weight training."

"I'm making up for lost time."

His expression softened as he cupped her cheek with an unsteady hand. "You're hiding from the loss of your parents."

"Fine," Regan snapped, rubbing at her eyes that had suddenly filled with tears. "What would you like me to do, sit around all day crying?"

"If that's what you need to do, then yes," he murmured, brushing away the stray tears. "Cry, scream, but don't hide."

"I can't, Ty. I can't stop and spend all day sitting around here looking at my boxes and being reminded my own parents chucked me out… I just can't."

"Then don't," Bass answered, all eyes going to him. "Don't sit around here. Come home with us."

"To Dark Shadow?" Regan answered hesitantly. "But Ty—"

"Tyler could have returned home days ago. He's here for you, and I support that if that's what you want, but from where I'm standing, it seems like you need a change in scenery. If only for a little while."

Regan glanced at Tyler then Jackson. Katalina wasn't sure if he wanted to throttle Bass or agree with him.

"I've already welcomed you to Dark Shadow, but I never said I welcome you as a River Run wolf," Bass added.

Katalina's chest hurt with pride and love. The words Bass was saying weren't an easy gift to give. There were members of their pack who didn't agree with the alliance, that were struggling with the move to the new site. But it seemed, just as Bass had promised her, he was going to make their world fit, even if it killed him. And Katalina's heart healed a little more, and she was certain Regan's did too.

"Well, I think things can be decided in the morning. For now, what you both need is sleep," Karen ordered, eyeing Tyler and Regan. "Jackson, make sure this one doesn't sneak out of your house alone again."

"I'll try my best. Though I didn't let him out the first time," Jackson answered.

"Can't keep up with my wolves, hey?" Bass smiled.

Jackson crossed his arms over his chest. "I wasn't expecting the idiot to try to kill himself."

"Come on, you," Katalina jumped in, dragging Bass to her side. "Stop winding up my father."

The use of *father* seemed to calm Jackson a little as she'd hoped. The trials of an alpha's daughter and mate were never simple. She imagined she'd spend the rest of her life fielding jokes and defusing tension.

"Take it easy, Tyler. We'll speak tomorrow," Bass said. "Jackson," he continued, with an incline of his head.

Katalina hugged Regan, then Jackson goodbye, then smiled at her grandmother who'd she'd forgiven, but hadn't quite healed the relationship between them yet. “Rest up, guys. We’ll see you tomorrow.”

Walking from River Run to Dark Shadow, Bass was quiet beside her. Katalina left him to his thoughts as she gazed at the clear, star-studded sky. It wasn’t until they were winding through the trees, their wolves in their gazes to see in the dark, that Bass finally said what had been rolling over in his mind.

“Something Tyler said has me thinking.”

“What’s that?” Katalina asked, already knowing she’d not like the answer.

“*He wanted blood, so I gave him mine.* Tyler was half right; the man wants blood.”

“But spilling Dark Shadow blood is pointless. The man’s not one of us anymore.”

“Exactly. So let’s give him the right blood.”

“Bass, I don’t like what I think you’re saying.” Katalina came to a standstill and faced him. “The man’s with Indiana. And killing him won’t bring Megan back.”

“No, it won’t,” Bass agreed. “But it doesn’t mean it won’t help. We’re animals at our core, primal and savage. Blood for blood. That’s how it works. Only Noah’s never had that blood and it’s eaten him up inside.”

“But how are we going to reach a man who’s surrounded by our enemy? An enemy, I might add, who has destroyed half our home and continues to wound us.”

“We aren’t,” he replied, his gaze fierce and determined, causing Katalina’s stomach to flip. She knew what he was planning, she knew, and it terrified her.

“No. No, Bass, you can’t.” She took hold of his hands, squeezed, pleading with her eyes. “No.”

“I can. I need to, for Tyler, for Regan.”

"Bass, it's too dangerous. Dark Shadow needs you. It needs its alpha here and in one piece."

He cupped her face and brushed his thumbs over her cheekbones. "Katalina, don't you see, this is what my father trained me to be. To be a shadow that walked through enemy lines unseen. My entire life I was trained to be the weapon that would walk as if a ghost and destroy Jackson once and for all."

"But you didn't kill me, Bass. That's not who you are. That's not how your fate played out."

"It's not all of me, no, but it is a part of me. I need to do this, for Ty, and to repay a debt Dark Shadow owes."

"Then take others with you." Her heart was in her chest, but it slowed its beat, each loud, steady boom like the tick of a clock. She'd known the day she'd met him loving him wouldn't be simple, that becoming part of the wolf world would test her in ways she'd not known, but it was a reality Katalina couldn't have avoided. And one she wouldn't want to, despite all she'd seen and done.

"I'm only a ghost if I'm alone. Have faith in me, my winter wolf, faith that I'll come home. That I'll come back to you."

Standing on her tiptoes, Katalina pressed her mouth to his, drawing his life into her body, his scent, his taste. She clung to him one last time before letting him go. "You're going now, aren't you?"

He nodded, stepping back into the shadows and almost becoming invisible to her already.

"Be safe. Come back to me" she whispered. He'd disappeared from her sight, becoming one with the night. Her shadow wolf.

"I love you." His voice drifted from the trees. "Always."

CHAPTER 58

Bass was well aware his move could leave his pack without an alpha. Leave them scrambling and vulnerable to attack as they dealt with the loss, but he was also aware of the voice telling him it had to be done, and the task had to be completed alone. It was a voice that had been with him for as long as he could remember, an internal compass of sorts guiding him through life. It was the voice that told him his father's leadership was wrong. That the fear that hovered over his childhood and pack wasn't right or normal. It whispered in his ear—an angel or devil he wasn't sure. Bass only knew he'd been ignoring that voice as of late and doing so had created a rift between him and Katalina, a rift he hoped this move would help heal, and hopefully heal those connected to his pack.

He'd not ignored the voice consciously, but self-doubt had dulled its intensity. Too many losses and not enough wins had left Bass feeling like a failure, feeling like maybe he was no better than his father after all.

Today, though, it had been clear. He knew deep down to his core that this was his job to do, and his alone. His father might have been cruel, he might have treated Bass as a weapon and not a son, but his father's actions had their uses. And today Bass would use them.

Journeying to Indiana in wolf form took most of the night. He had little time left until dawn, and contemplated waiting out the daylight. But there was an urgency in his blood, a need to return to his mate, his pack. So Bass slipped through the trees, a living ghost. His fur was as black as night, his feet silent and nimble—a lethal blade on the hunt.

Getting passed Indiana's patrols was the easy part; finding Richard was the difficult task. It was a job that would have to be done by sight and not scent as Bass couldn't recall the man's smell. He remembered the man's face though, remembered his cruel eyes, the flatness to them as if he felt no emotion at all. And his smile. He remembered it distinctly—a smile that said I'm untouchable, a smile morphed into charm if need be, a mask to fool the unsuspecting victim.

Scanning the quiet area, Bass took in the scene. He understood in a way why Castor wanted Dark Shadow as his own. Even burned to the ground the land was nicer. Kyle, it seemed, hadn't been much nicer than Castor as an alpha, and its people lived mostly in tents, though there were a few cabins. These Bass planned to check first. Knowing Richard as Bass did, he knew he'd never slum it in a tent. No, Richard would want the best that was on offer.

Shifting, he padded quietly on human feet, dashing from the cover of trees to the wall of the first cabin. Carefully, Bass peered inside the grubby window but found Raven and her grandmother asleep inside. The darker side of himself contemplated slipping into their cabin and slitting their throats but that voice, or maybe it was Katalina's this time, told him *no.* Cold-blooded murder wasn't what he was about.

Skipping the middle cabin because it made sense to have the alpha in the center, Bass headed for the far side and third cabin. His heart was a steady drum in his ears, his mind filled with cool, killing calm. This part of himself was the predator at his core. The wild wolf, the part that could have so easily been made into a mindless weapon.

Looking through the window, Bass found his target. The question now was how to leave without alerting anyone else.

Richard had company in the form of a woman laid curled on her side beside him. She wasn't touching him, wasn't curled around his body or facing him, which told Bass she wasn't Richard's mate and most likely wouldn't mourn his death. For a moment, Bass allowed the imagine of Katalina wrapped around his body in sleep to fill his mind. He used the image to remind himself what was at stake, to remind him of the mistakes he made would hurt more than himself.

Deciding on a plan, Bass selected a few stones from the ground and tread quietly to the edge of the cabin wall. There he threw the rock against the wall near where Richard's head lay asleep. On the second throw, he heard movement inside, throwing the last of the stones onto the ground in front of the door, Bass took a steady breath and waited, back to the wall, vengeance like a song in his blood.

Richard, as he hoped, got out of his bed and came to inspect where the noise had come from. The cabin door bashed open, causing Bass to cringe and pray no one else came to see what the noise was about. Dawn was fast approaching. Already the sheer blackness of night was giving way to the gray of daybreak.

Moving with the speed of a serpent, Bass reached out, wrapping his arms around the man's throat in an attempt to cut off Richard's air supply and render him unconscious. He was slightly shorter than Bass but wider in build. Bass struggled to hold him as Richard fought back. Clamping a hand over the man's mouth to muffle his yells, Bass locked his arm around the man's throat, squeezing to the point he was worried he'd snap his neck.

Richard slammed himself and Bass into the cabin wall behind him, knocking the air from Bass. The noise seemed like a thunderous boom in the quiet of early morning, but no one came running and finally, Richard faltered, his movements becoming heavy, his efforts sluggish until the man slipped unconscious.

Bass only paused for a second to drag in a breath when Richard fell limp to the ground, but the creak of a board had him jumping to his feet, spinning around. Heart leaping in his chest, Bass lunged at the woman who'd shared Richard's bed, covering her mouth before she had time to scream and knocking her unconscious.

"I'm sorry," he whispered as she gave up her fight, and he laid her back onto the bed.

Every second longer was becoming more and more dangerous. Dragging Richard up and heaving him onto his back, Bass quickly ran for the trees and the cover of shadows, only stopping briefly to snatch up a discarded rag, and a pair of shorts that hung on a washing line.

Running with the speed only an alpha possessed, Bass covered as much ground as possible before he had no choice but to stop and bind Richard's hands and mouth. Ripping the rag in half, he first tied the material around Richard's wrists, then gagged him. The man was coming to when Bass picked up a discarded branch and snapped it so that one end was jagged. As realization dawned on Richard's face, Bass smiled and slammed the branch through Richard's gut, making sure the hit wasn't fatal but would render the man from shifting.

"Can't have you shifting on me now, can we?" Bass said softly.

"Castor will have your head for this," Richard mumbled around his gag, panting with pain.

Bass laughed. "The man wants my head anyway."

"And your bitch."

Bass slapped Richard across the face, causing him to fall backward and jar the branch in his gut. He cried out, face scrunching up, and eyes filling with hatred.

"You'll treat my mate with respect, and Castor will find that she's not so easily tamed and will not bend under his will. Or anyone's will for that matter." Bass dragged Richard to his feet, shoving him forward. "Get walking. We've got a long journey ahead."

"She'll bend eventually," he mumbled. "You all will."

Bass didn't answer. Instead, he pushed Richard from behind, reminding him whose will he was currently under. Bass would face whatever fate was bringing him. It would come one way or another, but one thing was for certain, he'd sooner die than bend. Katalina right along with him.

He was no one's weapon but his own, and he'd stand as the shield of his pack until his last breath.

CHAPTER 59

Waiting until morning before she informed her pack's inner circle, Katalina then popped outside to call Jackson. After ending the call, she couldn't decide on his reaction to Bass's plan, and while a huge part of her had wanted to tell him in person and stay with River Run until Bass returned, she also knew her place was with Dark Shadow. The pack needed to see Katalina strong and not concerned.

"Are you all right?" Nico asked, taking her hand as he stood beside her.

"Yes and no," she answered, leaning her head on his shoulder. "I know he's still alive and not in pain, so that's a start, right?"

"Bass and his crazy schemes. I'd thought he'd given them up."

"I think he had, and that was a problem. Because the place those plans come from is the Bass we need to get through this war in one piece."

"I think you're right," Nico answered with a sigh. "They've voted to keep this news from the rest of the pack. No point causing unrest if he'll be home soon."

"When, Nic, *when* he'll be home soon."

Nico slung an arm around her shoulder, pulling her close. "Sorry, I didn't mean he wouldn't be returning, just the time part. Want to come and hang with Livy and me? I think she's cooking pancakes as we speak."

"Pancakes sound awesome." Katalina smiled, remembering there was family in Dark Shadow too. "I hope she makes that chocolate sauce she did last time. It's a wonder you're not fat living with Liv."

It was late afternoon and she was into her second chick-flick with Olivia when Jackson called her phone. Heart lurching at the tone, she quickly snatched it up and answered.

"Hello?"

"Bass is here."

Her breath rushed out of her. "Oh, thank God. I'll come right over."

"He's asked for a change of clothes."

"Sure thing." She hung up and faced Nico and Olivia's expectant expressions. "He's back, gone straight to River Run, so I guess that means he was successful. I've got to grab a change of clothes then go over."

"See you later," Olivia said, hugging her.

"Thanks for the pancakes and distraction."

"Anytime." She smiled.

"I'll go tell John while you get the clothes. Then we can go across together," Nico said.

Katalina nodded her agreement, jumping to her feet and heading straight out. Her anxiety wouldn't settle until she saw Bass with her own eyes, until she saw for herself that he was unharmed.

CHAPTER 60

He wasn't sure there were words enough to thank Bass, nor was he certain if thanking him was even right. Regan had been quiet since Katalina had told them what Bass had set off to do, and while Tyler knew this probably wouldn't be a magic fix, it would hopefully go a little way to healing the bad blood between Regan's parents and Dark Shadow.

"Are you okay?" Tyler whispered to Regan as she stared at the man on his knees who'd killed her sister.

"I imagined killing him many times after she died" was her quiet answer.

"It's just as much your kill as theirs." Tyler took her hand.

"No. I soon realized thinking that way wasn't healthy."

"I remember your sister," Richard said with a cruel smile. "She begged at the end, as you will when Castor is done with you."

Jackson shot forward, kicking him in the face. The man's head whipped backward as he fell back, hitting the ground.

"My sister was a child when you murdered her. You're nothing but a coward who preys on those weaker than yourself," Regan spat. "Get rid of him, Ty. I don't need to see his face again."

Tyler looked back as Regan walked into the house, torn between wanting to comfort his mate and follow through on her wishes.

"I'll go to her," Katalina said softly, touching his shoulder. "Go deliver him to her parents."

Tyler followed as Bass dragged Richard to his feet. The man had blood soaked through the front of his T-shirt, a branch protruding from his middle. The walk to Regan's parents seemed twice as long as it had the night before. His face was swollen and bruised from Noah's attack, his back wounds hurting more once again. But he'd accept no help. He had to do the walk without aid.

Jackson was with them, though he hovered behind, as if respecting this was something he and Bass had to do alone.

"Noah, Linda," Jackson boomed as they arrived.

Regan's parents came to an abrupt stop in the doorway when they took them in. Noah's landed on Tyler first, and he wondered if the man felt any remorse for the attack; if he did, it didn't show on his face. Regan's mother at least looked horrified, though that could be from the bound and bloody man Bass slung at their feet.

"The debt Dark Shadow owes is paid," Bass said, waving a hand over Richard.

"Fuck you," Richard spat, the word garbled from his gag but clear enough.

"Is that?" Noah whispered, as his mate clung to him.

Tyler stepped forward, forcing himself to stand tall, to move without showing pain. "You can no longer hold Megan's death over Regan. The blood debt is paid, her killer brought to you. I'm not asking you to forgive Dark Shadow, or even like me. Hate me all you want, but don't hate Regan."

"We don't hate her," her mother gasped.

"Then stop this nonsense, because no matter what Regan says, you're her parents and your absence hurts her, and I think deep down you don't want that. Deep down her absence hurts you just as much." Tyler turned and walked away, leaving Jackson to kill Richard once and for all. Bass fell into step beside him, touching his shoulder briefly, drawing some of Tyler's pain into himself.

"Thanks," Tyler murmured, breathing easier. "For more

than just easing my pain."

"You don't have to thank me, Ty. I'm your alpha, and Megan's debt needed to be paid. My father was responsible for a lot of bad blood, and today, I hopefully erased some of it."

"You shouldn't have gone alone," Tyler said, glancing at him.

"I work best alone. My father made sure of that. If I hadn't met Katalina, I think I would have walked my entire life alone."

"You had Nico."

"Yes. But I never let him in, not like I have now. I never let any of you in. I couldn't if I was to survive."

"I think we're coming back with you to Dark Shadow, unless Regan's changed her mind."

Bass smiled. "She'll always be welcome."

"You've no idea how relieved I am to hear that." The weight spilled from his shoulders, the pressure releasing from his heart.

"You've accepted Katalina as your own. What kind of man would I be if I didn't return the favor?"

"I just hope her parents come around."

"Even if they don't, it will be okay, Tyler. Because you'll make it so."

Tyler nodded, even though inside he was full of self-doubt and worry. Regan was his heart. He loved her more than anything and hoped it was enough. He hoped their love would carry them through the uncertain times ahead and give Regan strength as she navigated Dark Shadow.

Going forward, Tyler took comfort in the fact his alpha was doing the same, hoping and praying his love for Katalina and his pack would see them all through. See them to the end of this war.

Chapter 61

"Do you have an iron?" Regan asked, studying the dress she'd pulled from the drawer with a mixture of frustration and annoyance. Tyler had cleared out two of his drawers so she could put some of her clothes away. The rest still sat in boxes in Jackson's barn.

"No, but I think my mom has," he offered.

"We need some more furniture, Ty," Regan said, scanning what had been Tyler's home and was now theirs, for the time being at least. Zackary had moved out and in with Cooper and his parents. He hadn't seemed bothered by her being the reason for his move. In fact, Regan thought he was secretly pleased; Cooper had video games after all.

"We'll get some," he promised. "A wardrobe for your clothes and a shelf for your books."

Her gaze went to the hole in the roof covered by a tarp. "I don't dare unpack my books in here," she replied.

It wasn't that she expected higher standards, she just missed her old room. Her things on the wall that reminded her of Megan, a place where she could escape to.

"This isn't forever, Regan. Dark Shadow's being rebuilt."

"I know." She sighed. "I'm sorry. I'm being a bit of a bitch, aren't I."

"You'll never be a bitch to me," he replied, crossing the room and taking her into his arms. "Do you want me to take the dress to my mom's to get ironed?"

"Yes, please." She kissed him, then put the dress into his arms.

"Won't be long."

"Oh, Ty," Regan called before he closed the door.

"Hmm?"

"Get her to iron your shirt too, okay? We should look respectable for our mating celebration."

Tyler smiled, poking his tongue out at her. "Whatever you say, boss."

Feeling happier then she had a moment before, Regan marveled at the simple joy Tyler sparked inside if her. Facing the mirror, she smiled at her reflection before going to work on her hair and makeup.

It had been Katalina's idea to hold a party for the couples from both packs who had recently found their mates and after feeling guilty for so long for loving Tyler, it was nice to finally be able to celebrate him, and all he'd given her.

Her parents had also been invited, Katalina giving them the invitation herself and knowing her, a lecture along with it. Regan didn't hold out hope that they'd attend, but a small part of her, the little girl she'd once been, wished and prayed nonetheless.

It had been two weeks since the day Bass had thrown Megan's killer at their feet and she'd heard nothing from them, but Regan had made her choice to leave her past behind that day. That also meant her parents, if that's where they wished to stay.

Dark Shadow overall had been okay. No one had shunned her, and most of the time, she felt welcome, but it was the moments she found herself alone that got to her. At those times, Regan was lost in a foreign land, not unwelcome, but not at home either. She missed having a house with a kitchen, missed waking up in the morning and pouring herself a cup of coffee in private. Dark Shadow was run vastly different to River Run, and it would take some getting used to. But she was determined to do so. Her training continued with River Run, though she'd admitted Tyler was right so had slowed down on her obsessive ways. Mia often met her on the Dark Shadow boarder, and they'd go run together. It seemed more or less her two packs were slotting together nicely, yet Regan still didn't feel quite right.

Bass had said she'd needed a change of scenery and he'd been right, but coming to Tyler's didn't feel all that fresh. She only hoped once they moved to the new Dark Shadow site that she'd feel more settled, and truly have her fresh start.

"One dress all ironed, and one mate in a crisp shirt," Tyler said on entry. "Oh, and Mom says she can't wait to see you later."

"Your mom is a force of nature." Regan smiled. Lauran had gone out of her way to make her feel welcome and a part of Tyler's family. It helped soothe the hole her mom had once filled.

"And not to be reckoned with." Tyler came up behind her and bent to kiss her nape. "I like your hair up," he murmured, kissing up her bare neck.

Regan closed her eyes, tilting her head to give him better access. His hand skimmed down her shoulders, sending shivers across her skin.

"Can we be late to our own party?" he breathed against her skin.

Regan moaned. Oh, how she wanted to say yes. "You'll mess up my hair. It took me ages to get it just right."

"Fine. Get dressed before I decide I don't care."

Regan laughed, taking the dress from him. She ran to the small bathroom to dress, just in case the sight of her in her underwear had Tyler changing his mind.

"Are you looking forward to this party?" Regan asked as she came out of the bathroom, dress on but not zipped up. "Can you zip me up, please?"

"I'd rather not," he murmured, running a finger up her

spine, before doing as he was told. "And yes, I am. Plus, I think Katalina has a few surprises up her sleeve. Bass was moaning earlier. She's not allowed him to see the party site. I wonder what she's planned."

"Knowing Kat, it'll be epic." Regan smiled. "Okay, how do I look?" she asked, spinning around.

Tyler's gaze traveled from her head to her toes and back again, becoming hungrier by the second. She'd never felt more confident and sexier than when Tyler looked at her like that. "Like every man will be jealous you're on my arm and not theirs."

"You don't look all that bad yourself," she answered, kissing him lightly. "Let's go."

CHAPTER 62

Her nerves were steadily increasing as the minutes ticked by. Katalina had done a lot of planning and scheming over the last few weeks, dragging Tim into it with her, much to his horror. While Tim didn't find anything she'd requested out of the ordinary, the fact she'd told him he couldn't tell Bass or Jackson scared the hell of him. She'd admit the pair could be rather frightening when you didn't know them.

Katalina had drafted a crew of helpers all sworn to secrecy, mostly made up of the thirteen-to-sixteen-year-olds of the packs that relished the thought of keeping secrets from their alphas.

"Everything looks amazing," Luna reassured her as she joined Katalina in admiring their hard work.

"Yeah, Bass is going to freak when he sees this," Cooper added.

"Freak good or freak bad?" Katalina asked, glancing at the boy.

"Hmm." He shrugged. "Can never quite tell with him."

"I feel so much better." Katalina laughed.

"I've never seen you scared of him before," Zackary added. Katalina still worried about him, and it was statements like that, which made her think she was right to do so.

"I'm not scared of him, Zac. Bass has never been scary to me. I just… I hope everyone likes what I've done and doesn't see me as trying to push my ways onto them."

"Your ways being the normal way?" Zackary said sarcastically.

Katalina smiled, nudging him on the shoulder. "Haven't you realized," she whispered, "they're not very normal here."

"Shut it," Cooper joked. "Come on, Zac, let's scram before the alphas arrive."

"That's it, ditch me to face them alone," Katalina called.

Zackary saluted her before grinning and racing after Cooper, and just like that, she felt stupid for worrying about him.

"It really does look amazing," Luna said.

"Thanks," Katalina said, hugging the girl. "And thanks for all your hard work, everyone, but I suggest you all clear out and get changed for the party."

The area cleared quickly, leaving Katalina to survey their hard work. Tim had built a pavilion of sorts in the center of the area. Its hexagon shape fit well as the center piece. Lights lit the area and music had been set up inside, which was currently drifting through the air. All around the pavilion were picnic benches, and fairy lights strung above them on poles or hung in the few scattered trees. On one side of the pavilion stood tables with food, and on the other, drinks ready to be served. But the most significant thing was the placing of her creation, in being that it spanned both sides of the packs' land. She'd chosen a spot far enough away from the living quarters of both packs, and luckily the stream bent away, curving further onto River Run and meaning she didn't have it to contend with like she had with Regan and Tyler's cabin.

"I don't know whether to kiss you or throttle you."

Katalina turned at the sound of Bass's voice. She'd asked both Bass and Jackson to meet her at the same time, slightly earlier than the party was due to start.

"I'm afraid if he throttles you, I might have to stand back and let him," Jackson added.

"What have I said about the two of you ganging up on me? It's so not fair," Katalina replied.

Bass laughed.

"You leave us little choice, daughter, when these are the kind of stunts you pull."

Katalina crossed her arms, feeling a little worried.

"I have one question for you," Bass said. "Is there still room in our budget for a house of our own?"

"Of course, I'm not stupid. Though we might be living off beans and noodles for the next year."

With a shake of his head and a boom of laughter, Bass raced forward and lifted her into the air, spinning her around. "This is amazing, Katalina. As always, you astound me."

Squealing with laughter, Katalina hugged Bass as he set her back down, and then turned to face her father. "So?"

"Half of this land is mine," he observed.

"Yeah, I used my alpha-daughter privileges."

Jackson laughed. "You've done a great job. I'm sure both packs are going to have a wonderful time tonight."

She let out a huge breath, relieved that part was over with. All she had to get through now was the rest of the party and the unveiling of Tyler and Regan's cabin. It was safe to say Katalina wouldn't be resting easy any time tonight. As if reading her mind, Bass kissed her cheek then whispered.

"Try to enjoy yourself tonight. You deserve it."

Shortly after, guests began to arrive, and all seemed amazed and happy with what she'd accomplished. Music played, drinks served, and food eaten, the atmosphere full of joy, and while Katalina had planned this party with the packs in mind, she'd really done it for her friends. For the couples who'd found each other against all odds, and as a reminder to each other and the universe that they'd persevered and would keep doing so no matter what was thrown at them.

Bass spun her around the dance floor, other couples from both packs around them and as she tipped her head to the sky smiling, Katalina was sure she could see her parents smiling down at her, telling her she'd done well.

CHAPTER 63

Tyler had always thought his mother was not to be messed with, the one he'd never dare cross, that was until he met Katalina and witnessed the feats she performed. The party wasn't only for them, but for Nico and Olivia, and Cage and Anna. Though Tyler would always remember this night as his and Regan's, as the night both of their packs came together to celebrate a love he'd once tried to ignore.

He'd never seen Regan happier. Her dress fanned out as she twirled and twisted around the dance floor, the smile on her face did things to his soul, the happiness in her eyes mesmerizing.

And it seemed Katalina hadn't finished with the tricks up her sleeve.

"Come with me," she cooed, taking Regan from his arms and spinning around with her. "I have a surprise for you."

Tyler shook his head at her giddiness, eyeing Bass.

"She's had a few too many to drink," he responded.

"Well, tonight's the night for it," Tyler answered.

"But she really does have a surprise for you," Bass continued. "Well, from both of us, and Jackson too, I guess. Though—" Bass glanced across the party. "—he seems a little preoccupied with admirers at the moment."

"Eww," Katalina said a little too loudly. "I did not need to hear that, Bass."

Following Katalina and Bass, Tyler walked hand in hand

with Regan as they made their way through the trees away from the party.

"I hope your plan isn't to murder us in the woods," Tyler joked, "Because I warn you, I'm moving a little faster than I was. Can't lift my left arm above my head like, but…."

"Stop being silly. I've something to show you," Katalina replied, skipping as she went.

Regan laughed softly beside him, leaning her head on his shoulders. "What's out in the middle of the forest, Kat?"

"You'll see," she sang. "We're almost there."

Tyler couldn't help noting they were heading toward the spot he and Regan used to meet. It stirred up old memories and by Regan's sudden quietness, he guessed it was doing the same for her.

"Okay," Katalina said, spinning to face them dramatically. "Close your eyes. Bass, grab Regan's hand and guide her."

Bass met his gaze, then Regan's. When Regan held out her hand for him, Bass took it with a smile and gazed at his mate. "You're incorrigible, my winter wolf."

She smiled lovingly back, then turned her sights on Tyler. "Give me your hand then, and close your eyes. No peeking."

"Be careful with him," Regan warned Katalina, before closing her eyes.

"Promise," Katalina replied.

Eyes closed, Regan's hand in his right, Katalina in his left, Tyler took careful steps forward, counting ten before Katalina guided him to a stop.

"Okay," she breathed, sounding suddenly nervous. "Open your eyes."

Tyler sucked in a breath, Regan going deadly still beside him. He took in the cabin first, then noted the spot it had been built on. His chest felt suddenly tight, emotions churning inside of him looking for a way out through his eyes.

Regan gasped beside him, her hand going to her mouth. "Is this?" she whispered.

"All yours," Katalina finished.

Tyler met Regan's gaze. Her eyes brimmed with tears, the expression on her face one of sheer shock and happiness. "Ours," she gasped, staring at him.

"Want to go inside?" Katalina asked them quietly.

"Yes," Regan answered, tugging on his hand as Katalina walked ahead.

There were several steps that led up onto a large porch that swept around to the side, two railings fenced it in, decorated with lights. They paused at the front door, which had been painted green and had a small diamond window in it. Warm yellow light spilled from the glass, welcoming them in.

Katalina opened it and stood to the side. "Welcome home, guys," she breathed.

"We'll give you a minute to look around," Bass added, pulling Katalina to his side. "Take your time."

Following Regan inside, he closed the door and turned to find Regan who was crying softly. "Did you have any idea they were planning this?" she asked.

"None whatsoever. I'm a little lost for words actually. Katalina must have planned this the moment we were found out."

"How she got them to agree to this…." Regan shook her head and gazed around. "This is so amazing!"

As they walked in the front door, they were greeted with a door to their left and right and straight ahead opened out into the main living space. Regan opened the left door first.

"Oh my god, we have a bathroom big enough for a tub," she squealed, jumping up and down. "I can't wait to have a long soak in it."

"I can't wait to watch you have a long soak in it," Tyler added with what he hoped was a charming smile.

Grinning, Regan walked back out, going this time for the right door. Tyler followed her, enjoying seeing her reactions to their new home. Seeing sheer joy on her face made his chest fill with love. It was surreal to imagine the cabin as theirs, to picture himself and Regan living there. It was almost to good to be true.

The right door was a bedroom, big enough for a double bed, and a wall of storage was on one side.

"You've somewhere to hang your clothes now," Tyler noted.

She opened one of the closet doors. "Kat's even hung my clothes up that were at Jackson's. And this is my lamp," she said, running a hand over the lampshade on the bedside table.

"Shall we see the rest?"

Her smile was giddy. "Yes."

The rest of the cabin was one big living space, with a kitchen to the right, the center unit being big enough to serve as a breakfast bar as well. The cabinets where white gloss with chrome handles, the bench tops black.

"Well, now I know why Katalina was grilling me on what I'd want in my dream house the other week," Regan said. "Not once did I think she was planning this."

On the left of the room were shelves already housing Regan's books, a fireplace in the center of the wall, and a large corner sofa closest to the front door. Here and there Regan touched a few things that Tyler knew were the things she'd had to leave behind in Jackson's barn, and then she stopped in front of the large double doors at the end of the room.

Regan opened them and disappeared into the darkness.

Tyler heard her gasp, and then he was gasping right along with her. His arm wrapped around Regan as they took in the outside, a large deck went out over the stream, railings all around, strung with lights too. The cabin was beyond anything he could have ever dreamed, and while he would have quite happily lived in his small shabby cabin, Regan deserved far more. And now she had it, and Tyler would be forever grateful.

"We're on River Run land now," Regan whispered.

"Yup, and right behind you is a clearing that will lead to the new Dark Shadow," Katalina said as she and Bass came from around the side of the house and onto the deck. "What do you think?"

Regan ran from his embrace and flung her arms around Katalina. "I love it so much, Kat. Thank you, thank you."

"Yeah, it really is amazing. I'm kinda lost for words really," Tyler added. "But thank you, guys. We couldn't have dreamed something better ourselves."

"Well, I have been picking Regan's brain a little, so I hope you don't mind that everything is in her style," Katalina said.

"Anything Regan likes, I like," Tyler replied.

"There's a bottle of champagne in the fridge if you'd like to toast to your new home?" Katalina said.

"You really do think of everything, huh?" Regan shook her head. "I'm in awe of you, Kat."

The bubbly was popped and poured and as they clinked their glasses together, toasting him and Regan lots of happiness, Tyler's eyes stung with the need to cry. It was as if there was so much happiness inside of him it had nowhere left to go. Regan's joy burned through him from their bond and for the first time since the attack, Tyler didn't worry about his and Regan's future. Nor did he fear she'd not be accepted, because they were standing in a gift that meant far more than having a place to call home. It was a symbol of their love, of the bonds between them and the packs their love tied together. It was a gift that said, *we accept you, we stand with you, we'll face the future together.* And that, Tyler thought, was the most precious gift that could have been given.

Chapter 64

She'd danced until her feet hurt, smiled until the creases in her cheeks felt like permanent lines, yet there was something missing. The two people who'd been invited but hadn't shown. She found herself searching the crowd for them as the night drew on. Caught her heart with a hopeful spark that made her feel silly and naïve whenever she imagined it was them. She'd told herself a thousand times they didn't matter, that they were a part of her past and she belonged in the future with Tyler. But her heart hadn't quite got the memo.

Regan was ready for home, ready to fall into her new bed in her new home and focus on all the good she had in her life. Glancing at Tyler talking with a group of men across the clearing—some she knew, some she didn't—Regan willed him to look at her. He looked content, and Regan felt a little guilty for wanting him to take her home.

His eyes met hers, a small private smile on his lips just for her. She didn't say anything or indicate for him to come to her, but of course, he knew. He always did, even before the mating bond.

Shoulder pats and handshakes were given out and minutes later, Tyler was walking toward her.

"I'll be back in a sec," Regan murmured to Anna beside her.

"No, you won't," Anna answered, smiling.

Tyler pulled Regan into a one-armed hug, kissing the top of her head. "Are you ready to go?"

"Yes. Do you think it's too early to leave?"

"I think we can leave whenever we want."

"But I don't want to appear rude, that I haven't enjoyed myself, because I have. It's just…."

"I know, Regan. There's no need to explain yourself to me. If it makes you feel better, we can say I'm in pain."

"Are you?" she asked, cupping his face and searching his eyes to make sure he didn't lie to her.

"A little," he admitted. "I've been ignoring it."

"Well, you shouldn't be doing that," she scolded.

"I was having fun. I didn't want to leave."

"I've had fun too. Are you sure you don't mind leaving?"

"Not at all. I'm looking forward to trying out our new bed." His smile turned playful, eyes seductive.

Regan raised an eyebrow. "Thought you were in pain?"

"Not enough pain to miss out on christening our new bed."

Heat flooded her cheeks, and far deep places. Her reasons for leaving had nothing to do with her absent parents now.

"Let's go say goodbye," she suggested, tugging his shirt.

Bidding everyone a good night took far longer than Regan had anticipated. She was showered in hugs and well wishes by people she didn't even know, but who obviously knew Tyler. Finally, after Tyler's mother hugged her for the fifth time, she and Tyler were heading over to Katalina and Bass.

"Hey, guys, we're off," Tyler said on approach.

"Already?" Katalina moaned. "It's not even midnight yet." She had a plate of food in her hand and seemed to be leaning on

Bass for support.

"Some of us were on death's door a few weeks ago," Tyler pointed out.

"You're off to bed soon too if you don't sober up," Bass added to Katalina sternly, though there was a smile on his face.

"I'm eating," she replied, waving a sausage roll in the air. "I've only had punch. You'd think I'd be less of a lightweight with wolf genes."

Bass chuckled. "I think the punch was spiked to wolf standards."

Regan surveyed the party. "You're not the only one a little tipsy, Kat. And thank you again for everything, the party, the cabin.... Seriously, you should go into party planning or something."

"Please don't encourage her," Bass groaned.

"Regan," Tyler gasped. "Look." He guided her around, his one good arm on her shoulder, and whispered in her ear, his lips brushing her skin, "Better late than never."

"Told you my lecture would work," Katalina said, poking Bass in the side. "Looks like you're not leaving after all."

Regan had no idea what to say, or even which emotion rolling through her was most prominent. If anything, she felt numb from overload. Hovering under a tree together, her parents held each other's hands as they scanned the party, most definitely feeling out of place.

"Come with me," Regan whispered, taking Tyler's hand as she took a small step forward.

Her mom spotted her first, a smile lit her face then fell away and was replaced with worry. She nudged her father in the side and whispered in his ear.

"I'm terrified, Ty," Regan whispered as they approached.

Her stomach did flips.

"I'm right here with you. Always." His hand squeezed hers, and she settled slightly, knowing she'd never have to face difficult situations alone again.

"Mom, Dad...," Regan said as she and Tyler approached. She wasn't quite sure what else to say. A part of her was very angry at her parents and she wasn't sure them showing up was enough to fix the hurt caused.

Her mother's gaze flickered from Tyler's to hers, and unexpectedly, she launched herself forward and flung her arms around Regan.

"Oh, honey, you look so beautiful. And look at this place. That Katalina sure knows how to throw a party."

Regan stiffened with surprise, then her body relaxed, and her arms were going around her mother like they had a thousand times before. "She sure does." It didn't matter what had gone down between them. She was Regan's mom, and nothing could change that.

Her mom released her and then took a step back and looked to Tyler. "We're really sorry for the way we treated you," she said hesitantly. "I hope you're on the mend."

"I'm getting there," Tyler said. "Your daughter is taking good care of me." He smiled at Regan's mom, then turned his gaze on her father.

Regan didn't think she'd ever seen her father visibly shrink. She'd always known he wasn't a dominant wolf but in the eyes of the little girl she'd been, he'd always been a strong man, her protector. Tyler owed her father nothing. He'd done nothing wrong while her father had made mistake after mistake. So, when he stepped forward and offered a hand to her father, she didn't believe it was possible to love Tyler anymore then she already did. He surprised her daily with his generosity and good heart, yet underneath, Regan knew there lived the nature of a fierce wolf, ready and willing to protect its own.

Regan's father faltered for only a moment as he stared, stunned at Tyler's outstretched arm, and then he was clasping it back, shaking his hand and meeting Tyler's eyes.

"I owe you an apology. Quite honestly, I'm ashamed of my actions toward you and my daughter. I'm not really sure what to say or do to fix what I've broken."

"You already have," Tyler answered.

And while her father's words meant a great deal to Regan, there was a part of her that would need more time to forget what had happened. But tonight, she was choosing to focus on the positive. Her parents had come. They'd been the one thing missing and now they weren't. Her chest hurt from the crowded emotions coursing through her. Tears sprung into her eyes and she did her best to push them away.

"I'm so happy you came," Regan breathed, and then she stepped forward and hugged her father, and then her mother joined in too.

"We missed you so much, Regan," her mom sobbed. "You can come home whenever you like. Both of you, of course. We're so sorry."

"Actually," Regan said, stepping back from their hug and linking her arm with Tyler's. "We've got our own place now, a gift from Jackson, Bass, and Katalina. They built us a cabin on the pack's border. You should see it. It's so beautiful, Mom."

"Oh, well... wow. I can't wait to see it," she replied.

"You could come over for dinner sometime.... I mean, if you want to of course," Regan offered, a little afraid they'd say no.

"That sounds good, Regan," her father replied stiffly, then relaxed a fraction. "Real good. Your mother will love it."

"Yes," her mom agreed, smiling broadly.

An awkward silence settled over them and Regan hated how robotic it was between herself and her parents, as if neither of them knew where they stood anymore. She only hoped it would fade with time.

"There's plenty of food if you're hungry," Tyler offered, pointing to the tables near the pavilion.

"Actually, we only stopped by to wish you well," her father answered.

Regan's mother took her father's hand. "Yes, you know your dad, Regan. He's not exactly a party animal." She laughed hesitantly.

"That's okay," Regan replied. "It means a lot to me that you came."

"We're calling it a night anyway," Tyler added. "My wounds are playing up."

A look of guilt slid over her father's face while her mom fidgeted with her hands nervously.

"Well, we won't keep you," Regan's mom replied. "And we really are happy for you, Regan, both of you." Her mother's words settled over her, easing the storm of feelings inside of her.

"Yes," her father agreed. "I look forward to getting to know you, Tyler." A few tears spilled down Regan's cheeks and she shucked in a shaky breath.

"Me too," Tyler replied.

"Bye." Regan gave them both another quick hug, fighting back the emotions bursting from her. "See you soon," she added, her voice cracking.

Regan clung to Tyler as they walked away. The night had been perfect in so many ways, yet an emotional roller coaster, and she felt mentally drained. But as she left the party, it was on a high, and feeling ever so lucky to have Tyler beside her, his steady presence an anchor to the world.

"You've been rather quiet since the party. Want to talk?" Tyler asked as he handed her a cup of tea and took a seat next to her on the sofa.

Regan was silent for a minute, taking in all that was around her—all that was hers and Tyler's. She was quiet, but it wasn't that she was unhappy. Quite the opposite. It was as if her mind had gone into shutdown to absorb all that had happened over the night, over the course of the last few weeks. It was the first moment she'd had time to stop and reflect, to really let the realization sink in that Tyler was hers and not a secret. That they shared a bed in their own home, she had a kitchen, and a deck that looked out onto the spot that would always be hers and Tyler's. A spot that reminded her of his patience and persistence, his love that he conveyed even then, with one look from his wolf. Not once had Regan allowed herself to dream she could have it all. Her pack, her mate, and her family. It was too good to be true, and she wasn't used to the feeling. Of being complete. Of having all the parts of her broken heart healed and together.

"I'm all right, a little overwhelmed, I think. I'd hoped they'd show but never expected it."

He put his right arm around her shoulders and leaned his head on hers. "Tonight was definitely a lot to take in. I keep waiting for someone to walk through the door and say 'oh, sorry, there's been a mistake. Out you go.'"

"That would be awful," she agreed.

"Do you know what I think we should do?"

"What?" she asked, laughing at his silly tone.

He sat up a little, gazing at her and wiggled his eyebrows, making Regan laugh further. "Go try out the bed, just in case it is all taken away."

"Is that all you ever think of, getting me naked?"

"Hmm." He sucked in his lips. "Pretty much. But you can't blame me. Have you seen yourself naked, Regan?"

She slapped his leg. "You're terrible."

"Got you laughing though"

Regan put her cup down on the coffee table, then turned her attention back to Tyler. "Who says we have to go to bed?" She smiled at him slyly as she pulled at the zipper on her dress. "There's a perfectly good couch right here."

He watched her with hungry eyes as she dropped one shoulder strap, then the other, and then the whole dress to the floor.

He moaned. "So damn beautiful."

Climbing into his lap, Regan straddled him as she unbuttoned his shirt, taking her time, enjoying each step of their dance. It was a dance only for him, one that spoke of love and loyalty, of friendship and protection. One she'd never imagined dancing or even deserved having.

Tyler had done more than heal her heart. He'd shown her what she'd always possessed despite it being hidden beneath. He breathed joy and adventure back into her veins. He was her mate, her home, and the breath that gave her life.

Epilogue

Their home had become a casual meeting place for both packs. For unexpected matters, or ones that didn't require the formal etiquette of the official meetings that took place at the pavilion Katalina had organized. The edge of their deck had railings and bench seats, enough room to fit both pack's inner circles. Today, however, not everyone was there. Jackson had arrived with William and Cage, his only warning a text message to Regan minutes ago. Moments later, Tyler had received the same from Bass and he'd arrived with Katalina, Nico, and Jacob. Jacob being the new second voted in by the entire inner circle, and Dax had taken his place as enforcer.

"What's going on?" Regan asked Katalina as she walked up the steps onto the deck. Her gut swirled with anxiety as she slid her hand into Tyler's.

Regan knew something was wrong because gatherings were normally a more relaxed affair with drinks and nibbles, but not today. Today Jackson slammed a piece of paper down onto the table in the middle of the deck, his expression grim.

"I've received mail," he said. "From Castor." Dread rolled through Regan.

"What kind of mail?" Katalina asked as Bass's face paled.

"The kind that asks me to choose sides or die," Jackson answered.

"And your choice?" Bass asked calmly as if they were

talking about the weather.

"I made my choice a long time ago, son. The evidence is right there in your hand."

Bass looked down at his hand linked with Katalina's, lifting it upward. Regan did the same, glancing at her and Tyler's joined hands. She guessed Jackson was right; the moment he'd stood by Katalina had been a catalyst to all that unfolded since, and both he and Bass had solidified that choice further when they stood by her and Tyler.

"War's coming then," whispered Katalina.

And every set of eyes met one another's in silent answer.

War is coming and we'll face it together.

Acknowledgments

Someone recently pointed out to me what an achievement it is that I have created books alongside the very real scary problems happening right now in my life. "How do you do it?" she asked. And I said, "I don't know."

Yet her question stayed with me and this is the answer I found. I do it because writing is the one thing in my life that is truly me. Weaving a story makes my soul shine, it leaves me with a high that dulls all the chaos. I love this job, I love my readers, and when life has me on my knees, I remember these things.

I have a team of people who help me. They are my pack. Without them I'd not survive this storm, and wouldn't be able to create more books. I thank every single one of you for having my back!

Thank you to my father for his design work, for keeping up with my website and formatting my books. To my mother for everything that you do, the list is so long! To Becky and her team at Hot Tree for editing and promotions.

To the wonderful readers who help beta and proofread.

To every one of you that's checked in to make sure I'm okay over the last couple of years. For every message and comment. For your reviews and kind words.

And finally, to my children. The 4 most beautiful souls I know. You are my reason for being. The reason I get back up every time I'm knocked down. Every book is for you. To show you no matter how hard life gets, dreams are still possible. Happiness can still be found. **I love you.**

Author Bio

Rachel M. Raithby started her writing career in 2013 and hasn't looked back. She draws her inspiration from the many places she has lived and traveled, as well as from her love of the paranormal and thriller movies. She can often be found hiding out with a good book or writing more fast-paced and thrilling stories where love always conquers all. She resides in a quiet town in New Zealand, with her 4 children.

Her books include,

The New Dawn Novels

Winter Wolf, Wolf Dancer & Wolf Sight

The Deadwood Hunter series

Lexia, Whispers of Darkness, Holocaust, Betrayal & Surrender

Novella's

Death's Echo & Beast Within.

Connect with Rachel @ www.rachelmraithby.com

CPSIA information can be obtained
at www.ICGtesting.com
Printed in the USA
LVHW080003070819
626792LV00017B/912/P